ENMA

Alex Hughes

Order this book online at www.trafford.com
or email orders@trafford.com

Most Trafford titles are also available at major online book retailers.

Printed in the United States of America.

ISBN: 978-1-4269-9779-2 (sc)
ISBN: 978-1-4269-9780-8 (e)

Trafford rev. 09/30/2011

www.trafford.com

North America & international
toll-free: 1 888 232 4444 (USA & Canada)
phone: 250 383 6864 ♦ fax: 812 355 4082

For Jenny

Prologue

"**S**am, get the door."

The orphan was quick to comply.

Above the door, there was a wooden sign that read: *KINDER ROSE ORPHANAGE*, in cursive lettering.

Sam swung open said door to meet quite a surprise.

Knelt at the doorstep was a pale, raven-haired woman, an unconscious child limp in her trembling arms. They were both dripping with rain and blood.

It was then that Sam gave a frightened shriek. Not at the blood-he was accustomed to that-but there were strange, dark things, nearly invisible in the night, sprouting from either side of the woman's back. They drooped wearily at her sides. It took him a moment to realize they were wings.

A social worker, Lora, was at his side in a heartbeat. A shout escaped her as well.

"Sam, go inside." She ordered.

He didn't move. He could only gape at the dying angel bleeding at the steps.

She didn't press him.

"Please . . ." the angel wheezed. She inched closer painfully.

The social worker gasped and took a step back. Sam came forward.

"Sam." Lora cautioned, holding his shoulder. He gave her a defiant look, but stayed put.

"Please . . ." the angel said again, this time lifting herself sluggishly to her feet. She held the child before Sam. "Help him, I beg you." Red oozed from her mouth.

Sam looked at the small boy she held. He was pale and raven-haired just like the angel. Rain spattered his cherubic face.

"He is an orphan."

At this, Sam shrugged Lora's hand off his shoulder and stepped into the rain. He reached out, wrapping the boy in his arms.

The angel pressed her forehead to the child's, a motion that seemed to relax her and calm her heart, love in her mismatched eyes.

Before Sam could ask the little one's name, the dark angel had gone, leaving nothing but stray black feathers and the pool of blood which stained the welcome mat.

Twelve Years Later

Orphenn stood in his place around the fire that smelled of the corroding garbage that it burned. The smoke carried the stench with it as it barreled upward out of the metal trash can. Orphenn stared blankly into it, flames mirrored in his red and blue eyes.

He was with a new group today, and he was withdrawn and silent. Not that it mattered-he never spoke to the old group either. And whatever group he joined, there was never anything different. Homeless bums gathered around a garbage fire for warmth. Nothing more about it.

To Orphenn, living on the streets was much more predictable than others made it seem. True, New York alleys were cold and cruel, but what else was new? Also true, Orphenn was probably one of the youngest hobos in the park. But he didn't mind. No one else did much either. Others like him mainly worried about themselves. Though Orphenn seemed to be accustomed to a world without kindness.

He stuffed his hands into his trench coat pockets. He loved his trench coat. It was filthy brown and torn, but it was warm.

The others were talking. The one called Smitty, who wore a flannel coat and a beanie, began questioning the others in the circle.

"Hey, uh, *Maria*," he beckoned to a severely underdressed, middle-aged woman with a fuming cigarette held between two fingers. "What're you planning?"

"Buzz off." She rasped.

Smitty insisted. "No, come on, I mean, what're 'ya waitin' for? When 'ya gonna get yer life goin' again?"

She softened. "Just waiting for a miracle, Smitty. Ain't we all?"

"What 'bout you, R.J.? What you waitin' for?" Smitty asked a dark-skinned man across from him, who looked sullen and distraught. His plump lips quivered. R.J. responded slowly, in a tone that resembled weary excitement.

"I'm waiting. I'm waiting for my princess."

An awkward silence followed, with nothing but the crackling of the fire between them.

Listening to these people, Orphenn realized that every one of them *were* waiting. And that's all they would ever do.

Smitty again broke the silence. "Hey, you. Quiet Guy." He called. "Yeah, you, Silent Bob."

Orphenn's attention was lifted from the fire and he gazed through his long, lank hair at Smitty.

"What 'bout you, huh? What *you* waitin' for?"

Orphenn shook his head. "Nothing."

"Nothing? No hopes? No dreams? No love? Don't got no one? Ain't waitin' on nothing?"

Again, he shook his head.

"Not even a miracle?" Maria chimed.

"No."

"Oh, come on now, Silent Bob." Said R.J. "Everybody needs *somethin'*."

With one last shake of his head, Orphenn turned and left, erasing those words form his mind.

It was dark.

Sleep.

A voice said.

I need you to sleep.

Why? He said. Defiant, as always.

You will see, soon enough.

It was a feathery whisper in the darkness. He thought *what the heck*, and continued to dream.

A face appeared. Fine lips, pale skin, and big blue eyes. It was a woman, her hair as black as the abyss around her.

What is your name? She asked.

What's it to you?

It's taken a very long time to find you.

How do you know I'm who you're looking for?

You had just the right dreams. I know who you are.

Now that he thought about it, she looked eerily familiar. He hated to admit to himself that he was frightened by it.

My name is Orphenn. He relented.

She laughed. She only laughed.

Why are you laughing? Orphenn began to panic. *Why does everyone laugh?*

Her face became puzzled, and then faded back into the darkness, and was gone.

"Why is she laughing . . ."

The last images to dissipate were the woman's raging eyes.

"Why are you laughing?!" He shot awake.

He was back in the alley, where he slept with the stray cats every night, cold brick and cement, tin garbage cans and dumpsters.

He looked out to the street. There was a strange woman there, laughing at him.

"Who's laughing?" She sniggered.

He must have shouted in his sleep.

Chapter One

~

The Criminal

Orphenn was an orphan. At this time in his life, he began to believe that's all he would ever be. Ten years in an orphanage taught him that much. He was never even placed in the foster system, as so many had been.

No one wanted him. And he knew why.

Every time he saw his reflection, he said to himself: *My eyes.*

Orphenn's eyes were quite remarkable. One was an icy, Siberian Husky blue, and the other was a crimson red. They were mismatched, but not only in color. The pupil in one iris was a cat-like slit, and in the other, there were three small pupils, as if they had split into thirds from the original. Doctors were amazed he could even see. Though his eyes weren't the only of Orphenn's "oddities" as Lora called them.

The other orphaned children spread dozens of rumors about him: that he could talk to dogs, that he could become a ghost and possess someone, that he was from another planet, and even that he had hidden horns. Complete bogus, of course.

So Orphenn could bear it no longer-the ridiculous rumors, the taunting children, and the hundreds of parents who gave him nothing but a disgusted grimace or frightful glare before walking away with a more fortunate orphan in their arms. No family would ever adopt him, he knew. He wouldn't wait and see either, just in case, for he never was a very patient person.

He made the decision, at fifteen, to run away. He couldn't stay at Kinder Rose. Not that anyone would miss him.

Thus, for two years, going on three, he was homeless, and now he sits in the alley, his hair long, shaggy and tangled, and his face streaked with grease. He turned up the collar on his trench coat, as if to shield his ears from the laughter of the woman in the street.

"Who's laughing?" She antagonized the seventeen-year-old.

This woman was dressed in enormous heels, short shorts and a tube top. It was also obvious that a bra was missing from her apparently limited wardrobe.

Orphenn ignored her, and reached for his bottle of vodka. He was underage naturally, but he had acquired a taste for it a while back, after getting past its strong burn. He spun off the lid and took a large, satisfying gulp.

"Stupid hobo." She spat. She walked clumsily, as if she as well was intoxicated, further into the alley, stopping in front of Orphenn and lifting his chin up with a filthy hand. "But you're a cute hobo. How 'bout I take you back to my place?"

Strands of her greasy blonde hair fell into Orphenn's face. "Much better than sleeping in a trash can."

He doubted that.

He crinkled his nose. "You smell like a dog." He scowled.

With a girlish grunt, she put her hands on her hips. "And you would know? Looks like most of your little friends 'round here are pregnant *cats*."

Orphenn gave her an intense glare, his red and blue eyes like shards of crystal. "Sure." He shrugged. "I've known a few bitches in my spare time."

The woman shrieked angrily and slapped him across the face. She spun and stomped away in a huff, twisting her ankle a couple times in the effort.

Orphenn chuckled, and lay back down on the cement with his hands behind his head, and thought about his dream.

It was different from the other ones, which he had almost every night. They were all about angels. Always about angels.

He had a pair of wings himself, which he most conveniently discovered when he fell off the Empire State Building at the annual orphanage field trip. Also quite convenient, was that none of the social workers or other officials happened to look out the window when he fell, nor any of the orphans. All except Sam. Sam was always the observant one. He knew everything about Orphenn. Granted, there wasn't much to know. Not anymore.

He missed Sam. He was Orphenn's only friend. He had been adopted years ago, though. Nowadays he's your friendly neighborhood police officer, patrolling about New York City.

"Orphenn?"

Speak of the Devil.

"Orphenn, is that you?"

Orphenn jolted to his feet and gawked at the squeaky-clean man in uniform standing at the end of the alley. He grew excited, but not before first glaring questionably at the vodka bottle. "Sam?" He said, unsure.

The officer smiled.

"Sam!" Orphenn enthused, as he sped out to the sidewalk to greet his best friend with their secret handshake. Clap right, clap left, double knuckles, snap. "What are you doing down here?"

"What am *I* doing?" Sam jeered. "What are *you* doing? What, did you get pissed off and run away? You should be at Kinder Rose! Not on the streets!" Then he noticed the bottle in the younger boy's tightly curled fingers. "Oh, Orphenn. Don't tell me you've gotten into *that* again. I thought you quit."

"I had to run away." He defended, twisting the cap onto the bottle and setting it away next to a trash can.

"But why?"

"Because you weren't there for me anymore! I was treated like I was some kind of alien-well I always was, but even more so when you left! There was no one to stand up for me. You're my only friend, Sam."

No one to stand up for me anymore. When Orphenn spoke these words, he realized he was just like the rest of them around the garbage fire, and had the sudden urge to vomit.

"I'm so, so sorry I left." Sam apologized. "And I know I promised I would visit, but-"

"I considered *suicide* Sam!" Orphenn interrupted, leaving Sam speechless. "Something I believed I would *never* do!"

"I never thought you would either." Sam replied after a slight pause. "But I never thought in all my life that you would sleep in a trash can like *Sesame Street.*"

"I don't actually sleep *in* the can! Why does everyone say that?"

"I know you're capable of so *much more*, Orphenn. *I know it.*"

At this, Orphenn could only stare at the older man.

"*I've seen it.*" Sam continued. "You may not look like much, I know that! But Orphenn, you can *fly*. No one else can say that. Or do you not remember all those times I covered for you while you snuck out in the middle of the night to use your wings?"

"I haven't forgotten, Sam."

"You could be saving the *world*, or something with the powers you have!"

"No, I couldn't."

"Why *not?*"

"Because I'm not *like* you, Sam!" His face was a mask of envy. "I'm not the kind of person that can accomplish much more than finding something to *eat* every day! You're a *hero!* You're saving *lives* every day!"

"You're ten times more *capable* of it than I am!" Sam countered. "You could use your gifts to help the task force! The Coast Guard, Air Force, Firefighters—the damn Forest Rangers for Hell's sake!"

Orphenn looked down at his weathered boots. "I don't know . . . That I could do any of that . . ."

Before Sam could reply, gunshots sounded out in the street.

Sam was in the street with his gun at the ready in seconds. Orphenn couldn't see what was happening-a herd of passerby surrounded the scene, blocking everything from his view.

More shots went off.

"Sam!?" Orphenn called.

He heard shouting and clattering as a firearm was knocked to the asphalt.

A tall shirtless man with baggy jeans broke from the crowd, running down the road as fast as he could. Sam sped after him.

"Sam!" Orphenn called again, picking up his feet to gallop after them. They ran for what seemed like hours. They dodged through a playground like an obstacle course, then the man began to slow down, though he persisted until he came to a bridge overlooking the ocean. He began to stroll across it nonchalantly, as if he were on a brisk weekend walk, rather than being pursued by an officer.

"Sir." Sam cautioned, Orphenn panting beside him. "Sir, I'm going to have to ask you to come away from the bridge."

The man gave him a strange smirk.

"Sir. Step *off* the *bridge*." Sam seemed to realize the command came out wrong the moment he said it.

"Oh, crap." Orphenn muttered.

The man laughed maniacally and hopped onto the bridge's steel railing. "Whatever you say, officer!" And he fell over the edge.

Sam jerked, as if wanting to go after him, but Orphenn had already pushed him aside, got a running start, spread his wings, and dove after the criminal.

He kept his wings close at his sides, shooting down toward the man like a speeding bullet, until he got close enough to touch him. He grabbed his arms around the man's waist, snapping his wings out to catch the air. He began to ascend again, but it was difficult. Not only was the man heavy, but he struggled and squirmed like a whining kitten.

"Ugh! Cut it out!" Orphenn yelled, flicking him in the head.

The man continued to struggle, but Orphenn managed to wrangle him to the edge of the cliff where Sam waited for him.

Sam's eyes widened in awe as Orphenn hovered back to land, his wings beating lightly to keep him a few feet off the ground. He socked the man in the head with a fist as strong as stone to cease his wriggling. He was out cold.

It was then that Orphenn noticed Sam's stricken stare. He tossed the man to the ground, where he lay unconscious, but still breathing.

"What?" Orphenn held his arms out quizzically as he folded his wings and dropped lightly to his feet in front of Sam, wings suddenly gone as if they had never been outspread. "You're looking at me like I just kicked a puppy."

Then Sam smiled. He pulled out a walkie-talkie and spoke into it. "All hands on deck."

"Huh?" Orphenn raised one eyebrow.

"*Aye aye, Captain.*" Buzzed the communicator.

"Oh, it's our code talk. Between my partner and I." Explained Sam. "He should be here with the cruiser in a few minutes."

"Ah." Orphenn stuffed his hands in his trench coat pockets, feeling a bit jealous that his best friend had a new partner.

"I knew you could do it." Sam said, catching Orphenn off guard.

"What do you mean?" He clicked his tongue. "Oh that? Flying? It was nothing."

"Was it?" Sam shook his head. "You captured a murderer."

"Oh . . . I guess I did."

"Not only did you save his life, but you prevented him from escaping and striking again if he survived. You saved other lives, too."

Orphenn blushed, idly scratching the back of his neck.

The cruiser honked its horn behind them.

After stuffing the murderer in the back seat, and watching his only friend drive away with his new partner, he took a deep breath and began to walk back to his alley.

There was still a mess of people when he arrived. Sam had gotten there before him, and was shooing people away from a dead body.

Orphenn was suddenly regretting only punching that criminal once to knock him out. But at the same time he felt incredibly glad that he was lucky enough to be the one to punch him. *That's beside the point.* He thought. *He's locked away now, forever. That's what's important.*

"So what happened?" Orphenn asked after Sam politely asked a nosy woman to leave the premises.

"Apparently the poor guy was having an affair with the murderer's wife." Sam answered.

"I feel bad for the wife." Orphenn sympathized.

The old friends bid farewell, and separated, one with a job to do, the other with dreams to ponder.

Then, through the crowd, there was a still, dark figure on the other side of the street. As the crowd cleared, he saw it more clearly.

Everything seemed to come to Orphenn's eyes in slow motion, so stricken with astonishment he was. No sound came to his ears. The remaining onlookers slowly left the street, leaving remnant shadow trails on his retinas.

It was a woman, clad head-to-toe in black, her neck draped with chains. Her jeans were torn and she wore a strapped black leather jacket and matching knee-high boots. Her hair was long, reaching the small of her back, sleek, and the color of obsidian. Her bangs were cut straight across, and shiny sunglasses covered her eyes. She was leaning against an odd-looking motorcycle, arms folded and legs crossed at the ankles.

Her face looked so familiar . . . . eerily familiar, like the woman in his dream before had looked. In fact, she had the same face as the woman in his dream.

Orphenn saw the woman slip her shades off her face and squint in his direction.

She had intense, mismatched eyes.

Chapter Two

~

The Angels

Her green and blue eyes shot like lasers beneath the shadow cast over her face. She lifted her chin to the sky, and let the light shine on her features, still gazing intently at the homeless person across the street.

Now, all the people had gone from the avenue, leaving nothing but a stretch of asphalt between the woman and the orphan.

Her face had a new look of certainty.

"Keiran." She said. She pushed off her motor bike and stepped forward, chains jingling. The air of relief surrounding her and the excitement in her eyes astounded Orphenn. No one had ever looked at him like that.

"What?" He speculated, their contrasting eyes meeting.

The woman reached out to him. He hadn't realized how close he actually was to her. Had he subconsciously walked slowly toward her? The sense of familiarity she gave him seemed to be drawing him in.

She rested her hand on his neck. He wanted to jerk away, but his legs felt like weak stilts. She looked deep within his abnormal eyes, as if searching for something hidden inside.

She was a stranger to him, and yet, Orphenn already felt a strong connection to her.

She stared for a bit longer. Then with an unexpected smile, she pulled his face closer, and touched her forehead to his.

Orphenn considered running away like a frightened bird, but it was a far away thought. The woman's affectionate gesture strangely calmed him. Like it was something he was used to.

"You've gotten so tall." The woman whispered, kissing his cheek lightly.

"Who are you?" Orphenn questioned, nearly dazed, hoping against all hope that this was not an alcohol-induced hallucination.

"You don't remember, do you? You're sure? You don't know who I am?"

Orphenn thought hard for a moment, but shook his head. "I feel like I should . . . . But I don't."

"Oh, Keiran." She lamented. "It's true . . . You've lost your memory. It must have been that last portal . . ." she trailed off, rubbing her temples in an effort to remember.

"Portal?"

"What's your name?" She abruptly changed the subject, steepling her fingers. "What did they decide to call you?"

"Orphenn."

"*Orphenn?!*" She gaped, as if he had said his name was Mega-Man. Then she straightened, tapping her chin in thought. "I didn't think they'd take what I said so literally . . . When I said you were an orphan, I thought they'd at least come up with their own name for you . . ."

"Who are you?" Orphenn repeated. "Wait, wait, wait, wait, first-How do you know me?"

"My name is Cinder." She answered, suddenly serious. After a pause, she said, "You're my baby brother, Orphenn."

"*What did you say?*" He nearly hissed, grasping Cinder's studded wrist in astonishment. "You mean . . . I have family?"

She nodded.

"How many?" He demanded.

"There's only the four of us left."

"Only four . . . ." He echoed. *That's more than I've ever had.* "Where are they?"

"You're the only one still here."

"In New York?"

"On Earth." She looked at him expectantly, as if waiting for him to tell her she was a nut job.

Instead he said, ". . . So you came to get me?"

"You believe me then?" She seemed relieved.

"Hey, I've heard stranger things," he lied. Hearing he had a family out there was the strangest thing that had ever come to his ears. "Hell, I'm pretty strange myself."

"Come on, then." She grinned, motioning to her motorcycle.

"Uhh . . ." Orphenn hesitated, taking a step back. "Are you sure you wanna take me?"

"What are you talking about?"

"I'm not really . . . . Normal. I mean-I can-I'm . . ."

"We'll worry about that later, when we get to Aleida." Cinder assured. "Maybe you'll demonstrate your 'abnormality' for me then."

"Aleida . . . We're going on *that?*" He tilted his head toward the odd motorcycle. Cinder said she was the only family he had on Earth. Did that mean they were going to some other planet? A strange unknown galaxy?

"Yup."

That 'yup' was surprisingly helpful.

At this point, Orphenn was ready to believe anything. Well, almost anything. If you told him Abraham Lincoln was standing right behind him riding a unicorn he might be like 'Wha?' But you get the picture. Anything was better than another night in that alley.

Cinder mounted her bike, slipping her shades back on her nose. "You ready, Baby Brother?"

Warm butterflies rose in his stomach at the affectionate nickname, but he looked down at his boots passively. "How can I be sure you're my sister?"

"Our eyes should be proof enough." She placed a comforting hand on his shoulder, adjusting her sunglasses to look him in the eyes again. Her right eye was watery blue and slitted, and her right was emerald green with a split pupil. Just like his, apart from the color.

Orphenn never believed himself worthy of anything, let alone a family and a nickname.

"Don't worry yourself, Orphenn." Cinder soothed. "Nobody's normal where we're going."

"Promise?"

"Promise."

He hopped on the bike seat behind her, still feeling anxious. Then he recalled the antics of earlier that morning, when he had captured that criminal. He had saved a life today.

He was filled with a new hope as Cinder revved the engine. "There's so much to do!" She enthused. "You have to meet Celina and Sven, and-oh! I hear his *daughter* is about your age now." She elbowed him playfully.

He laughed bashfully. "Who's Sven?"

"You'll see when we get there-he can help you remember."

There was a pause before Orphenn said, "Cinder?"

"Yeah?" She flipped up the kickstand with her heel.

"Um . . . Yeah, just wondering . . . What is Aleida?"

"Home."

That's all the answer he needed.

The bike surged forward in a flash, and was gone.

Orphenn could've sworn he saw a rush of space and stars like a Disneyland tunnel ride, but it was gone in a wink.

And in the next instant they were surrounded by white light. It temporarily blinded him, and Orphenn hid his face in Cinder's leather-strapped back. Now he understood why she wore the shades.

He felt suddenly shaky and nauseous, like he'd been set on tumble dry. His breath came in wavered gasps until he was able to calm himself and say, "Where are we?"

"Denoras."

Orphenn squinted, his sight coming back to him.

Denoras was magnificent. Still, as he looked about, everything was white . . . A white city. The architecture was the most unique Orphenn had ever seen. There were arches and statues everywhere, and each building looked as if it was carved from swirling marble or granite-almost fragile in its beauty.

The Palace itself was massive, and tall, with many towers atop it in random placement. They could be seen from the outer gates of the capital city. The largest and tallest was a clock tower soared above the others, with majesty that stood out from the rest.

Cinder drove her vehicle slowly (with a much disoriented Orphenn clung to her waist) along the smooth cobblestone-like pavement into the White Square, the heart of Denoras. There was a tremendous monument of white marble in the center of the plaza. Orphenn couldn't quite tell what it was at first, but gasped as they came closer to it. It was a statue depicting two women, with mighty wings blooming from their shoulders, and a fountain spurting at their feet.

He was again reminded of his nightly dreams. But neither this nor the amazing attention to detail that must have gone into creating this work of art was what shocked him-what made his jaw fall open was that the two figures had the same sculpted face-twins, that looked exactly like Cinder.

Orphenn nearly inquired about it, but was interrupted before he had the chance.

"No vehicles beyond this point, ma'am."

Orphenn turned his eyes up to the guard, who was curiously eyeing Cinder's ride. She switched off the engine and come to a halt. The guard's armor almost blended in with all the whiteness around him. Then Orphenn realized there were guards like this one at every corner in the square, hardly noticeable.

The guard lifted the brim of his too big headgear to peer down at the biker and the orphan. "I'll have to ask you for some identification."

Sam popped into Orphenn's head at the sight of this official. In fact, he looked a lot like Sam.

Cinder only chuckled at the guard's request. This seemed to catch the attention of another nearby guard, who came to stand beside the first. "What's goin' on over here? Who's this?" He gave the two on the bike a quizzical look.

"Got ourselves some *criminals*, sir." Warned the apparent neophyte, reaching for his firearm.

"Oh, you're such a drama queen." Sighed the second man, who was obviously much older and more experienced. "We'll just need some proof of ID before entering the palace."

Cinder turned her face to the veteran, tipping her shades down to show her eyes. "How's it goin', Pliley?" She nodded.

Officer Pliley started, nearly jumping. "Lady Cinder!" He jerked to glare menacingly at the younger officer. He jumped too.

"Ah!" The newbie exclaimed, "Lady Cinder! *The* Cinder! *The Mysterious Drifter! The Renegade Angel!* I've wanted to meet you all my life!" He was bouncing on his heels now. "You're in textbooks! You're famous, you-"

"That's enough, Hollei." Pliley chastised. He shook his head. "Rookie."

Hollei complied, busying himself by glancing at the angel monument, then at Cinder, then back at the monument, then at Cinder again, over and over, all with a goofy smile plastered to his face.

Pliley rolled his eyes at the rookie, then turned again to Cinder. "You haven't been home over three years now, Your Grace. What brings you back?" He asked casually.

"Family business." She answered, tilting her head toward Orphenn on the seat behind her, who was still clutching her zipper-covered jacket and wondering why they all treated her with such reverence.

The guards went dumbstruck at the word 'family.'

"Go right ahead." Hollei gestured, nonplussed.

Cinder advanced, parking her bike at the foot of the palace's wide entry stairs. "Sorry about that. Normally we Enma only have to show our eyes to receive unquestioned entry." She apologized, helping Orphenn off the seat. He limped up the steps alongside his sister, without even enough energy to ask what she was talking about.

"Who's the kid?" Hollei asked, once Cinder and Orphenn were through the great columned entrance.

"I don't know." Pliley admitted.

"He was awful quiet, wasn't he?"

"I suppose . . . There's been a lot to take in."

*   *   *

Orphenn's irregular footsteps echoed through the alabaster halls. The white columns were high and magnificent, the interior just as breathtaking as the outside of the palace, everything crafted from polished snow-white marble.

"You doing okay?" Cinder glanced back over her shoulder, her own steps jingling throughout the hall. "That trip must have done a number on you."

"I think I'll be fine." He rasped, flattered by her concern. The idea of being cared about was still new to him.

"Cinder!" A voice called from down another corridor.

Cinder's boots stopped, as did Orphenn's. He stayed closely beside her. He gazed at the huge gray and white dome overhead, so big it was like a second sky, and listened to the rapidly approaching footfalls.

Cinder knew she was coming before her voice ever broke the silence, just as she knew Cinder had returned before she ever climbed up the palace steps.

"Celina." Cinder muttered, holding her arms open for the rushing woman in white who was about to be wrapped in them. They embraced, rocking back and fourth like a pendulum.

Celina was dressed all in white-billowing white robes of silk and sparkling linen, and a ribbon that held her raven hair, even longer than Cinder's, from her face in a large ponytail. She also wore a silver coronet, with a single white jewel embedded in the band where it rested on her forehead; Orphenn came to infer that she had important social standing. Her face, like the two women in the monument, was a mirror image of Cinder. Her eyes were like theirs as well. One was the natural blue, and the other rusty brown.

Orphenn chastised himself for only just realizing that the women in the monument were facsimiles of the twins hugging each other right in front of him. And then once again for realizing that also like Cinder, Celina was his sister too.

It was nearly evening, and the sunlight shone bright through the wide windows, making the hall glisten, just as the twins' smiling eyes did when they pulled away from their embrace.

Cinder lightly winked in Orphenn's direction, and Celina looked to see what she was motioning to. At the sight of Orphenn, she gave a loving smile. Then her face seemed to change slightly. She ran to her long lost brother and clasped his hands in hers. She kissed his fingers and held him in her arms. "Keiran. You've grown."

Orphenn hugged her back. "So I've heard." His throat felt like sandpaper.

He felt an instant bond with Celina, just as he had with Cinder.

"He goes by Orphenn." Cinder stated.

"Orphenn!" Celina held him at arm's length. She looked at him as if she was about to tell him how horrible that name was, but thought better of it when she saw the innocence in his face. "Orphenn, then."

"I-I've lost my memory . . . . She says . . ." He wheezed.

Cinder touched his shoulder. Celina touched his cheek. "I know." She sympathized.

"Do you think . . . . That you could tell me about everything I've forgotten?" He looked at them both with pleading eyes, still in a state of disbelief. He'd never seen a place so beautiful, seen faces so beautiful as his sisters' whom he already loved deeply-a beautiful feeling he never thought he could feel.

"There isn't much we could tell you about what *you* remember." Said Celina.

"But we can tell you everything we know until Sven arrives." Cinder offered.

"But we will tell you nothing until you've had a bath."

"And a change of clothes."

"And a haircut. It's very unruly."

"And some medication. You look peeked."

"And some food. You're a bit thin."

Orphenn smiled, for the first time since . . . He couldn't even remember.

Orphenn felt wonderful. He was clean, and for once he didn't smell like an orphanage or a garbage can. Or a feral cat for that matter. Celina lent him a fresh linen bathrobe until his tailored jumpsuit was completed. His hair had been nicely styled-long in the front, short and spiked in the back, with a long rattail trailing down his back. He was given effective herbs to help his aching head and bones (which were pretty badly battered by his trip through dimensions) and as he sat by the hearth in a cushy wingback chair, he was served a decadent meal by a pair of white-aproned chamber maids.

Celina sat in another chair across from him, Cinder in another beside him.

"How are you feeling?" One of the maids asked politely.

"Lovely," He replied with his mouth full.

"Your suit should be ready by morning," said the other maid, "pity, though. That bathrobe does wonders for you." She winked.

Orphenn swallowed, and cleared his throat, blushing. "I've never felt so pampered." He said. "Your work ethic is definitely efficient."

"Thank you, Young Prince." They said in complete unison with a low curtsy, before hopping out the door, giggling the whole way down the hall.

Celina grinned widely. "You're quite the charmer aren't you?"

Cinder smiled too. "Flirt."

He ignored their mocking and asked, "Why did they call me 'Young Prince?'"

"Well, you are the brother of the Supreme Commander. What else are they supposed to call you?"

Um, how'bout my name? He thought. "I don't know. Anything but *Young Prince*. I feel like Bambi. Wait . . ." He pondered. "*Supreme Commander?*"

Celina nodded. "That I am."

So that's what the coronet stood for. Celina was a political leader of some kind. Supreme Commander . . . Orphenn pondered. *Sounds so . . . Supreme.*

Orphenn tried to hold back an imminent yawn, but pitifully failed. No amount of herbal tea could hide his exhaustion. He rubbed his eyes.

"Let's get you to your chambers, little brother." Celina said, noticing his drooping eyelids. "Come with me."

"Huh?" He drowsily stood from the chair and began to walk with Celina down the white hallway.

"Goodnight, Cinder." Celina waved.

"'Night." Cinder replied. And as Celina and Orphenn exited, she stared reminiscently into the fireplace.

"No, but wait . . ." Orphenn protested as they padded along the marble. "You were going to tell me . . ."—A yawn broke his sentence—". . . About everything."

The two ascended a tall spiral staircase to the next floor, and trod across the wide open landing to Orphenn's new bedroom.

"All in good time, Keir-Orphenn." She stumbled, remembering his new name. "All in good time." She patted his shoulder, and unlatched the door, easing her brother inside.

The room was decorated fully in white, silver, and ashy gray, with accents of pastel blue. The four-poster bed looked incredibly appealing beneath the half-moon shaped stained glass window, set high on the wall.

"Sweet dreams." Celina wished, softly closing the door as she left.

She stood in the hallway for a moment, until she heard the muffled growl of a motorcycle engine.

Cinder's eyes watered from forgetting to blink while staring into the flames. Her eyelids fluttered as she rose form her seat, and strode out the door, down the hall, and into the night.

When she reached her bike and started it, she took a moment to reach into her jacket. From it, she produced a wooden-framed photo. It was a picture of the Avari family.

Mother and father, triplets, and one other son.

"I never knew you were so nostalgic." Celina noted. She had subtly come to the bottom step, beside Cinder's idling vehicle.

Cinder started, but only slightly. "Celina. I didn't see you there." She stuffed the frame quickly back into her jacket. Then she killed the engine to let Celina speak.

"Why are you leaving again?" She demanded. "For God's sake, you only just got here! Why don't you stay?"

Cinder stammered. "I just-I don't know. I guess it seems kind of like tradition now. Out there on the road, just me and the gang."

"Tradition? To visit for a bit then disappear for a few more years? What about Keiran? Won't you stay for him?" Celina looked ready to cry, even beg on her knees if she had to.

Cinder fiddled with her chains, then gave a relenting sigh.

"Okay." She stepped off her bike. "For Keiran."

Celina smiled, teary-eyed.

Chapter Three

~

The Day Star

Gelina woke at the break of dawn, just before the trill of the tower bells. She stretched in her elegant, massive white bed.

She hastily dressed, and galloped to Cinder's practically unused chambers. She broke through the double doors, not caring to knock.

To her devastation, the room was empty. Not to mention the bed sheets that were strewn haphazardly across the mattress. Cinder hadn't even had the consideration to tidy up before she ran away-which she usually did on the almost nonexistent occasions that she stayed in the palace.

Which meant it was still possible she hadn't gone yet. Celina could still catch her before she left.

She hopefully sprinted down the hall, down the stairs and out of the palace. She was filled with relief at the sight of Cinder's bike still standing at the steps. She shaded her eyes with her hand to squint across the square.

There she was. She was standing below the monument with a tall man with long crimson hair, a scarred face, and tears in his eyes.

Orphenn was having his usual dreams-but this time, strangely more vivid. He could see two of the angels clearly now: Cinder and Celina. But the third was still a blurry silhouette along the skyline. He relived the experiences of the previous day, mainly Cinder's calm voice. Random bits of what she'd said to him reverberated through his subconscious.

>   *You'll see when we get there . . . .*
> *He'll help you remember . . . . Maybe you'll demonstrate . . . .*
>   *. . . . Our eyes should be proof enough.*
>   *Nobody's normal . . . . Promise.*

Home.

Home.

Orphenn? You doing okay Orphenn?
        Orphenn. Get up.
                He's here, wake up.

"Orphenn!"

"Wha-huh?" Orphenn shot awake, almost butting heads with Cinder in the process. Cinder laughed, holding him steady. "Sven's here."

Orphenn rubbed his eyes and smiled, bubbling with excitement. She said before that this Sven would help him remember. Now that he was absolutely sure this whole adventure was not the result from the bottom of his vodka bottle, he was so ready to remember.

Celina let herself in through the already open double doors, holding a bundle of leather. She threw it to him, and as he caught it, she said, "Your suit's ready. Try it on."

Orphenn met his sisters in the parlor. When he entered, they nearly squealed in delight.

"Orphenn!" Celina cooed, "You look strapping!"

"Yeah!" Cinder agreed, "You look like my Baby Brother again, instead of a little homeless boy!"

His suit was black and gray leather, and expertly tailored. Even *he* thought he looked good. He thought he looked like something from a Matrix movie.

And then he noticed the tall man at the fireplace, with his back to the rest of the room. He wore a long, high-collared, black trench coat. It was then that Orphenn realized: "I miss my trench coat." Without realizing he had said it out loud.

The man chuckled, turning to face Orphenn. He had deep crimson hair that was shoulder length and slicked back, the ends frayed and spiking out around the base of his neck. There was a loose strand that rested on the bridge of his nose. His face had sharp, hawk-like features, and pointed ears, accented by a wide scar that stretched across the right side of his face, starting at his jaw line, painted across his right eye and splitting his highly arched eyebrow. "So this is the Orphenn I've heard so much about." He assumed, stepping closer. His voice was deep and grumbly, like boots on gravel. His pale skin was covered in other scars, pointed ears like an elf, and his eyes were harsh, like they could bore through steel. His split-pupiled eye was a black that matched his trench coat and the slitted one a snake-like yellow.

Orphenn nodded. "And you're Sven?"

Sven's scar cracked his smile. He had sharply pointed canines.

Orphenn was not intimidated by Sven, for the sole reason that he was overwhelmed with eagerness. He stomped closer and gazed hopefully up at the striking man. "You can help me remember?" The boy nearly shouted, never taking his eyes from Sven's.

Sven's frightening disposition abruptly changed. Now he smiled with an air of kindness. "How can I deny that face?" He said.

Orphenn suppressed the urge to do a happy dance, and waited.

Cinder and Celina watched, grinning, arm in arm, as Sven pressed his palms to the sides of Orphenn's head, thumbs meeting at the boy's brow. He looked in the teenager's eyes with the commanding force of a god, reaching into his memories and breaking the chains that bound them.

When Sven's eyes shut, Orphenn's opened wide. He didn't see what was before his eyes, only what was being liberated in his mind.

He drew in a sharp breath. Memories and flashbacks were flowing across his vision like someone had opened the flood gate in his brain.

He remembered so many things at the same time, countless things-already his head was prone to burst.

He remembered his old house, his parents, his favorite toys. A familiar flash of space and stars, the Earth.

He remembered the third angel. She was beautiful. She was the third identical sister. She, Cinder, and Celina were triplets, and she was the youngest. He remembered her name. Cira.

He remembered being in Aleida before, years ago. He remembered a sparkling river. It was colorful-he remembered thinking it was like diamond water, comparing it to the rainbow colors in a puddle of oil in the parking lot. He remembered drinking the water.

And then nothing.

Orphenn staggered backward. It happened so fast, so much to take in at once. He began to ramble, his head throbbing. "Ugh . . . The third . . . Angel . . . Cira . . ." His eyes clamped shut, brows furrowed, pulling at his hair. "Sam . . ." He felt a hand grasp his wrist, and he jerked away from his fit, blinking.

"I'm sorry." Someone said.

His vision dripped back.

He had fallen to a sitting position on the floor, Sven holding one of his hands, and both his sisters holding the other.

"I know it's a lot to take in." Sven grumbled, "You had quite the stash crammed back there, kiddo."

Orphenn shook his head to clear his thoughts. "I remember you!" He looked at his sisters joyously. "And I remember you, Sven . . ." For some reason he felt a bit like Dorothy in Kansas again. "I saw you with Celina, by a big tree once . . . ." He stared off absently. "I remember Mom and Dad. Mom always smelled like lavender and her clothes were always warm . . . ." He gave Cinder and Celina an intense glance. "I remember Cira."

The two looked almost hurt.

Orphenn gasped in realization. "She's the one that spoke to me in the alley . . . . She wanted me to sleep . . . ." He gasped again, face puzzled. "Why isn't she in the monument outside the palace? Where is she?" He finally grew silent, but neither of them replied.

Sven at last said, "Looks like we got a little story to tell 'ya."

"Where do we start?" Asked Cinder incredulously.

"The beginning, perhaps?" Sven chimed.

"I can show him everything." Celina reminded.

"That's right." Sven nodded. "Forgot about that gift you have."

"What was it again?" Cinder inquired, "That television one?"

"If you'd visit more often, you'd know what it was called." Celina retorted with her nose in the air.

Orphenn began to feel a tad left out. He had seen an amazing ability from two of the three people there with him. Cinder could create and travel through portals; Sven had the gift to reach into someone's memory, and Celina was about to brandish her power. No one had seen yet what the orphan could do. But he practiced his patience. Now, it was story time.

"I call it Dreamfasting, or Memoryfasting." Celina informed. "I need only to touch you."

As the group helped Orphenn to his feet in order to join hands in a circle, Cinder noted, "You know Celina, when you're not being totally annoying, you do make things a lot easier."

Just as she ended her comment, the parlor room around them spun into nothing, a children's play park taking its place.

Orphenn could smell the wood chips, the grass, feel the breeze through his hair. It was almost like they were there, inside Celina's memory. It was precisely as she described it. She was *showing* him the story.

"*We lived on Earth.*" Celina's voice came to their ears slowly, like they all were underwater, yet it reverberated, like they were in a tunnel.

Three young girls, maybe ten or eleven years old, faded into view. They were playing on a see-saw, one on either side, the third in the middle. They all had the same glacial blue eyes, and their mother had obviously dressed them up to match that day. Orphenn couldn't tell the difference between them.

"*How precious.*" Sven's voice echoed like a rock thrown into a cave.

"*On this day, our lives would change forever.*" Said Celina.

The sun was low in the sky. Its light seemed to spiral and swirl, until a figure began to form from the rays.

A glimmering woman made of bright orange light slowly flowed toward the triplets, every movement she made correct, and fluid. She had robes of golden light, and eyes like shining topaz. A sparkling trail of dust followed her every motion. She looked like some Greek goddess.

The sisters were frozen by awe. They looked on in fear, but also in reverence. She was the most beautiful thing that had ever come to their eyes.

Her hair and her robes appeared to float, as if the laws of gravity did not apply to her.

When she spoke, her words were like molten gold. "There is something I need your help with."

"What is it?" Asked the bravest sister.

"It is my daughter. Your Mother Earth."

"Is she sick?"

"And in grave danger." The being of light kneeled to the girls' level.

"In danger of what?" Asked the sweet sister.

The sun maiden pointed to the sky. It was the Day Star, as the sisters had named it. It was so bright, it didn't have to be dark to see it twinkling against the sky.

"The Day Star?"

"She is a very powerful star. And she is very angry. She is about to die. And when she does, Earth will die with her. More of us as well."

"You mean a Supernova?" Asked the most intelligent sister. "A star at the end of it's life cycle could take out an entire galaxy!"

"Her death could mark the end of the Celestial Family." Said Mother Sun.

As the sisters began to look worried, Celina came in: "*She assured us there was a way to save the planet. When we asked how, the sun set and she was gone.*"

Mother Sun gazed behind her, and she faded away with the setting sun.

Celina continued. "*When the sun disappeared behind the mountains there was a strange flash of white. Our bodies were wracked with pain.*"

The three little girls were writhing in agony, wood chips flying.

"*What did she do?*" Orphenn demanded. "*Why did she hurt you?*"

"*She started everything. She gifted us.*"

Screaming, the sisters began to sprout wings.

"*We mutated.*"

Blood and black feathers lay among the wood chips.

"*At the last breath of twilight, we heard her whisper. 'Save her.' She said.*"

The memory faded, and the scene changed. They were now floating high over Staten Island, sky above, ocean below. The girls were practicing their gifts.

"*We all were gifted with flight. I had gentle powers of telekinesis and some telepathy.*"

The triplet that was absolutely Celina burst from the ocean and flew to the other two, ripping the oxygen mask from her mouth.

"*Cira was gifted with fire. She was telepathic and telekinetic as I was, but much more powerful, having one of the elements on her side. She also had frequent premonitions and was a talented psychic.*"

Random hunks of metal, plastic and wood floated around young Cira—objects her mind was moving, like puppets on strings. Flames licked up her arm and formed a ball of fire above the palm of her hand.

"*Cinder had . . .*"

Celina and Cira turned on the other, synchronized. Celina's scuba equipment shattered to pieces of sharp metal to mingle with Cira's sharp-looking collection of debris, hers happening to be on fire, and they aimed their elements at Cinder, and in unison they hurled blazing fire and metal at their sister.

"*I guess . . . Everything in between.*"

Performing an aerial spin, Cinder's body twisted into nothing and out of sight, dodging the attack. She reappeared fluttering between the other two, startling them. They laughed, the Day Star shining brightly over their heads.

"*She could disappear and reappear in the blink of an eye. Only later did we recognize it as teleporting between dimensions. She could even port to the other side of the world and come back seconds later.*

"*It had been a few months since these gifts were 'bestowed' upon us. We hadn't told anyone what we could do. And we never did.*

"*A few years passed. There were days when we worried about the Day Star, and thought about Mother Sun. But nothing ever happened.*

"*Until the twilight on the eve of our seventeenth birthday. We saw her again.*"

"*I remember. She had touched my shoulder. She was so warm.*" Cinder added.

"*Yes. She had told us only that 'It was time.' And pointed to the Day Star.*"

Cinder began again. "*My sisters were confused at first, but Mother Sun looked at me, and I knew what to do.*

"*The sun set. I took Cira and Celina by the arms and ported, with the Day Star at the forefront of my mind.*

"*In a split second, it had grown completely silent. We could breathe, and we felt fine. Just has Cira had predicted: Mother Sun had protected us from the cold outside the sanctity of the Earth's atmosphere.*

"*Then we saw her.*"

Everything they described played out like a cinema all around them.

"*She was massive.*" Celina said. "*And beautiful. We looked, and for once we didn't see Earth as a planet. We saw her as a living, breathing entity with a visible pulse.*"

Sven and Orphenn looked at it, and saw it just as they had seen it. Celina was right. You automatically, almost instinctively fell in love with her. It was like feeling a growing baby's heartbeat for the first time and already knowing you loved her.

"*It made us want to protect her even more.*"

Cinder started again. "*We planned on trying to attack the Day Star, who was now a raging supernova, growing brighter by the second.*"

The Day Star appeared to be a woman like Mother Sun, except she shone a hot, frightening white. Her liquid face contorted in anger. She appeared to be very slowly straddling her way towards Earth.

"*But there were things Mother Sun could never have protected us from. There is no oxygen out there. Fire needs oxygen to live. Cira was useless without her flame. There was nothing for my sisters to hurl with telekinesis, and the angry thing had no mind that Cira could read.*"

Orphenn spotted Celina motioning to Cinder in the memory, panic in her eyes.

"Celina had an idea. I tried porting to find any random chunk of ice to use to her advantage, as some sort of weapon. It shattered when she tried to use it. It was then that I tried a new trick, at the last minute."

Cinder performed what looked like a mastered Kung Fu move, bringing the heels of her hands together in front of her, and holding her hands open like the jaws of a crocodile.

Day Star's last thread of life looked about to snap, just as a sort of wisping darkness like black fog stormed from Cinder's claw-like hands. It acted like a black whirlpool, even darker than the starry abyss around them. It submerged Day Star, as if billions of dark hands grasped her and overwhelmed her. The darkness absorbed her, and she was gone with the portal. Earth was safe.

Where did she go? What did you do? Cira had asked. She had sent the thought to Cinder's mind, as speech cannot be heard without air. Cinder answered with another thought.

I ported her. She's exploded now, somewhere far away.

There was a moment of cold, absolute silence for the death of the Day Star.

Celina wants to know where you learned that. Cira smirked.

"I ported us home just in time for our birthday party." Cinder said proudly.

"When we got there, we had the usual party-presents, cake, ice cream." Celina interjected. *"But the real present was a surprise for after all the guests left."*

"Mom and Dad had told us a secret." Cinder intoned. *"Nine months later, we had the most beautiful little secret we ever could have asked for."*

Celina directed her words at Orphenn. *"You were born on October twenty-fourth."*

She showed a memory of the infant Orphenn in their mother's arms, with the triplets and their father surrounding the hospital bed, close at her sides.

"They've all been in there for a long time, haven't they?" Xeila noted.

"Well," Jeremiah reasoned, "you've heard the rumors. They've got their long lost *brother* in there."

"Sure, but they've also got Dad in there. I need to talk to him. And Celina has an urgent visitor."

"The visitor can wait. And so can you."

"You said that about marrying me too. Look where *that* got us." Xeila clutched the doorknob.

"Wait. Don't be rude, Xeila-"

She flung open the door.

Chapter Four

~

The Big Picture

Celina, Cinder, Sven and Orphenn stood in a circle on the floor, hands joined, eyes closed. Sven had a loving smile, like he was having a pleasant dream, and the others had tears coming like waterfalls.

At the sound of the door slamming the wall upon opening, Celina's eyes jolted open, red and swollen from crying. The others did the same, barely managing to keep from shouting in surprise at the sudden change in environment. The instant Celina's eyes opened, the group tumbled back into the parlor, as if the memory were a carpet tugged out from underneath them.

Standing in the doorway before them were a man and a woman. The man was tall, with long blonde dreadlocks, the top layer bound in a ponytail. One eye was a hazel that exactly matched the color of his hair, and the other was slitted and soft violet. The woman was russet-skinned with a shock of white hair, feathered and layered, its length just brushing her jaw line. Her hair was brighter than the white of Denoras, though she was anything but old. Like Sven, she had long pointed ears, fanged incisors and black and gold eyes. "Dad, I have to talk to you." She stepped inside to stand by Sven.

"Pardon the intrusion," Jeremiah beseeched, to compensate for the woman's rashness, though his manners went nearly unnoticed.

"Yes?" Sven replied, almost sadly. "What is it, Poppet? You get any news?"

"No, nothing." She shook her white head.

Sven is a father? Orphenn pondered incredulously.

"By the way, Xeila," Celina stood tall beside Orphenn, who was even taller. "I've been meaning to thank you. If it weren't for your mission—"

Xeila stopped her. "I didn't find my sister. I didn't accomplish anything." She lamented. Sven blinked slowly.

"On the contrary, my friend." Cinder countered. "Thanks to you, we've found our brother." She rose to stand beside Celina, and yanked Orphenn to stand closer to her side.

Sven and Xeila now stood straighter, as if in respect.

"You're very popular among the chamber maids." Jeremiah interjected, traipsing into their circle. "You're Orphenn, right?"

Orphenn flushed and nodded, shaking his hand.

"I'm Jeremiah. And the rude brown one here is my fiancé, Xeila."

The Rude Brown One nudged him in the side. "Well, I'm glad for that, at least. That I could help in some way."

"I promise we'll get Pigey back." Sven said to her. "Don't beat yourself up."

Xeila nodded, swallowing back the lump in her throat. Then she looked at Celina. "Chairman Matthias gave me the message to tell you that you have a visitor waiting for you on the top floor. He says it's urgent."

Celina nodded acknowledgement.

Xeila turned with Jeremiah toward the door, but stopped to reach for Sven. "Daddy?" She invited.

Sven gave a weak smile. He tapped Orphenn's forehead. "Catch 'ya later, squirt."

With Jeremiah and Sven on either arm, Xeila left the room.

"I suppose I should see who's waiting for me." Celina said after a brief pause. Then she left as well, leaving Cinder and Orphenn alone in the parlor.

Orphenn leaned up against the fireplace mantle. "I had no idea Sven was a father." The thought of parents still sped up his heartbeat, especially at the realization that he could remember his own now. He knew they were gone, that he'd never see them again. But already he felt a filial bond with Sven, and at the same time felt guilty for it. He could feel the tears in his eyelids once again, and he chastised himself for being so emotional. He turned his back to Cinder and swallowed hard, restraining his laments.

Cinder grinned, happily. "And he's a damn good one too. He was all they had when their mother was killed." Her smile faded, remembering. "He reminds me so much of our Dad."

Orphenn sensed the danger of sentiment in her words. *I'm such a baby*, he thought as he quickly changed the subject to avoid a sappy speech, his strong front already delicate. "Who is 'Pigey?'" He raised an inquisitive eyebrow, spinning to face Cinder.

"Huh?" She gave him a curious look. "Oh. What Sven said? It's Pigeon. A nickname for his youngest daughter. Eynochia is her name. She's been missing for at least a week now. I only found out this morning when I spoke to Sven at the monument."

"Ah." Orphenn comprehended. "That's why he had such a . . . . Sadness about him. Even as he called me 'squirt' he seemed . . . . Tired."

Rammes Cain stood staring through the window pane at the downpour. He felt undermined. He was sure the Master thought herself more important to the cause than she believed him to be, when it was his ideas and meticulous planning that started that war years ago! His own brilliance. Ardara would have won if not for those creatures.

He thought, maybe he should break the partnership. Though his affiliate would spit fire if he ever brought up the notion. But he knew he didn't want to share what was left of Ardara's power with her any longer.

He needed a plan. With Master Ardara out of the way, the once great nation and conquest could rise again without hindrance.

Another thought came to his head. *She does seem to like wine. A drop or two of arsenic in her glass should do the trick. And those henchman of hers as well. Especially that favorite one, Dacian. I never liked him.*

"Oh, I'm afraid that wouldn't work out so well." Ardara's laughter was like a feathery whisper.

Rammes spun around with a start.

She stood there, dressed in revealing maroons and violets, and hooded, with black hair that hung in her face, and eyes like scorching blue daggers.

Dacian stood behind her, smugly leaning against the doorframe.

Rammes hated him. That arrogant look on his face, his one red eye.

"Don't you find it annoying when she hears your thoughts?" Rammes hissed at him.

"I would," Dacian shrugged, "if she did."

Ardara began to pace, high heels thumping the floor. "You see, Rammes-even if you did carry out your cute little assassination plan, it wouldn't have succeeded. Not only would Dacian have smelled the poison long before you had the chance to use it, but, also thanks to Dacian, I am, like him, immune to poison. Isn't that odd?"

"So do plan to kick me out? I won't succumb so casily. It's *me* that wants to leave *you*." Rammes defied.

"I want things back the way they used to be." She said lightly, yet viscously. "When Ardara had full control."

"You're so obsessed." He spat. "You were full enough of yourself to name our entire campaign after yourself. Now-"

"Actually," she interrupted, "I named *myself* after the *conquest*. I thought up the name over a glass of stolen wine, and decided it fit me better than my birth name. Though I bet you're correct about the obsession bit."

"You're insane."

"Anyhow, the point is, Rammes Cain, that *you* were never part of the *big picture*." She widely gesticulated, arms out as if a great window were plastered across the middle distance.

"You have no idea what you're talking about. You were *weak*. That's why our campaign failed."

"*Your cowardice sent our plans into ruin!*" She began to grow angry. "That, and the people of Verlassen had a secret weapon.

"The Enma," he chastised, "were severely outnumbered. We butchered them. There was no way they could've won, but they did. I never understood it."

"No, you didn't, because you ran away before you could see the beings that helped them!" She screeched.

"What?"

"They were *huge*, like massive clouds of light that rained down from the sky! Oh, how they swept across the battlefield-you should have *seen* it. It took *seconds*. *That's* the power I want . . . With it . . . Anything is possible."

"Is this really wise?" Rammes mused. "Disclosing all your plans to me? When I could be a potential enemy . . . ?" As he said this, he subtly drifted backward, to take up a firearm from his desk. He pointed the revolver at Ardara.

She cackled, stalking closer.

"Don't be a fool, Rammes Cain."

"It's a bit late for that." Dacian snorted.

Rammes pulled the trigger.

Ardara only flicked her eyes at it, and the bullet froze in the air. She idly stared at its silver casing, then her eyes abruptly jolted back to Rammes, sending the bullet darting back at him. It submerged itself in his abdomen. He gave an earsplitting shriek, and the gun fell from his hand.

Ardara held out her palm and the gun was brought to her grip before it hit the ground, like her mind had attached a string to it and she was the puppet master. As soon as the revolver floated to her hand she cocked it, and with three more shots, she ended the life of Rammes Cain. Though she fired seven more times.

When the shots stopped, her eyes were crazed, but she calmed herself. "Damn." She breathed dismissively. "I got a bit carried away. I would have preferred to electrocute him. Ah, well." She shrugged, dropping the emptied gun to the floor. She willed Rammes's lifeless body to levitate above the floor, and it did so, dripping with blood, with only a flash of her eyes. And with a swish of her hand, the body was tossed out an open window. "You are dismissed."

Ardara relaxed her mind when she reached the throne room. There was a huge window behind the looming throne, letting in what little light there was in this land. "Now," she exhaled, sinking into the plush of her throne cushions, "it's time to try again. Bind the girl." She said to Dacian. "Make certain she does not interrupt me again."

Dacian complied, turning to the iron cage that lay beside Ardara's throne. Crouched inside was a silver-haired girl with skin like the shell of an almond. Her clothes were in tatters, and she hid her face in her arms, rocking back and fourth, even though the cage wasn't locked, or even shut. In fact, it was wide open.

Dacian clutched the girl's wrists and brought her forcefully out of the cage. She never struggled, only scowled as Dacian chained her arms to shackles that hung from the towering ceiling, her waist to the wall, and her ankles to the floor. Her black and green eyes burned with hatred.

Ardara began to stretch her mind, closing her eyes. "I do have one thing to thank you for . . . . Pigeon. Lovely pet name." She said to the unresponsive prisoner. "You did remind me to take care of some political business." Now she held her hands out before her, as if waiting to touch something, though she stayed in one place.

Orphenn felt a headache coming on.

"Now to ensure you don't go into one of your fits again." Dacian murmured to Pigeon, lifting her chin so she looked straight at him. He parted his lips slightly and drew closer as if to kiss her, but instead, a noxious black vapor misted from his mouth. He breathed it out, and it seeped into her mouth and nose. He pulled away when her mismatched eyes rolled back. He released her jaw, and without the support of his hand, her head fell to her shoulder, her body going limp in the chains.

"I hope you haven't killed her," warned Ardara, still entranced, "I am *not* fond of her father."

"Just a sedative." Dacian laughed.

Ardara stood slowly and her fingers curled, like she had taken hold of something invisible.

Orphenn's head throbbed, then he felt a strange smack, like someone had clapped a pair of symbols next to his head, their resonance knocking him to the floor.

Ardara fell backward onto her wide throne, like someone had shoved her. The hood slipped off her head as she landed, rubbing her head as if suffering from a migraine.

"Are you okay?" Cinder worried when Orphenn collapsed.

"Yes, I'm fine . . . . Just this weird . . . . Head thing . . . . Kind of dizzy . . . ."

"Let's head over to the infirmary. You might still need to recover."

Ardara shrieked infuriately, huffing to her feet. Dacian was already beside her.

"What happened?" He demanded.

"It's that *vermin's* fault!" She jabbed an accusing finger at the unconscious girl hanging from her chains. "I was too late. Sven's already gotten to him and shielded his mind from me, just as he's done with every other Enma he could get his hands on . . . . I hate that man . . . ." She almost whispered. "And not only that . . . . I'm deathly afraid of him."

"Why?" Dacian scarcely remembered her admitting her faults. She always wore a façade of fearlessness.

"He could do horrible, unthinkable things to a psychic mind such as mine . . . . Things I don't even want to imagine. I want to lock him up with his stupid brother." Her eyes were wide with realization. "And even scarier than *that* . . . . I feel I am strangely attracted to him."

"You really have lost it this time, Master."

She flashed an enlightened grin. "I've just had an epiphany. I need you to take advantage of your gift. Find me the source of the Enma's power. I will achieve my goal soon enough."

"So tell me about your mission, Poppet." Sven said. "What did you think of Ardara?"

Xeila was reluctant to answer as they halted beside a tall column near the palace steps. "That's what I wanted to talk to you about." Jeremiah held her hand as she spoke: "The place is a wasteland. The woman's a psycho. You know what happened with her-I heard her talking to someone, though she was totally alone. She said out loud where a boy named Keiran was, though I didn't know who he was at the time. I told Celina, and that's how she found him, and told Cinder to bring him here.

"In Ardara's throne room, there was something-sounded like a dog yipping and growling and carrying on, and I was sure it was Eynochia."

"Of course it was." Sven remarked. "She would know your scent anywhere. Even with your chameleon gift, she knew you were there. Didn't matter none that you were invisible." His certainty comforted Xeila, even though he hadn't been there with her in the castle.

Her face grew sad. "I could have taken her and left, I could have rescued her. But I had let my guard down." She paused to pull her hand from Jeremiah's, and slip out of her jacket. Now that her arms and neck were visible, the other two could see that a large, nauseatingly colorful bruise was forming up her right arm, neck and chest. The tone of her skin made it seem even more gruesome. "But I didn't see Dacian coming up behind me." She snarled just as Sven did at the mere thought of Dacian.

"He hurt you!" Sven jeered. "*I'll kill 'im.*"

"How could he have attacked you?" Jeremiah cut in fiercely. "Weren't you in your stealth state? How did he see you?"

"He must have seen that tiny refraction my body gives off to the camouflage . . . . That's all I can think of." Xeila concluded. "He threw dust at me and saw where I was. He only touched my neck."

"And it did *that?* We're going to the infirmary this instant, Xeila. That man is *toxic.*" Jeremiah took her jacket and her arm, starting to walk her back up the steps. He looked back. "You comin' Pops?"

Sven was gazing intently up at a top floor window. It was wide open, and the drapes swayed with the breeze.

"Go on up without me."

Orphenn and Cinder were in the infirmary when Jeremiah and Xeila arrived. Orphenn had a tall glass of water, nearly spilling it when he saw Xeila.

"Oh my God! Wha—"

The door swung open again, beholding an even bigger problem than Xeila's injury. Orphenn nearly collapsed again, and this time, he did spill the water. The glass shattered when he dropped it.

It was Sven, with a bleeding Celina dangling in his arms.

Chapter Five

~

Enma

She was bleeding from her eyes, her nose, her mouth. She was pale, and she looked thin, and limp. Her black wings hung down, the tips of her feathers brushing the floor. Sven folded them gently to her back and set her down on the closest bed, moving her hair from her bloodied face as the others swarmed around them.

The medic pushed her way to the bedside as Sven lightly removed the coronet from Celina's forehead.

Orphenn and Cinder too stricken to speak, Xeila and Jeremiah gaping, they clung like magnets to the bedside.

"What happened?" Cried the panicky medic.

Sven almost screamed. "It was that *traitor!* Again! That filthy, vile, traitor! I swear, it seems like he's *bent* on hurting me, though I doubt he even knows!" With a raging cry he turned away, with his scarred face in his hands. "I'll kill him. *I'm going to kill him.*"

"Traitor? What traitor?" The medic questioned ignorantly.

"Dacian." Sven, Xeila, Cinder and Jeremiah all hissed in unison, leaving the medic and Orphenn clueless.

No more was said.

It had been a few hours. The medic came in occasionally to check on Celina. Orphenn still had no idea why she was hurt. She had stopped bleeding, but was still very pale. Sven, Xeila and Jeremiah sat together on a bed across the room, conversing. Orphenn sat on a stool by Celina's bed, Cinder seated on another bed to the back of him.

Celina breathed slowly. Her eyes were sunken and darkly circled, and her skin was pasty white. Her red-stained robe had been exchanged for a gray infirmary gown.

"I want to go back." Xeila whispered. "I want to try again."

"No, Xeila." Said Jeremiah, who was seated behind her, rubbing an antitoxin cream onto her bruised skin.

"You'll get your chance, Poppet." Sven assured.

Orphenn held Celina's hand, and laid his head on the bed, remembering a time back on Earth, when he had had a nightmare. Celina had let him sleep in her bed with her. He relished the memory, now even more grateful to Sven for liberating his mind. "You never finished your story." He informed both her, and Cinder.

This caught the others' attention. "Why don't we continue, then?" Sven suggested.

"Where did we leave off?" Cinder said.

Orphenn closed his eyes. "I was born."

She resumed immediately.

"Cira, as you know, could see the future-not voluntarily-she couldn't control the premonitions she had.

"A few years after you were born, her visions became more frequent. She was constantly suffering from headaches and nightmares."

Orphenn recalled waking up to Cira's screaming one night and traveling to her bedroom to investigate, but his mother had arrived before him and ordered him to go back to sleep.

"Her visions began to show her things she didn't want to see. She told me about it once, when she had woken up screaming again. She said she kept dreaming about people hurting-being tortured, burned, struck by lightening, crushed by boulders. They showed her nothing but death and pain. Later I would find out her dreams were also glimpses of the future.

"One night I found her crouched in the corner of her bedroom, rocking back and fourth, muttering to herself. Her wings were splayed out. We typically used a cloaking ability to hide them, so this was unusual."

So that's why my wings were only seen when I wanted them to be. Orphenn thought. *I had an ability I never knew about.*

"When she saw me, she stood up, and glared at me. She didn't look like my sister. The moment she started to speak, I knew she had gone insane, honestly mad. She kept saying that she'd seen another world, and that someone named Ardara was telling her she needed to conquer it. She trailed off about it, saying Ardara wanted her to kill Earth. She wanted me to come with her, to be her partner. She said we would be the most powerful beings in that world, that it would be a fast, simple takeover. I asked her, 'What about Celina?' She said we would make do without her. Her eyes were crazed, and violent. It scared me. I tried to talk sense into her, but she refused to listen and started in with, 'You don't love me,' 'I'm alone. None but Ardara understand me.'

"Electricity shot from her hands-the lightening power she'd mastered. It jolted all up the walls and ceiling, and the power through the whole house went out. When Celina came to investigate, we started to smell smoke. The area surrounding Cira caught fire, and soon the whole room was ablaze.

"We ran from her, even though she was only slowly walking toward us. Something about her was just so . . . . Menacing.

"I was grateful, at the time, thinking our parents had gone out that night. I remember you were at your friend's house near Time Square . . . ." Orphenn was shocked-he remembered too. His friend's name was Brenna. He wondered if she remembered him.

"We rushed outside, and she calmly came out the front door after us, like nothing at all was wrong. Her face was blank, but again, I could tell by her eyes that she was enraged. With just a wave of her arm, the entire house exploded. There was a huge cloud of fire. I had no choice but to port all of us away to escape the blast.

"But Cira had known that I would do exactly that. She forced a thought into my mind. As I only have to think about a place to teleport to it, this turned our course onto a completely different path.

"We saw the solar system pass us by like hyper speed, then the galaxy, and billions of stars, until we reached a planet so much like Earth, it was hard to tell the difference with just your eyes. It was called Verlassen.

"We landed in a courtyard, outside a city. It was the capital of the most powerful country in this world, the Verlassen Empire, which had entire control of the planet, apart from one little wasteland. Cira knew just where to go. She ran away from us. I tried to run after her, but Celina stopped me. 'Find Keiran.' She said. So I ported back to Earth to retrieve you and bring you here. We thought if we used you to persuade her, she would come to her senses-she loved you so much . . . ."

Orphenn's eyes began to sting with the beginnings of tears, remembering when Cira would read him story books when Mom was away, complete with all the different voices and enthusiasm.

"The plan didn't work. And Cira nearly killed you. She was blinded by rage and madness.

"We had no choice but to run. We stayed one night hiding in the wilderness outside the capital city. The next morning we were woken by gunshot. We only just escaped the men that pursued us, who called themselves 'Ardarans.' We later discovered that Cira had gained the loyal support of that country's power-hungry leader: Rammes Cain. In what seemed like only hours, the Ardarans started raiding neighboring lands and conquered them easily with the power of Cira's gifts, and the power of Rammes's military. In days, they together, literally, had taken over the world.

"In the days that followed, there was nothing but war. In the midst of hiding, Celina and I found ourselves in the center of a battlefield putting us and you in immediate danger. The only escape route was a shortcut through a calm river. It was hidden in the dense surrounding thickets and no one caught us. The river sparkled with color, and its water was warm. We drank our fill from it."

"I remember that!" Orphenn announced, immersed in the story.

Cinder nodded and continued. "But before, in the chaos, I had been wounded-shot through at least three times. I couldn't stand keeping you in such danger any longer. I used the last of my energy to take you back to Earth.

"My first intention was to leave you with Mom and Dad, hoping they were living somewhere safe with a friend of the family. But when I focused on them and ported, with you in my arms, we were brought to the ashy remains of our old house in New York. I found their bones among the rubble.

"You were unconscious for that bit, thank God. You had passed out from the pressure of the portal. That's why you lost your memory.

"With our parents dead, and no other family, I was left with no other option but Kinder Rose orphanage.

"The boy took you in his arms like you were his brother instead of mine. It hurt. But I had to live with it. I had to hurry back to Celina. I could only tell them one thing. 'He is an orphan.' And apparently, that's what they decided to call you. I had to leave before I could give them your name. I was surprised I had the strength left to port back to Celina, back on the planet that Cira had also renamed 'Ardara.'

"I was weak, and losing power. I was dying."

Cinder's and Orphenn's eyes had been leaking tears since the bit was told of Cira's old love for Orphenn. Xeila was bawling. And so was Celina. She had finally woken.

"I was so scared for you," She said to Cinder, carefully sitting up. "I thought I would lose you after we had already lost our brother."

Cinder started again. "The both of us suddenly began to go into convulsions. Painful seizures that lasted several minutes.

"My wounds were miraculously healing, though my body was racked with pain. Our eyes changed. We found ourselves with new abilities. We had mutated for a second time."

"We discovered it was the river we drank from that had altered our DNA. After several experiments on frogs and squirrels and things." Celina added.

"Then we were so scared; you had also drunk from that river. We feared you didn't survive the mutation."

"It was then that I had an epiphany." Celina enthused. "If we could convince the remaining faithful Verlassians to drink the water, we would have a mutant army-and easily overthrow the still human Ardarans."

"This is where we come in, isn't it?" Sven interjected.

Cinder smiled. "Sven was the first to volunteer. Sadly, there were few of us. Even children had to go through mutation. But they were all successful, which gave us new hope that you had survived. Thankfully, we found that injecting the water directly into the bloodstream was much quicker and less painful than simply drinking it."

"Convenient, that they had to figure that out *after* I had to drink it." Sven griped playfully.

"We called ourselves the Enma," Celina said, "and our rebellion was named *Aleida*. In the Ancient Tongue, it translates to 'winged one.'"

"And what does '*Enma*' mean?" Orphenn queried.

"Hope." Cinder answered for her.

Celina smiled and continued. "We trained our militias in secret, perfecting the skills of each and every mutant. When they were all trained, they were organized into squadrons based on capability and skill. Only after our first few victories were we able to acquire a few airships, but that was later on.

"I was proclaimed Supreme Commander after our first victory. It was a rather epic event. Everyone wanted for both me and Cinder to lead them, from the proven success of our own leadership and strategy, but Cinder had turned them down. To this day, I don't know why she did. But I digress.

"The war against Ardara lasted six years. During that time . . . ." She paused, allowing tears to fall down her cheeks, "I was betrayed by my best friend. He was my squadron's sharpshooter. He killed my squadron, destroyed my airship, and ran to the side of Ardara. So I was forced to join Cinder's squadron. And with heavy hearts, and rapidly depleting numbers, we raged the last battle."

"Each member of my squad as well were killed in that battle." Cinder proceeded. "And we were severely outnumbered. When it seemed like the end, and we had lost all hope, there came strange lights in the sky."

"It was Mother Sun." Celina clarified. "She and the rest of the Celestial Family-Saturn, Jupiter, and so forth-came to our aid. Even Earth came, to fight for her children on Verlassen."

"Ardara was conquered at last. Sent to fester in her barren wasteland. She is in exile, though her few remaining supporters are still loyal to her. They were exiled as well."

"Then the planet was renamed for the last time."

"Aleida." Orphenn murmured. "After the battalion that saved the world."

Celina nodded. "Cinder and I were regarded as saviors and angels by all the people here-most of them who had been kept as Ardaran slaves in the war. And now, every Enma is revered and respected as an icon. A symbol of freedom.

"By these same people, I was named Queen of All the World, though I prefer to keep the title of Supreme Commander.

"Cinder and I would have shared power, but she refused. She's intent on being a drifter."

"That's beside the point here." Cinder defended.

"The point *is*," Xeila sniffed, "That Ardara is planning a comeback."

The others all listened intently.

"I heard her talking to Rammes about it." She clarified. "But I only heard something about a source. I had to retreat before I heard any more-but at the last minute I caught something like '*the Enma's power source . . . .*'"

Sven gave Celina an intense glare. "So *that's* why!" He exclaimed, bolting to his feet.

"Oh, God . . ." Celina cursed. "That's why he came."

"Who!?" Xeila squealed.

"Dacian!"

"He was *here?!*" Orphenn yelled, squeezing Celina's hand.

They all stared at Celina now.

"He beat you senseless!" Sven shouted.

"You saw it?" Roared Jeremiah.

"I got there in time for him to jump out the window and escape!"

"That bastard!"

"He barely touched me," Celina objected.

"And yet you're bleeding in a hospital bed?!" Orphenn demanded.

Celina looked at him, sad, and hurt. Orphenn realized with a shock that her eyes looked normal. They were both the same universal blue, no odd pupils, just one black orb in each iris.

"He used a new gift." She said. "He called it 'Diffusion.' He took the mutations from my blood stream, and removed them through the pores of my skin. He stole the Enma right out from my body."

Chapter Six

~

The River

Gelina slumped to the white door at the end of the hall, on the top floor of the palace. She straightened herself and took a deep breath before regally stepping inside. The face that turned to meet her drained the blood from her cheeks. "What are you doing here." It was not a question, but an order.

"Have we met?" Dacian replied seriously.

"Answer me."

"I was given a mission." He said cautiously.

"What do you mean? You're telling me you don't remember?"

"What are you babbling about? I was given a mission," he repeated. "And I shall carry it out quickly and efficiently." He produced a syringe from behind his back. "That's why I'm the favorite."

"What are you doing?" her voice wavered when he crept closer. He caressed her face. He twisted her hair. Her heart skipped a beat. So did his.

What is this? Dacian thought. In revolt, his hand clamped her shoulder, hard as granite. She whimpered.

"This is new. A skill I like to call Diffusion."

Her skin began to burn, fire in every pore. Like pasta in a strainer, Dacian pulled a substance out of her skin that glistened with life and color. It gathered in a bubble at his fingertip. He drew it into the syringe with a smug grin.

Celina coughed violently. She cried red tears and blood poured from her mouth, nose, and ears. She fell to the floor, her blood clashing with the white.

He bent over and took a handful of hair from the back of her head, her hair ribbon loosening and falling out. He tugged her head up and gazed into her red-streamed face. Her one brown eye faded to pale icy blue that matched her other. The hurt in them gave Dacian a strange feeling of guilt-something he could never recall feeling before. He hated it. In frustration, he buried his fist into her abdomen, forcing more blood from her mouth.

"Why are you doing this?" Celina gasped. The pain in her voice once again filled him will unexplained grief. In a rage, he was about to slam her face into the wall, but before he could do so, the door swung viscously open.

That intimidating man, that rigid Enma stood there with a look of absolute loathing.

Dacian released Celina's hair, and her head fell to the hard floor.

This is getting too complicated he thought. He veered around and leapt out the open window into the night, starting the engine of his hidden cruiser and zipping away.

Sven had no time to track him down. But he would. One day he would.

Sven shouted, pacing like a tiger in a cage. "That's what he had in that syringe." He concluded. "He's stolen your essence, and now he'll take it to Ardara."

"But Ardara hates Enma." Jeremiah reasoned. "She said precisely; 'disgusting, filthy, hybrids.' What would she want with Celina's essence?"

"She will do anything for power." Celina stated. "Even mutate herself."

"It's been hours." Orphenn informed. "She must have already changed by now."

Sven slumped into a chair, his face resting in his palms. "So what do we do?"

"We wait." Celina said determinedly, flipping her legs over the side of the bed and standing up. "We don't yet know what will happen." She motioned to a nurse maid to fetch her robes. "Rest assured, my friends. To this day, we are the only ones who still know where our true source is."

"Celina, lay back down, you're weak. You can't even hide your wings." Cinder warned.

"Thank you." Celina said to the maid when she returned with her white robes, calmly ignoring Cinder's order. She stepped behind a screen to change and said, "Orphenn? Would you care to talk a walk with me?"

"Certainly." Orphenn agreed, as she came back to tie her hair.

As she took her coronet from the bedside table and slipped it back on her forehead, she reached out to her brother. "Come along."

Orphenn and Celina trod through a thick forest. They walked arm in arm, as Celina needed a bit of support to stay upright.

"Are you feeling alright?" Orphenn asked, concerned. "You're a bit shaky."

"I'm just a little nervous." She answered.

"About what? Where are we going?"

"You remember the River, yes?"

"The River? The sparkly colorful one that mutated us? That's where we're going?"

"Precisely."

"And . . . . You're the only one who knows where it is?"

"Sven and Cinder and I. The only living ones that drank directly from the water, like you."

"Instead of being injected?"

"Right."

"Are you going to drink from it again?"

"I'm a bit frightened, but yes."

"Why?"

"I don't know if so many mutations to one body would hurt me, kill me . . ."

"*Whoa.*" Orphenn halted. "You've got me freaked out now."

"On the other hand, the Enma could simply return to me, like it was never taken in the first place."

"And what are the odds of *that* happening?"

"Relax." Celina said, bringing Orphenn to a steady walk again. "Besides. We're here."

"Huh? I don't see anyth-" He stopped as the trees and brush they passed unveiled a sunlit clearing. The water moved so calmly, Orphenn couldn't have heard it until he stood on the bank. He was so used to the rushing waters of the Americas-he'd never been to such a peaceful place.

The River was just like it was in his memory. "It's so colorful . . . ." He reminisced, "Like there's glittering treasure at the bottom or something. Even though you can see right through, and there's only rocks."

"I know, it's beautiful . . . ." Celina released Orphenn's arm to pad across the mossy grass to the river bank. Orphenn hurried to her side as she lowered herself into the water, folding her wings.

"I'm not so sure about this, Celina . . . ." Orphenn kneeled anxiously at the bank, gazing after her.

"Have some faith in me, Little Brother." She waded into the middle of the River, her white robe rippling after her.

Orphenn was awestruck. The light in the water seemed to swirl around her as she entered the water, almost like it was conscious of her, welcoming her.

Orphenn splashed in as well, but stayed close to the bank, fearful. The water was warm, and its luminosity also seemed to spiral around him.

Celina turned to face him. "It's like a loving cradle . . . ." She described, pooling water into her palms. ". . . . So warm." She tipped her hand up to her mouth and gulped it down.

She only gave a soft gasp as her eyes and pupils flickered, and changed subtly back to their mismatched blue and brown and odd pupils. Her wings began to fade to transparency, veiling themselves as her energy recuperated. She closed her eyes and smiled, tears falling.

"What, no seizure, no agonizing pain?" Orphenn laughed gratefully. "What happened?"

Celina took a deep breath. "Amazing . . . ." She let sunlight shine onto her face. "This planet . . . . So alike, yet so different from Earth. It remembered me . . . . It knows who I am . . . ." She dipped her finger into the water, stirring it around, and the light followed it. "It's alive, Orphenn . . . . It's alive."

When they returned to the palace, everyone still sat in the infirmary with Xeila.

Cinder sped to them when they came to the door. "Celina! Your eyes! Your wings!"

"How?" Xeila questioned.

Sven rose form his chair, looking back and fourth between Orphenn and Celina. "Did you go to . . . . ?"

"The River. Yes."

"You idiot!" Sven gently bopped her on the head. Orphenn guessed he was one of the only people that could get away with that. "Do you know how much you risked? You are so lucky you didn't die, Celina, or I woulda smacked you. Right upside the head!" He shook his head, and the whole room was smiling. "Did you get your original powers back?"

"Yes."

"Miracle."

Orphenn looked longingly at Sven's long, whooshing trench coat as they walked further into the room. Sven turned, noticing his glance with a chuckle. "Here, kid." He unbuttoned the coat, and threw it to Orphenn, revealing his bare torso. He was lean, and speckled with scars.

Orphenn bounced up and down when he put it on. It fit him surprisingly well.

"Dad, you need a shirt." Xeila chastised.

"I think not." He replied with vigor.

After a fit of laughing, Orphenn asked Celina, "Do you mind if I take a walk?"

"We just got back from a walk." She said.

"Yes, I know. But I'd like to explore a bit."

"Very well." Celina relented.

He smiled. "Thanks. And thank you for the coat, Sven."

"No problem. Don't get lost."

Thunder rolled, and dark clouds swirled around the sunless land of Ardara. The ominous castle tower stood tall, its point reaching into the eye of the storm. Lightning struck from the clouds, the shaded castle surrounded by an almost constant cage of electricity. Inside the frightening monument, Ardara herself stood waiting.

"Master." A low voice beckoned from the window.

"Dacian." She grinned, and turned to gaze up at the speaker. There was only a dim shadow, standing on the windowsill, silhouetted every time the lightning flashed. He was wet and dripping from the downpour outside, and held a peculiar glowing object.

"I found it. I found the source."

"Brilliant." She sighed, gesturing for him to step inside. As he did so, he presented his superior with a rain-dropped syringe, a luminous liquid bubbling in its tube.

Ardara gazed adoringly at Dacian, and then at the syringe. "The essence . . ." she whispered. Her eyes fixed on it as she took it into her shaking hands, its light illuminating her pale skin. She ran her finger up the thin needle. She clutched it tightly, and closed her eyes, as if she was absorbing it through her hands. Without warning, she stabbed it into her arm, injecting the lustrous substance into her bloodstream.

Dacian's face cracked in a wicked smile. His master's laugh burst out of her quivering body, her own mad grin spreading across her face. The pupil in her left eye split into three smaller ones while her right thinned into a cat like slit. As this occurred, her left eye faded from icy blue, to crimson red.

Eynochia watched helplessly. She hung in her chains, nearly hyperventilating from despair. Ardara was becoming Enma, right in front of her, and there was nothing she could do. What new abilities would she gain, that she would undoubtedly use to hurt others? She was already powerfully talented, and as insane as she could get. But even more terrible than that, Eynochia had no clue where Dacian had found that essence. And what did that even mean? The *essence?*

When Ardara stopped convulsing, she clumsily staggered to her feet, her long cloak falling off her shoulders onto the floor, uncovering her revealing mauve leather jumpsuit. Dacian supported her as she recovered, taking a momentary reprieve. Eynochia watched in suspense as she stood up straight with more strength in her stance than before.

"Tell me, Dacian," she said with a nefarious grin, examining the now empty syringe, "from whom did you diffuse this mutant gene?"

"Avari, Celina." He said her full name as if reading from a document.

Ardara laughed like a psycho in a loony bin. "How perfect!" she enthused, but her joy was cut short when Eynochia screamed at Dacian.

"You *cretin!* How could you!? She loved you!" she pulled on her chains, growling.

Ardara glared at her. "Be *quiet.*" With a slight reach of her hand, Eynochia's chains shone red hot. She screamed and struggled as they scorched her skin where they bound her. But this left the chains softened by the heat, and she broke the weakened links when she tugged with the strength of three men twice her size. They still hung from her body by the shackles as she gave a roaring howl, her face elongating, teeth sharpening, hands changing to claws.

Dacian charged at her, taking a steel spear from his back and twirling it in his hand. "Not this time."

Her body produced guttural cracking noises as it contorted, her silver hair spreading down her back and limbs, as she became a white wolf.

Dacian hadn't enough time to raise his spear before Eynochia slashed him. He fell back, bleeding. Ardara did nothing as the wolf barreled out the window.

"She is of no use to me anymore." Ardara explained. "Though I am expecting a little visit from Sven later on."

Eynochia crawled, wheezing out of the moat surrounding the dark castle. She spotted the cold corpse of Rammes Cain still floating there.

She climbed onto the banks and ran out into the rain.

Orphenn walked in the opposite direction he and Celina had taken him in the forest, sticking to the sodden trail. He was immediately glad for his new trench coat; it was beginning to get chilly, and the dark clouds to look ominous. Despite the worsening weather, he decided to take a seat on a nearby log, and allow his mind to drift. Rain began to dribble on his head, but he didn't mind. He closed his eyes and listened to it.

He heard something jingle, and then the crunching of leaves. His eyes shot open. With a start, he noticed a blur of white among the lay of forest colors.

It was a huge wolf, at least the size of a small pony. Blood spattered its white fur along the shackles of the chains hanging from her. It also dripped from her razor-like teeth. Its eyes of green and black were rolling, eyelids drooping with exhaustion.

Where did you come from? Orphenn asked it. He remembered asking the same question to a wolf back at the zoo. But this white wolf answered.

Here. She came closer, obviously willing to trust this boy who could speak to her. She sniffed at his trench coat, as if she recognized the smell. Then she warily lay her big head on his lap. When her eyes closed, she seemed to shrink, and her fur fell away. There was now an unconscious girl on his lap, with no clothes. Only her bloody chains covered her dark, russet skin. This might have sent him into shock, but *What they hey,* he thought. *Stranger things have happened.*

Orphenn hastily threw off his trench coat and wrapped her in it. To save time, he unfolded his golden wings and flew back to the palace.

"Where *is* Orphenn?" Cinder said. "It's *pouring* out there!" She stood at the large window, staring out.

"Should we go find him?" Xeila wondered.

Then something caught Cinder's eye. She flung the curtains aside.

"Oh my God."

"What is it?"

Cinder swung the window open wide.

"What are you doing? It's freezing!"

Something flew in from outside, and Cinder shut the window again as it fluttered its glistening wings and landed on its feet. It was Orphenn.

The whole room, even others in the infirmary rose in excitement at the sight of the girl in Orphenn's arms, but all was silent as he folded his wings away.

"She's hurt." He said.

Chapter Seven

~

Pigeon

Sven sat beside Eynochia's bed. He tucked her choppy silver hair behind her pointed ears. The motion softly woke her. Tears gathered in her eyes.

"Daddy."

"Pige." He kissed her cheek.

"Eynochia, you're awake!" Xeila exclaimed, as she and Jeremiah rushed to her side. They kissed her cheeks as well, Xeila taking one of her hands.

Orphenn got up and went to the door, opening it. Cinder and Celina were conversing in the hallway.

"She's awake." Orphenn said to them. The three came back inside to gather around the bed.

Sven laughed weakly. "Lately I've been spending a lot of time in this infirmary. Hopefully it stops here."

Eynochia sat up very slowly.

"Careful, Pige, you're exhausted. That was at least a five-day journey you just ran in fourteen hours." He paused. "Just like your mama." He smiled.

"I'm so sorry, Dad." She apologized. "I should have listened to you."

"No, no. It wasn't your fault." He held her free hand.

Orphenn saw the joy in his eyes, and in Xeila's. There was no sadness there anymore.

After a while of chatter, Sven took Orphenn aside to speak to him in the hallway. Orphenn noticed he had on a new trench coat-and a quite nice one, black and gray with brown straps and silver buttons.

"Thank you, Orphenn." He said. "You know what's unique about you?"

Orphenn shook his head expectantly.

"You help people without even knowing it." Sven put a hand on Orphenn's shoulder as the boy was brought to tears. "What's eatin' 'ya, Squirt?"

He couldn't reply, but Sven understood.

"Aw, come 'ere, boy." He gave Orphenn a comforting hug. When he pulled away, he said, "You know what else is unique about you? If any other boy brought my daughter home in nothing but a trench coat, he'd be drowned in the fountain before you could say neuroendocinology."

Orphenn laughed so hard he almost cried again.

Sven looked to the door, as if dropping a hint. "Why don't you go talk to her? She'll have to stay in bed for a while with those bad burns. But the rest of us got business to attend to. Wouldn't want her to get lonely."

"Sure thing." Orphenn smiled, hoping his blush wasn't obvious.

Jeremiah came through the door into the corridor, Xeila, Celina and Cinder behind him.

"Hey, Sonner Boy! You ready to go?" Sven said to Jeremiah.

"Yeah Pops, just have to fetch a few things."

"Where are you going?" Xeila asked.

"We've summoned a meeting in Plenthin." Answered Celina. "Would you like to come, Orphenn?"

"No, thanks, I'll pass. I think I'll keep Eynochia company, eh?" He winked at Sven and reentered the infirmary.

After he disappeared through the doorway, the others huddled together for Cinder to port them all away, leaving nothing but dust in the corridor.

"Hello." Orphenn said, coming to sit in a chair by her bed.

"Hi." Eynochia greeted. She looked much like Xeila, with longer, more spiky looking hair, almost a mullet-like style, that was a softer shade of silver, rather than Xeila's bright white. She had the same left eye as her sister and father, that deep black, her right eye a gentle green. Even without the dark bruises, her skin was just a smidge deeper in color than her sister's. Xeila obviously took more of her looks from Sven's side of the gene pool. Eynochia's features were more subtle, less sharp and angular. She wore a two-piece hospital garment as to make it easier to access the wounds at her mid-section.

"How are you feeling?" Orphenn asked.

"Just slightly nauseous. Probably the aftereffects of Dacian's poison."

"He poisoned you too?"

"Just to knock me out-I was 'interrupting' Ardara's little psycho-mind-ritual crap."

"What a jerk."

"No kidding."

Orphenn noticed her picking at the edges of her stained bandages irritably.

"Looks like it's time to change your bandages. Just a sec." He retrieved a roll of gauze from the bedside drawer. He unwound the existing bandage at her wrist, and threw the dirty cloth away. He looked at the festering burn with puzzlement. "What happened back there?" he said, reaching into the drawer again and taking out a tube of ointment.

She explained as Orphenn applied it to the wound. "Ardara made herself Enma. I couldn't just sit there. I found out Dacian had taken Celina's essence. I was so pissed, I screamed at him. I'm thankful she's okay, though."

"Yes." Orphenn said, wrapping her wrist in gauze. "She drank from the river again. I went with her."

"That's amazing." She smiled.

"How did you escape?"

"Ardara used a new gift-she's all freaky psychic, so she already knew how to use it, right after she mutated. She heated up the chains she had me on, and they burned me. But that also made the metal softer, so I was able to break it. I slashed the traitor and jumped out the window."

Orphenn moved on to her other wrist and began to unwrap it.

"It seems like she did that on purpose." She pondered.

"Let you escape, you mean?" Orphenn queried, applying ointment.

"Yes."

"How did you even get captured in the first place? And why?"

"I saw Dacian in the woods. I ran after him, even after Dad told me not to. He paralyzed me with a special toxin when my guard was down and took me prisoner. Ardara kept me there because she thought I would know where the source of the Enma was."

"What was it like there?"

"It's a big dark metal castle in the middle of nowhere and it rains all the time. Don't know who in their right mind would build a *metal* castle in such a moist environment. It's rusted all to hell.

"They have Enma as their slaves-prisoners of war from years ago. They're tortured and hurt, and I wanted to help them, but they only respond to Ardara. I was only fed their leftovers. It's horrible."

Orphenn began to unwrap her waist bandage, again hoping she couldn't see him blushing. "But wait-" he said, "if there were so many Enma in her castle, including you, why did Dacian steal *Celina's* essence? What was the point of traveling all the way to Denoras? Weren't they best friends?"

Eynochia growled. "They weren't best friends. They were always together, I remember. They were in love."

"That's despicable! Why would he go out of his way just to hurt her? What's his deal?"

"I don't know. He's such a horrible man. I hate him."

Orphenn paused, thinking. "What if . . . . He's not? What if he's only following orders?"

"Only a horrible person would carry out those orders with a smug grin on his face."

"I guess you're right."

After a moment of silence, Orphenn lowered to re-bandage her ankles, and said, "So, Cinder told me about the war, and how few rebels there were. That even children had to fight . . ." he looked up at her. She looked down, knowingly, yet passively. "Were you one of them?"

"Yes." She answered sadly. "And Xeila too. It must have been so hard for Dad, to watch his own children be mutated."

"I can imagine . . . I was put in the hospital for my first week at the orphanage. They thought I had epilepsy or some strange parasite that changed my eyes. When they found out I was perfectly healthy, the doctors were stumped. Especially about my eyes. They thought I should be blind, at least. I don't think they ever once thought to check for DNA mutation. 'Course I guess an orphan didn't merit that much effort."

"Interesting . . ." she folded her legs up onto the bed when Orphenn finished her last bandage. Tapping her chin thoughtfully, she asked, "So what's your story?"

"Well," he began, perching on the bed beside her, "I stayed in the Kinder Rose Orphanage for ten years. I only had one friend. His name was Sam. The other orphans didn't take too kindly to freaks, nor did any of the adults. Even the social workers hated to work with me.

"When Sam was finally adopted, I had no one but myself. I would never be adopted, not even fostered, so I just ran away. No one missed me, as I expected. For a year or so, I lived on the streets with the homeless. I let my hair grow out to cover my eyes so no one would ask about them. Regularly I went to soup kitchens and other charities for food-I refused to steal. Granted, that probably gave me most of the hunger pains, but it wasn't worth saddening someone else's life.

"Only a few days ago, I saw Sam again. I helped him catch a criminal-he's a cop now. Right after that, Cinder found me and took me here.

"Then your Dad brought my memory back, and I remembered everything. I'll always be grateful to him for that."

"Hm . . ." She thought. "My father says you're quite talented. Though none of us have seen much of your gifts. I can't help but be curious. What kind of things can you do? Apart from your wings."

"Well . . ." Orphenn hesitated. "I can't say that I know much more about it myself, yet. I could somehow speak to you, when you were a wolf, but I don't know what that means."

"Hmmm . . . I'll make you a promise. Once I'm well enough, I'll be your mentor. But until then, I'm sure Dad will be up for it."

Orphenn couldn't comprehend the reason for the sudden oath, but he nodded and smiled. "Training? Perfect."

The portal hurled them back to Denoras in a maelstrom of black mist, all with eagerness and subtle nostalgia in their hearts. As they returned to the palace, Cinder drifted from the group, as she often did.

She strode across the white cobblestones and scaled the hedges that bordered the courtyard with ease, touching down inside the garden. She traipsed through the foliage and flowers, and came to a point where she could see her little brother beneath a drooping Wisteria. She went to sit beside him. "Hey Bro."

"Cinder! I thought you were at a meeting in Plenthin?" Orphenn picked a bloom from the blue wisteria and flicked it at her playfully.

"I was." She said.

"What did you guys talk about? Who else was there?"

"It was just us."

"Just the four of you? Then what was the point of going all the way to Plenthin just to talk to each other?"

"Plenthin is a desert oasis in the southern hemisphere. It's in the middle of the Desert of Mara that's famous for its scary inhabitants. You know, monsters and creatures, most of them carrying deadly poison. No one goes there, not even the Ardarans. And there's no indigenous people either. Absolute privacy. There is one air dock for passing ships, but we preferred to talk in the jungled areas beyond it."

"What about . . . . The monsters?"

"Jeremiah put up a barrier to keep them away from us. That's why we brought him."

"He can do that?"

"Oh yeah. Just one of his gifts. As for what we talked about, I think Celina would be better at explaining it."

"I see." Orphenn began to absently pick at the grass at his feet. "So . . . The Enma . . . . We still have an army, right? I mean, just wondering . . . What with Eynochia saying she heard Ardara's plans for a comeback. Are we prepared?"

"Of course we are. What do you think Sven is here for?"

"You mean you have ranks and combat training and everything?"

"I should think so."

"What is Sven's rank? Like General or something?"

"Even higher up. Sven's our Field Marshall. Right below Supreme Commander."

"Oh wow. How long did it take him to get there?"

"Well, the war only lasted a few years. Celina actually chose the best from our rebellion to be the higher-ups. She hand-picked the Enma with the most powerful or practical gifts, and the rest were just soldiers. But really, the ranks don't matter to anyone much. Celina never was very organized."

"Who were all of the higher-ups?"

"Most of them are dead now. Sven wasn't always a Field Marshall, in fact he once was just a Captain. But that first year was totally chaotic. Many of our ranks were killed. He was promoted eight times in that one year."

"What a sad way to be promoted."

She nodded and continued, "Now, Jeremiah is Major General, Xeila is Lieutenant General and Eynochia is Staff Sergeant."

"What are the powers of those? And the lower ranks?"

"Most of them transform into animals, including Xeila and Eynochia."

"Oh! Speaking of Eynochia-she said she wants to put me through some training . . . And guaranteed that Sven would volunteer to mentor me until Eynochia's well enough."

Cinder pondered for a moment. "Well, training is certainly what you need."

"Do you know where Sven is?"

"Let's go find him."

Chapter Eight

~

Training

Sven walked down the palace main hall toward the parlor, but was cut short by a swirling shadow that appeared in front of him. The portal dissipated, revealing Cinder and Orphenn to stand before him.

"Orphenn says Eynochia wants to train him." Cinder announced.

"I'm in!" Sven enthused without a second thought. He stepped forward. "Gather everyone up and meet me in the training grounds outside. Don't keep me waiting, Drifter."

Orphenn stood in the center of the field. Sven stood a yard or two away, and all the others stood in line on either side of him-Xeila and Jeremiah to his right, and Cinder and Celina to his left. Celina had abandoned her formal robes for the moment and was sporting a white jumpsuit.

The breeze began to strengthen to a heavy wind. Sven's trench coat flailed behind him, a black and white one of heavy leather, and Orphenn suddenly wondered where he got all these trench coats.

"Shall we begin?" Sven asked Celina, flashing Orphenn a smile.

"Xeila!" Celina called.

"Yes, Commander." She answered.

"Starting with you, we'll show Little Brother what we're capable of. Go!"

At Celina's command, Xeila surged forward, and before their eyes, she transformed. Her body tensed, chrome scales fanning around her eyes, and saber-like fangs grew from her teeth. Her fingers elongated into razor-sharp claws like filed steel.

She gave a menacing snarl as Jeremiah came forward. An adamant crystal formed on his arm like diamond armor. It grew on his other arm and across his chest as well; then a sharp crown around his head, outlining his face and eyes in glittering gem.

Sven swung his arm in the air. A tail of what looked like sparkling dust followed his hand as he spun around and pointed a golden pistol at Orphenn. The glistening dust gathered at his other hand and produced another pistol, a silver one, which he held in his palm and also directed at the teenager.

Orphenn, now thoroughly freaked out, thought to himself: *So. Xeila can transform, just like Cinder had mentioned. It looks almost snake like . . . Well, some kind of reptile, that's for sure . . . Chameleon? Jeremiah can create some kind of crystallized armor-looks formidable. Sven can summon weapons from thin air . . . I have yet to see what else they all can do . . .*

At Celina's signal, she and Cinder both unfurled their wings, with spans of at least thirteen feet across, and black feathers like that of a raven.

Each Enma took an offensive stance, ready to strike. Though Celina's stance was something more confident-both hands held behind her back. Orphenn wondered what that was about.

"This is training . . ." Orphenn thought out loud. He let his golden wings fan out behind him.

"Ah, our little bird has come to show us his abilities." Sven mocked. "Should we teach him a lesson?"

With a hiss from Xeila, they charged, and Orphenn turned to escape. Before he could take a step in the opposite direction, he collided against something, then looked up to realize it was Jeremiah.

Is he a teleporter like Cinder? Orphenn started, rearing back just as Xeila caught him and turned him to face her. Her face was beginning to morph into a serpent-like shape, the fangs and claws making her all the more frightening. She shoved him backward into Jeremiah's stone grasp. With the strength of a god, he hurled Orphenn into the sky. "Fly!"

Celina and Cinder immediately shot upward to follow their brother.

Orphenn was flung higher into the sky than he had ever flown. He careened and plummeted toward the ground. His eardrums seemed to implode at the affect of Sven's gunshot, the bullet whistling as it barely missed him.

Orphenn screamed, struggling to catch the air on his wings.

"You've got wings, dip wad!" Sven shouted, then shot again. "Use 'em!"

The bullet again whirred just past his head. He was shocked into flight-his wings finally carrying him on the wind.

"Those almost hit me!" Orphenn squealed.

"Don't let down your guard!" Sven ordered, discarding his pistols into dust for a newly appeared rapid-fire machine gun. A wicked smile cracked his face as he opened fire at the golden-winged angel.

Orphenn squealed again, banking low in an effort to dodge the bullets. He barely escaped them, just as Cinder appeared with Celina through a dark portal. The two flapped to either side of their brother.

Cinder clutched his arm, and from his elbow down, it disappeared into a portal from her hand. Another portal materialized above his head, and his hand reached out of it and bopped his forehead.

"Holy-" Orphenn hastily pulled his arm from the portal, watching and rubbing his wrist as Cinder keeled over laughing, barely managing to stay in the air.

"Don't get distracted!" Celina smiled.

"Let me help you out there, Celina!" Sven called upward. He grinned maniacally and from the air, swirling in that summoning dust, came hundreds of small throwing weapons-needles, knives, daggers, and the like-and without any indication or hand motions, she raised them to arrange behind her, and with minds of their own, each little knife and needle shot in Orphenn's direction like a flock of ravenous bats.

He descended, wings struggling to keep him aloft.

Celina can manipulate objects . . . . Mentally? He pondered. *What's that called . . . ? Oh . . . Telepathy? No . . . . Telekinesis!*

Finally gaining his balance, he glided, inches away from the marble of the palace's back wall.

Celina never took her hands from behind her back. She sent the blades slicing through the sky toward Orphenn. He dove to dodge them, and landed in the branches of a tree.

Countless became embedded into the railing, centimeters shy of Eynochia's fingers. "Wow, you guys!" she beckoned. "You all are really good at *missing!*" She had decided earlier to come out on the balcony to watch Orphenn's progress. Apparently it was pretty tough training.

Orphenn clung to the branches of the tree, catching his breath. Only a slight moment's reprieve though, for more shards of metal cut through the leaves, lodging themselves in the trunk and branches.

Attempting to escape, Orphenn swung to the other side of the tree and climbed to the top.

The wind had died down . . . . so what was this rocking back and fourth when he reached the top? A tremendous crack sounded as Orphenn rose with the tree slightly higher into the air.

"Hey, whoa! What the-" Orphenn looked far below to see that Jeremiah had bare-handedly uprooted the entire tree from the ground. He then let the tree drop, as well as Orphenn, and stood back to watch as it tipped and started to fall.

"Whoa!" Orphenn leapt out of the tree and soared with the accuracy of a hawk, and touched down to the ground just as the tree did behind him. Dirt and grass and leaves flew everywhere. Cinder and Celina arrived at Orphenn's side, picking the debris from his hair.

Sven turned to Jeremiah and nudged him. "Nice work, Jerry."

"Just a warm-up." Jeremiah remarked, his crystal armor cracking and receding. This put a smile on Xeila's face, now free of fangs or claws.

"Aw, that's my boy!" Sven laughed.

"And you, Orphenn," Jeremiah said, stepping over to the seventeen-year-old, "that was pretty good for your first time."

"Although, I did try to go easy on 'ya." Cinder shrugged.

"*Obviously.*" Orphenn sneered, recalling her little portal trick.

"*I* didn't." Sven snickered.

"Also obvious. You almost shot me!"

"Good thing you're quick on them wings, eh?"

The laughter in the training field could be heard from a few stories up, on a slightly damaged balcony. Sven had reclaimed all his weapons by now, leaving gauges in the marble where the blades had been imbedded.

Orphenn glanced up at Eynochia, who was smiling at him and leaning on the balcony's railing.

He fluttered up to meet her, gingerly sitting on the hole-scarred railing and tracing one of the gauges with a fingertip. He wiped sweat from the back of his neck. "That was one *hell* of a training session." He sighed.

A week or two passed of Orphenn's training, growing more vigorous and violent each day.

He found that Xeila transformed into a white chameleon-like serpent, though not completely-her body stayed in an in-between phase and couldn't morph any further; unlike Eynochia who could transform totally into a white wolf.

Jeremiah was not another teleporter-he was incredibly *fast*, and inhumanly strong and seemingly weakness less as his adamant armor.

Cinder could mold shadows into weapons and use them to her desire. She and Celina could take advantage of the strong link between them, automatically knowing what the other was thinking and acting on it.

Sven's many varieties of weapons were drawn from a large armory inside the palace, for him to summon whenever he wished.

One day he made the decision to orient Orphenn with weapons.

After a short discussion, he tossed the boy a loaded revolver.

Orphenn caught it in wary hands. "But I . . . ."

"No complaining." Sven interjected.

"*Complain!*" Orphenn whined.

"*Search your* feelings, *Little Bird.*" Sven teased, drawing a broadsword from thin air. 'Little Bird' was a new pet name for Orphenn. Sven seemed to be fond of giving everyone his own nicknames.

"But . . ." Orphenn moaned, "Guns can kill-"

"Boy," he countered before Orphenn could finish his objection, "sayin' guns kill people is like blamin' misspelled words on your pen." He took a look at his sword and grimaced.

"Oh, not *this* one," he chastised, flipping the weapon away, and it faded away in shiny dust as another sleeker one appeared in his hand. He spun the hilt in his fingers. "Now shoot."

It actually turned out pretty well.

Sven had deflected the bullet with the blade of his sword, and it shot into the ground.

From that point on, target practice became a part of daily training. Though the targets were now scattered about the place, rather than just shooting at Sven.

Orphenn was also trained with the sword and spear, and the bow. But out of all of them, he enjoyed the firearms the most.

Chapter Nine

~

The White Herons

Ardara stood at her machine, staring into the chamber. The machine had buttons almost like an oversized typewriter, which operated the mechanical limbs inside the looming chamber. The metal claws soldered and sliced at a hunk of iron held on a tall pedestal.

Dacian stood beside her, watching intently. "New toy?" he questioned.

"I am building a device." She clarified. "A device that I hope will stunt an Enma's abilities, and harness their power. Rendering them . . . Virtually human."

"Don't you already use devices like that on all the slaves?"

"Yes, but this one is different. With your help, I'll create a way to remove the energy from a large power source."

"As in . . . Another way to steal an Enma's essence?"

"And more." She grinned.

Sven and Celina whispered to each other as the others continued to battle with Orphenn.

After bare-fisted combat drills, Orphenn advanced to the shooting range. He fired at his set targets, and when he struck all their bull's-eyes, he glanced all around him. The others looked pleased with his progress. Eynochia beamed down at him from the balcony.

"Okay, Birdie, take a break-ten minutes. When you get back, prepare yourself for one-on-one combat training." Sven ordered, and sent the gun targets away in dust, back to the armory. Orphenn immediately nodded and trudged off into the palace.

He met up with Eynochia in the doorway of his bedroom. "Finally out of that infirmary gown, are we? You look like you're feeling better." He greeted, nudging her shoulder.

"Yeah, I'm not so sick anymore." She replied.

"Let's see your burns." He took Eynochia's hand and rolled up her sleeve to examine the bracelet of sores around her wrist. "Still looks pretty bad." He commented, running hid finger along the edge of the scarring tissue.

Eynochia gasped.

The burn seemed to glow. The blisters shrank, and were gone, and the wound disappeared as if erased from a piece of paper.

"Orphenn!" Eynochia exclaimed, rubbing her healed wrist in astonishment. She hurriedly looked at her other burns on her other wrist, waist, and ankles. All gone. "You healed me!" she yelled. "How did you do that?"

Orphenn was speechless. "I . . . ."

"We have to show Dad!"

Orphenn's newfound gift was greatly appreciated. He put it to use healing the minor injuries gained during training sessions, which Eynochia could now participate in. Soon his skills were catching up with hers. He discovered she was an excellent fighter, though not as viscous as Xeila or as fast as Jeremiah. But she was accurate and efficient in her attacks, and ready for anything.

But what Celina announced one morning before all of Aleida caught all of them quite off guard.

The Supreme Commander rose up to the podium. A sea of people stood in the plaza, applauding and watching her on the massive hologram screens above her head. They showed her wave at the crowd and smile, and her people cheered.

Orphenn and the others stood behind her, all clothed in white for the occasion-all but Cinder, naturally, who wore her signature head-to-toe black garb. Beside them there was a gargantuan white tarp that hid something equally large beneath it. It stood almost as tall as the palace's highest clock tower.

The ocean of both Enma and human citizens silenced as Celina spoke, her voice like a welcome breeze about their heads.

"People of Aleida. Today, I have news that is both grave, and joyous."

There was not a sound.

She continued. "I know you all recall the Great War that took place less than two decades ago. I know you remember the hardship and the fear, and the loss besides. But I also know that you all remember how *fiercely* we triumphed." Here the swarm boomed back its acknowledgement, before Celina continued solemnly. "However, now you must be warned.

"Ardara is plotting a comeback. My sister plans to expand her conquest once again. And according to my sources, she plans to do it soon. Her rage is strong, and she is bitter and hateful in her exile. She will retaliate with more ferocity than she ever before mustered." Whispers and anxious hushes floated in the air.

"My people, don't let your hope be lost. I plan to bite back just as hard!" Celina held up her clenched fist, and loud encouragement rose from the audience. "I am reforming my squadron!" With this pronouncement she motioned the others to step forward. When they did, Celina ceremonially awarded each of them with a white uniform jumpsuit, and a diamond crest. She touched her own crest, which was pinned at the shoulder of her own matching uniform, and rose to the podium again. "With my loved ones at my side, the White Herons are reborn!" She pulled a thick rope cord, and the gigantic tarp slowly fell, and revealed what had been hiding beneath it. Celina smiled as a massive airship was unveiled.

"Introducing the new *Avian*-the Day Star! With this faithful vessel and our powerful army behind it, we can stop the Ardarans in their tracks! They'll never get as far as the Wasteland's border!" Again, she raised her encouraging fist.

"Aleidian victory!"

The crowd roared back: "*Aleidian victory!*"

"Does this mean all the other squadrons will be reformed?" Sven asked Celina later that afternoon.

"Not necessarily all the *same* squadrons. But yes. The Day Star is the first of seven airships to be built for future squads."

"Seven? There were only four before." Sven raised one short, arched eyebrow.

"The squads will be organized with only Enma members." Celina clarified. "All humans will be field soldiers."

"What about the remaining Enma that aren't assigned to squadrons?"

"Also field soldiers. I want the most powerfully gifted Enma put into squads. Their airships will protect them and give them advantage during battle. There aren't many of us left."

"Yes, but the human portion of Aleida's population is just as powerful! Sure, they can't fly or erect force fields, but I wouldn't underestimate them, Angel Face. They may be 'only human' but they're a force to be reckoned with, by damn! They got spark!"

"I suppose."

"If you're so worried about it, why don't 'ya just mutate a new generation? I'm sure there'll be willin' voluntaries. Enma like us are revered as gods, dang near."

"You now I would've thought of that. You also know that I traveled to the River a while ago. It returned the Enma mutations to me, and I realized that it remembered me. I also realized that it was running low."

"What?" Sven started, eyes widening. "The River is . . . . Dying?"

"I believe so."

"I get it now. With the River runnin' on empty, you don't want to use any more of its essence . . . . You're scared it'll dry up."

"Precisely. I'm trying to preserve us. Without the River, there will be no turning back. The River is this world's vitality. It's consciousness. Without it, everything will die. I regret ever using it."

After an interval of silent thought, she said, "I hope you're right about the humans. They'll need all the help they can get."

Orphenn and Eynochia lay beneath the stars that evening, taking reprieve after a particularly exhausting training session. Tonight he had been thinking a lot about his parents. When Sven brought his memory back, he remembered what they were like. His father's laugh, his mother's smell. He even recalled the way his father's hands would move, his mother's idiosyncrasies, every little mannerism etched into him.

"Say, Eynochia?" He said.

"Yeah?"

"What was your mother's name?"

She got up on one elbow and looked at him with glowing, green and yellow eyes. Orphenn noticed that seemed to be an Enma trademark, like a uniform characteristic, a telltale sign of mutation, apart from the mismatched color and pupils . . . They glowed.

"Oriana. Dad used to call her Orio." She laughed. "Why the sudden curiosity?"

"Oh, I was just . . . . Thinking." He turned his head to look at Eynochia, his own blue and red eyes glowing, blades of grass tickling his ear. Her eyes and hair gleamed in the moonlight. "What was she like?"

Sven came from the veranda to lie down beside the two teenagers, and spoke, as if his intrusion was perfectly appropriate. The youngsters didn't mind, though.

"She was like the silver moonlight shining on us right now. She was like the rain-the kind of soft rain that comes when the sun is still shining. So beautiful, when she looked at 'ya, you wanted to die. That was my Oriana." Eynochia gave a sad smile. "This is her." Sven said, handing Orphenn a crumpled photo. He sat up to look at it.

Sven was right. She was gorgeous. She had the russet skin and silver hair like her two daughters. Sven was beside her in the photo. It was obviously taken long before the war; both their eyes were the same color-deep, dark black. And Sven looked so much younger-his face was bright and free of scars. But even in the photo he wasn't wearing a shirt. *Same old Sven*, he thought.

Orphenn thought for a moment. "If it's alright to ask . . . How did she die?"

Sven sat up, slouching, moonlight on his bare, scarred back. He began, without preamble. "It was the last battle. She and I fought side by side like warriors. My little daughters had to fight too, and I hated it. We never left their sides." His shoulders shrugged, bony and lean.

"We were at the River, battling it out with some Ardaran soldiers. They had ambushed us when we had thought we were safe on the banks. We tossed them aside easily, but Pigeon's knee got hurt. I picked her up.

"While my back was turned, I heard Xeila scream. I spun around. It was Dacian. He had kicked Poppet to the ground and threw down Oriana too.

"That bastard had been in my squadron. He had murdered each member months before, apart from Celina and myself. We only escaped because the two of us were out on recon.

"Anyway. He raised his lance, and pointed it at my wife. I handed Pige to her sister and rushed to hold him back. I socked him right in the face. He turned right around and slashed me with his lance. That's how I got this." He touched the scar that ran down his face. "It seems like only seconds I blacked out. But it was long enough for Dacian to knock her across the head with the butt end of his lance and slit her throat.

"I knew she was dead. But even as she fell into the River I didn't wanna believe it.

"The girls were screaming on the banks, trying to get in the water and help her. I screamed at 'em, 'No girls, stay put! Don't look at Mommy. Don't look at Mommy, just look at me!' Though I can't have looked much better. Face cut in half, blood all over. But alive, at least. I ran through the water to get them, and hugged their faces close so they wouldn't see.

"The traitor was gone. Nowhere to be seen." Sven's face took on a twinge of awe, the memory fascinating him, even now as he retold it.

"Then the water started to move. It was shining with color and it rose, and lifted my wife into the air. I reached for her. But the water rained back down and she was gone. There was no more blood in the water. Not even a trace that Oriana had existed at all.

"By that time, the war was over. Guess that's why the traitor scrammed off so quick. The Celestial Family had come to help us. Should have been happy. But for the longest time I felt numb. It must have been years before I actually cried.

"And . . . . I been cryin' ever since." His voice cracked.

Orphenn was speechless for several moments. "Do you remember?" he finally asked Eynochia, mutedly, his voice quieted with empathy.

"I remember." She breathed tearfully.

Their pain tugged at Orphenn's heart, and he found himself crying as well.

For a long time it was silent. They sat, staring at the stars.

Eynochia chuckled. "Dad, it's cold. Get a shirt on."

The marshal smirked, chin still quivering, residual tears trailing down the scar at his lips. "Nope."

The next morning, the group was readying themselves for daily training, when Sven burst in, holding a leather belt with two holsters in his hand.

"Change of plans, ladies. Today's our first mission. Commander's orders." He walked to the table where Orphenn was tying his boots. "Got somethin' for 'ya, Little Bird. Put this on." He gave Orphenn the belt.

When it was securely strapped around his waist, Orphenn asked, "What's it for?"

"These." Sven summoned two glimmering pistols into his hands. One was gold, and the other was silver. "I want you to have them."

"Hey! You attacked me with those!" the orphan laughed.

"Yes. On several occasions. Here." Orphenn took the guns and admired the way their casings reflected the light, silver and gold. "And let me tell you something about these. This gold one-never runs out of ammunition. And the silver one *never* misses. That's why I only shot you with the gold one."

Orphenn twirled the pistols expertly before slipping them into their holsters. "Thanks."

"Don't mention it. You'll need them for the mission."

"Where are we going?"

"Ardara."

Chapter Ten

~

Ardara

The Day Star was an amazing airship. The exterior was colossal, entirely of steel construction and painted white to match the city. The inside was extravagant, exquisitely furnished, yet practical for mid-air battle; wide, open main hold and spacious cargo hold, and living quarters that rivaled the palace's own. Equipped with cannons, gas bombs, missiles and acute navigation radar, it was a marvelous weapon of war. Its predecessor, the Avian, was only half as much.

That day, a ribbon was cut at the end of the runway, dropping the signal for the Day Star to take off, with the White Herons at their stations inside it, and six other great airships trailing behind it. As the Day Star rose, and advanced, the others spread out and flew away in all different directions, like great birds of metal, moving as swiftly as if they didn't weighs tons and tons in steel and iron. Some were to set camp in strategic locations on the Aleidian map, and others sent on their own appointed missions.

"And we're off!" Jeremiah enthused at the helm.

"Like a dirty shirt." Sven chuckled.

"Celina?" asked Orphenn, looking down at the shrinking palace through a wide porthole.

"Yes Orphenn?" she answered from the head of the ship, where Jeremiah was steering and Xeila was navigating.

"Who watches Denoras when you're away?"

"I have some very trustworthy delegates who keep things organized."

"Oh." Orphenn looked around the main hold. Xeila was insisting on learning to drive, Jeremiah advising her against it, and Celina laughing at the squabbling couple. Cinder sat at the mess table, feet propped up on it, gazing blankly through a spyglass and looking at everything in the hold in boredom while munching on toast. "I see you." She raised her voice to echo in earshot, as she was yards across the floor of the large hold. She bent backwards on the bench to glare upside-down at Jeremiah through the lens. "Your head is *enormous*."

"And you're really bored." He sneered back at her.

She apparently refused to wear the white uniform she was given, as she was still sporting an all black ensemble, but she wore the White Herons' crest on her shoulder nonetheless.

Righting herself, she pointed the spyglass at Celina. "Why are we going to Ardara?"

"I want to find out what Cira's up to. Maybe free a few slaves." She looked back at Cinder, her face warped like a fishbowl through the scope.

"How long will it take to get there?"

"About a day and a half."

Cinder groaned.

Orphenn was intrigued to realize that Celina and Cinder regarded Ardara as if she were still Cira, still their sister. It was as if the last war and the one that swiftly approached were just petty quarrels between siblings.

Then he noticed Sven and Eynochia standing at the wide reinforced glass window that took up the majority of the south wall. Their shadows stretched down the floor. Eynochia touched her father's shoulder, then left to stand with her sister at the navigation table.

He walked over to Sven with a sudden curiosity. The man was still shirtless, his uniform top swung over his shoulder.

"Sven?"

"Hm?"

"I know it's a random question, but-why do you have so *many* scars? No one else's are that noticeable."

"Well . . ." Sven looked at him earnestly. "I guess I was the one that was fightin' the hardest." He gazed across at the sky outside the window.

"You look kind of off today." Orphenn noted. "You okay?"

Sven's eyebrow rose thoughtfully. "Yes. It's just so . . . Déjà vu. Being here. With my squad in our ship. It's such a familiar feeling."

"Hm . . ." Orphenn pondered. "Is it a *good* familiar feeling?"

Sven smiled. "It is now." He playfully ruffled the boy's hair.

Orphenn turned to leave, trotting his way back to the table where Cinder sat. He took a seat across from her, and for at least an hour, they sat there twiddling their thumbs and sighing.

"Cinder." He straightened urgently. She pointed the spyglass at him in acknowledgement. "I'm bored." He stated, as if she could solve his problem. Which she most likely could.

She set the spyglass on the table with vigor. "Me too." She motioned him to lean closer and whispered, "Wanna go for a ride?"

"On your weird-lookin' bike? Hell yeah!"

"Okay, but Celina probably won't approve-"

"Cinder." Celina beckoned, her timing impeccable. "There's a disturbance on the screens. Care to investigate?"

"Sure thing, sis!" Cinder said, seizing the opportunity to escape the ship momentarily.

"I'll come with you!" Orphenn declared, and followed his sister into the cargo hold.

Cinder's motorcycle was the only vehicle among the large barrels and boxes of supplies and other cargo.

As she mounted and started the engine, Orphenn stood aside, folding his arms. "Wait . . . Why don't we both just *fly* down to land? Better yet, why don't you just port us down? Why do we even need the bike?" he reasoned.

"Orphenn!" she gave him a look of mock criticism. "You know better! That's not as much *fun!*" she chastised. "Now get on!"

He did so, but couldn't help being a skeptic. "Uh-huh . . . So you're saying we're just going to *drop* from the sky, and still be alive when we get to the bottom?"

"No guarantees." She teased.

"Ah." He hid his anxiety behind a question: "So, do you just not like using your gifts? I haven't seen much of them, apart from training."

"Who needs 'em?"

At this, Cinder punched the throttle, and ported the bike outside the ship, despite what she'd said seconds before.

And then they were falling. They plummeted and plummeted, hair and clothes whipping in the wind. Cinder's face had a wide smile, but Orphenn was too caught up trying to hold on to think about his facial expression. He was about to give in and unfurl his wings before the ground caught up to them, when Cinder kicked a switch at the last moment.

Switch-activated, metal wings shot out from the sides of the bike, and they caught the air, mere feet from a crash landing, and pulled them higher, soaring on a breeze. Cinder let out a cheer of exhilaration. "See!" she shouted, "You didn't need to worry!"

She flew the motorcycle to a place where the ground was level and landed, wings retracting again. "Whew," she sighed, "*that* was fun." She hit the 'talk' button on her wrist communicator and spoke into it. "Alright, guys. Tell me where to go."

The squadrons' crests acted as tracking devices and showed up as white dots on the Day Star's radar.

"To the west of you is the source of the disturbance." Jeremiah's voice cracked through the speaker. "I'll tell you when you've reached it."

"What sort of disturbance is it?" Orphenn inquired into his communicator.

"Some sort of chemical reading. Could be an Ardaran factory or something."

"Alright. We're on it." Cinder turned the bike toward the west.

"Cinder." Celina came in, "Make it quick. We must carry on."

"Eh . . . In a minute." Cinder bargained. Forgetting her speaker was still on, she said to Orphenn, "We're goin' for a thrill ride!"

"You'll do no such thing!" Celina cawed.

Cinder's lips mouthed a curse when she switched off her communicator, and she gave a sarcastic "*Oops.*"

Orphenn chuckled. "I don't know, Cinder . . . Wasn't falling out of an airship thrill enough for the hour?"

"Nonsense, darling!"

"Fine." Orphenn sighed, passively. "Where we going, Cinder Block?"

"We're gonna he—*Cinder Block*?" She gave him a look of incredulity at the pun-name. Orphenn only smiled.

Cinder smirked back. "Alrighty, we're off then."

"Like a dirty shirt." Orphenn added. Then he gasped. *Did I really just say that?* Already, Sven was rubbing off on him.

Cinder's bike veered across the road and spun around, stirring up dust as it sped in the other direction. Accelerating rapidly, the wings extended, and the bike was sent hurling straight for the side of a rocky cliff. Already, adrenaline pumped in Cinder's blood, and seemed to pulsate from both of them.

The bike ascended abruptly, barely avoiding a collision. With a rush, Cinder suddenly hit the brake as they reached the cliff top, the bike balancing precariously, the back wheel hanging over the edge.

"Alright, now . . ." Cinder smiled deviously, then said carefully in a low hush, "Lean back . . ."

"Cinder. I'm not leaning back." Orphenn defied. He was still slightly unused to so much excitement in so little time. "You'll kill us-" but his objection was cut short when Cinder forcefully pushed her back against him, giving him no choice but to lean his weight backward, causing the bike to totter, and fall from its perilous balance.

Orphenn shouted in terror as the bike plunged backward, down toward the earth below. Cinder laughed loudly, a triumphant cackle. After a few seconds of torturing her brother with the steep fall, she punched yet another mysterious button, which set off a pair of high-powered jets that shot the vehicle into a more steady air current, and they floated on a safer, softer course, wings extended to let the bike drift slowly downward.

Orphenn, stiff and windswept, his long rattail tangled, muttered through clenched teeth. "Do you *have* to do that?"

Before she answered, she let the bike descend onto a dirt road near the foot of the cliff, where a small thicket of densely packed trees stood not far off. As the wings retracted, Cinder said, "You'll get used to it." She turned the bike around, then said, "Now I think we should get to that mission of ours."

Orphenn straightened in alarm. "Wait, we're on a mission?"

"Uh, yeah. 'Investigating the disturbance,' remember?" she laughed. "That fall really cleared your head, huh?"

"So . . . This is like a little mini mission that's part of our great big mission?"

His exaggerated gestures brought a smile to Cinder's face. "I guess so."

Then it was her turn to stiffen. She quieted her engine to better hear a noise in the distance. Orphenn heard it too. It was the roar of another motor, possibly several. "I know that sound . . ." Cinder realized, dismounting.

"Cinder, what is it?" Orphenn worried.

The only answer she gave was a smile as the roar grew louder, to the point that Orphenn had the urge to cover his ears. Before he had the chance, from the coverts, came another unique motorcycle, perhaps even more so than Cinder's, then another, and another, and when the last biker burst out of the forest, there were six, that surrounded the two Enma in a circle. They all dressed in black as Cinder did. Their ages varied as much as the expressions on their faces, though the only one who looked unhappy was by far the youngest. A boy, with long sandy-brown hair, cornrows weaved along one side of his head, and black and silver beads threaded onto the braids. Both his eyes were emerald green, and his scowling lip was pierced through with a silver hoop. He looked scornfully at Cinder and Orphenn. He held up his palm in a silent command, and every engine was switched off. It was peculiar to witness all of them follow the wishes of a boy who couldn't have been older than fourteen.

"Raven." He hissed.

"Sparrow!" Cinder called out eagerly. "It's been ages! I-"

"I know." He spat. "Where have you been the last three months? I was forced to take over leadership." Sparrow's words were full of hurt.

Another biker spoke up. "You know what they said, Sparrow. She found their little Young Prince, they been training him."

"And *he's* the long-lost *Keiran Avari?*" Sparrow's angry eyes flicked to Orphenn. "*This* is the brother that replaced me?"

"Sparrow. It's not like that. I wanted to come back. I had to stay for my brother. What would you have done?" she demanded, immediately regretting it.

"If I discovered that I had family left, you mean?" he came off his tall bike seat and walked to stand in front of Cinder. "I wouldn't want to believe it." His raging frown became something more sullen and genuine. "I would at first, secretly wish to go back to how it was-just so it wouldn't feel so strange."

Orphenn came in, with an air of wisdom. "Then you and I have something in common."

Sparrow's face flitted to look at Orphenn. His eyes were accusing. He quickly turned, pulling Cinder along with him by the sleeve of her jacket, the both of them disappearing into the thicket. When they were clear from view, Sparrow stopped.

"Raven!" he cried, with an infantile sob and tears in his eyes. He shoved her. "*I'm* your brother! *I'm your brother!*"

"Sparrow! Sparrow, hush." Cinder wrapped her arms around his head, and he sobbed into her chest. "I know. I'm sorry."

Orphenn watched, somewhat guiltily, as the two disappeared through the trees. A biker with a wide-brimmed hat and a mustache caught the look in his eye. "Don't pay him no mind, Youngun." He said. "He's still a youngun himself."

Orphenn nodded at him appreciatively.

The man continued. "The name's Gryphon." He dismounted, and reached his hand out to Orphenn. "You be called Keiran?"

Orphenn shook his head. "I'm called Orphenn now."

The remaining four bikers followed suit. A tall, lanky girl with long blonde Rapunzel hair, ratted from riding against the wind, shook his hand. "Ibis." She said.

The next three to introduce themselves were a pale woman with short white hair and swirling tattoos all up her arms and torso, who was called Dove; a bald, goateed man, covered in piercings, named Crow, and a long haired red-headed boy named Finch.

As Orphenn shook Finch's hand he noticed that each of their bikes had their names, "Sparrow," "Gryphon," "Ibis," "Dove," "Crow," and "Finch" etched and polished into the steel, and that each bike was different in shape and design. In curiosity, he shifted in Cinder's bike seat to glance at the fuel tank, and his thought was confirmed. "Raven" was inscribed there in ornate silver lettering.

"Sparrow did that." Finch said, noticing Orphenn's observation. "He's really good."

Orphenn smiled and nodded, tracing the curly "R" with a fingertip.

Without warning, Sparrow came in a huff out of the brush and mounted his ride. "We're leaving." He commanded, revving the engine.

The others, however hesitant, complied, and climbed onto their bikes to start their engines.

Sparrow spun his bike around, his back wheel leaving a half circle scar in the dirt, and jolted forward effortlessly. The rest of the gang waved and smiled before following after him, back into the trees.

The rush of air tousled Cinder's hair when they sped past her, and when the snarl of their motors died in the distance, she emerged from the coverts to go to Orphenn. As she approached, Orphenn tapped the gas tank.

"What's this? Raven?"

She paused a moment.

"And what's the story with Sparrow?"

She sighed. "The Flock. My Flock name is Raven."

"The Flock? The name of your little . . . drifter biker gang?"

"Yeah, yeah. When the war ended I lived a purely nomadic life. Those guys found me, helped me out. At the time, it was just Gryphon, Crow and I. I was made leader, since I was Enma, not to mention the '*Savior, Lady Cinder*,' 'ya know. Ibis, Dove, and Finch joined later. We found Sparrow after that. He was orphaned, like I was . . . . Like we were . . . . And he reminded me so much of you at the time, though he was younger. I couldn't leave him."

"So . . ." Orphenn pondered. "He's jealous of me?" he still had so much to get used to.

"It killed me to leave. But now there are more important things than running around in the back country with my gang."

"Is that what you tried to tell him? Back there when he dragged you away?"

"And other things. I tried to convince him to tell the Flock to come back to the Day Star with us. We need all the help we can get. But he refused and got angry."

"None of them are Enma . . . Can they fight?"

"*Can they fight?*" Cinder whistled. "You don't need genetic mutations to be powerful."

"Okay, you win." He surrendered. "Now, I really think we should get to our-"

"If you two are finished dawdling," Jeremiah broke in through Orphenn's communicator, "there is an investigation to conduct."

"We're on it. Sorry for the delay." Orphenn replied. "Oh, and, by the way, it was all Cinder Block's fault."

Jeremiah turned to Sven, puzzled. "Cinder Block?" he mouthed silently.

Sven shrugged.

The two siblings rode, and advanced calmly forward, onto a dirt road that led into a seemingly abandoned cluster of buildings. Farther down, the road forked, and Cinder turned to the right.

The houses were all ragged and old, weathered with years of neglect.

"Some kind of ghost town?" Orphenn wondered out loud.

"Yeah." agreed Cinder. "By the looks of it, I'd say no one's lived here since the war."

Just then, there was a sound of haste from behind them, and she killed the engine in front of an old house where someone had rushed inside and slammed the door.

"Or . . . . So I thought . . ." Cinder corrected, flinging one leg over the bike seat to stand on the dirt. "You stay here." She told Orphenn, then carefully made for the old white house, whose paint was peeling, and whose dusty shingles were dripping and moldy.

As Cinder came to the rotting doorstep, the door creaked as it came slightly open, cracking just enough for Cinder to see one half of a woman's face, staring at her from the other side of the door.

"I didn't think anyone lived in this town . . . . Who might you be?" Cinder said politely. When the woman remained silent, she said, "My name is Cinder-"

"I know who you are." The woman interrupted, almost too quickly to comprehend.

Cinder continued weakly, ". . . . I came down here from my airship to investigate a disturbance." She pointed at the sky, to the Day Star above their heads. "Do you know what I might be looking for?"

"I know. Just by your eyes, I know who you are." The woman replied unhelpfully. "You are Enma. Enma do not belong here."

Cinder's face was a mask of questions, but before she could ask any, Orphenn cried, "Uh . . . . Cinder?"

Cinder turned her back on the woman to look at Orphenn. His eyes were pleading, and he stiffly twirled his finger as if to say, *Around us.*

Cinder glanced at every building, each one of them with a face or a pair of loathing eyes glaring from an open door or window.

"Ooohh . . . . Damn . . . ." Cinder cursed nervously. She took a step down from the aging porch, still anxiously aware of each open door and window, just as Orphenn gave a frightened shout.

"Cinder! Behind you!"

The timid woman had stepped out onto the porch, revealing the long dagger she held between her fists, previously hidden by the door. Before Cinder had the chance to dodge, the dagger was thrust into her back. She let out a short, staccato scream of pain, before she vanished in a swirl of black mist, leaving nothing but blood on the blade of the dagger the woman still clutched in her trembling hand. It fell from her grip, and landed with a sharp ring. The woman shut herself away inside the house, without another word.

Cinder groaned when she reappeared again, on the bike seat ahead of Orphenn. "Talk about a backstabber." She grimaced.

Orphenn fretfully spread apart the tear in Cinder's jacket to look at the wound, intending to heal it, like he had healed Eynochia's burns; but when he looked, there was no injury.

He was sure he had seen blood on that dagger. He chose to ignore this for the moment. He might bring it up again at a more suitable time.

"What's going on down there?" Sven's husky voice broke through the speakers of the communicator at Orphenn's shoulder.

"Nothing, everything's fine so far." Orphenn answered quickly. He made doubly sure his mike was switched off, so no one else would hear what he said next. "Cinder, let's get the *hell* outta here."

"Took the words right out of my mouth." She acknowledged, then spoke into her wrist, "It looks like some kind of Ardaran settlement. A colony of supporters maybe."

"A colony?" Celina asserted. "There are no Ardaran colonies, they were all *exiled*."

"Well, guess *what*." Cinder retorted. "Now where's the disturbance?"

"You're only yards away from it." Jeremiah replied. "It looks like it should be inside that large building ahead of you."

Cinder and Orphenn gazed forward, and the structure that loomed over them was built in hard metal and bolts, with a tall, smoking chimney. The smoke gave off an acrid scent like burnt hair. The dark building stood out against the rest of the beaten down town like a black sheep in a flock of white. *Or more like a parasite,* Cinder thought.

"Yup." She confirmed suddenly.

"'Yup' what?" Orphenn asked.

"That is definitely Ardaran."

A bonfire crackled as it burned in the center of a large, metal room. In the heart of the flames, a heap of metal warped and reddened with the heat.

At the head of the room was a raised dais, with a long table, which seated three in tall, ornate armchairs: Ardara's three favorite servants. Dacian glowered from the center chair, violet-haired Nyx glued to his right arm, and Wynne, off to the left side, resting his chin in his palm. They each wore the deep red and black uniform, with matching headgear.

Many supporters surrounded the bonfire, laughing and gazing up at the putrid smoke barreling skyward into the chimney.

Dacian smirked and rose from his seat. In that instant, the vast crowd gravely silenced, anticipating their superior's next words. He straightened, and spoke.

"Comrades!" his booming voice resonated in the room even after his mouth closed. He walked around to stand at the end of the long table. "You might be wondering why you're staring at a noxious bonfire," he paused for a few chuckles to escape the crowd, and continued, "and for this, I have an answer." As he said this, he gallantly trudged down the steps of the dais, to meet the gazes of his audience at their level. They spread apart to give him a path, and as he walked to stand by the fire, he produced a wide ring of metal, about the circumference of a small soup bowl. It was one of Ardara's devices, used to suppress the mutant powers of an Enma. It would set around the subject's neck like a choker necklace. It would inflict immense pain if an attempt was made to use a gift or ability. Its welding and bolts along the outer plating were brown with rust. It had a glass compartment which likely used to hold liquid. On the inside, opposite the empty compartment were three thin spikes, meant to puncture the back of the wearer's neck, and inject the chosen substance from the compartment into the blood stream. "As you know," Dacian went on, "this device prevents a mutant from using any ability whatsoever. A historic innovation, and genius mechanics. But you know what? It's worthless." He tossed it into the flickering flames with the rest of the demoded technology. Then his serious expression faded. With a smug grin he produced another device, less bulky, shinier, and free of rust. "Master Ardara felt it was time for an upgrade." He twirled the ring in his hand. "*This* device does the same as the last, with an extra perk. While wearing this, it will not only *hurt like hell* to use any power an Enma may possess . . ." his voice had a surprising tone of viciousness, ". . . . It will kill them if they try." His audience gave him an enormous roar of approval. "It stops their heart on the spot. So, not only will the slaves be more manageable," he paused again for the crowd to laugh, "but any Enma attempting to invade the castle will be rendered defenseless-and, let's face it-dead." Now he laughed along with the supporters.

Nyx had a straight face and applauded from her seat, but Wynne rolled his odd eyes. His weren't mismatched in color like most Enma, though he still had the abnormal pupils; but they had quite a strange color. His were both a piercing pink, like that of a white rat. They clashed with his long platinum blonde hair that was held in a high ponytail. He glared at Nyx, that simpleton, with choppily braided violet hair, and black, fathomless eyes. She wasn't even Enma, but Ardara took an eccentric liking to her.

Without warning, there were three heavy *bang*s at the big double doors.

"Why are you knocking?" Cinder reprimanded.

Orphenn shrugged.

Cinder kicked the door wide open.

The Ardarans glared incredulously as the two Enma stepped in through the wide doorway. Orphenn instinctively reached for the holsters at his hips.

Wynne felt an odd dizziness come over him when his eyes found the woman in black, standing beside the young boy in white. He longed to know her name.

Dacian's face changed again, from a look of shock, to his signature smug grin. "Welcome!" he mused, holding his arms out in a semblance of warmth. Then they fell to his sides, and he said sarcastically, "Come to join the party?" he cackled.

Wynne sighed, again rolling his eyes. He wearily stood, and made his way to the door, still not completely over the dizzy spell. Dacian could really get carried away sometimes.

Dacian slowly walked toward the siblings with an arrogance that was almost a strut. "My, my. *You're* a young one." His red and black eyes passed right over Cinder and set on Orphenn.

"Leave the child be, Dacian." Said Wynne, who had appeared beside him.

That's Dacian? Orphenn thought. *The traitor I was told about?*

"Must you always make such a fuss?" Wynne complained. "Dismiss them and continue your long and boring speech, and we can all call it a day and go home."

"Wynnie!" Dacian exclaimed. "I'm surprised at you! Where's your Ardaran spirit?"

But Wynne gave no response, for he was frozen, staring at Cinder, yet not seeing her, as if having a flashback.

The supporters began to gather closer, all with mischievous or devious visages.

"Just let them go." Wynne insisted, sluggishly, only just recovering from the strange trance-like episode. It had only lasted some short seconds, but he was greatly affected nevertheless. Then he said more forcefully, the absence leaving his eyes, "Just let them leave, I swear I'll kick your ass."

Orphenn was beginning to like Wynne.

"Oh, Wynne. I'll let them go. But not without a fight!" Dacian scowled, his arm just a blur as he pulled his poison-dripped lance from his sheath at his shoulder.

Just as quickly, Cinder had formed a similar lance from a collection of shadow that gathered in her hand, and used it to block Dacian's blow, the weapons clashing just above Orphenn's forehead.

"You're fast." Dacian smirked.

In that instant, Orphenn drew his silver and gold pistols and pointed them at Dacian's head. He never intended to fire, but this gave Cinder the time she needed. At the wave of her hand, there was a maelstrom of darkness at her side that dissipated to reveal her odd motorcycle. Anticipating Dacian's intentions, she and Orphenn mounted, but not before Dacian yelled, "And how *convenient* that you decide to visit *now!* Try *this* on for size!" Despite Wynne's best efforts to thwart the other, the device Dacian had been holding unhinged, and he thrust it at

Cinder. It caught her collar and re-hinged itself, and tightened around her neck. She painfully screamed when the spines punctured the back of her neck.

She writhed and coughed, clutching her throat, and the bike's handlebars to keep her balance.

During all this, the raving supporters surrounded the bike, regardless to desperate orders from Wynne. The sight of Cinder's agony put the pink-eyes Ardaran into almost a state of shock. *Who is this woman? What in the world is she doing to me?*

The supporters swarmed, trying to tip the bike over, or to damage it to some extent to prevent escape.

Slightly regaining her composure, Cinder kicked the switch, and the wings shot out, knocking them all aside. She punched the throttle. "Fire!" she ordered Orphenn.

The motorcycle seemed to defy gravity, its speed and wings helping it to veer upward, and crawl up the wall like a fleeing spider.

Orphenn swiveled his torso to aim at the crowd below them, and pulled the triggers, intentionally avoiding shooting in Wynne's direction. He liked Wynne.

He saw a few in the crowd collapse, knowing his bullets were embedded in their bodies.

The last thing he saw before Cinder drove them out a high window, shattering the glass, was the wicked smile on Dacian's face.

Chapter Eleven

~

Mission

Back in the Day Star's cargo hold, Cinder slowly slid off her bike, barely retaining enough balance to stand. Orphenn steadied her.

She still clutched the device at her neck, wheezing. Orphenn reached behind her to sweep her hair over one shoulder. He saw that blood was seeping from underneath the device's bolts and rolling down her back.

She tried to gently unhinge the device, but yelped as the action sent agony shooting through her body.

"Cinder! Don't take it off!" Orphenn urgently whispered.

"The others can't see." She pleaded. "They'd be angry . . . . They'd want to do something, to try and help . . ."

"Why don't you want help, you freak? You obviously need it! You can't use any powers with this on, and you can't take it off!"

"They would insist on going back to 'teach them a lesson,' I just know it. They'd want to get even. Before we knew it, *all* of us would have these around our necks. I don't want that." She pulled the zipper on her jacket up all the way, so her collar covered her neck completely. "It feels like a noose." She complained.

It was late that next morning, yet still dark outside. Here, the clouds always hid away the sun. The land below was nothing but stone and dirt, no fertile soil or vegetation to be found, everything darkened by constant shadow, a dreary gloom. Rain patted the steel siding of the Day Star.

Orphenn went to stand beside Jeremiah at the wheel, staring out through the rain-streaked windshield.

"And it's *still* raining here." Eynochia griped.

"This is . . . . Ardara?" guessed Orphenn.

"Yes." Jeremiah answered. "These are the wastelands Ardara and her followers were banished to. The castle is nearby." He yanked a lever, and the airship slowed to a stop.

"Are we here?" Sven interjected, coming to stand by Orphenn.

Jeremiah answered by pointing toward the outside, out across miles of rubble, where Ardara's castle could be seen in the distance. The tower stood out against the gray clouds. "I can't take the Day Star any further without being spotted," he stated, "Cinder, can you port us past the moat?" he asked before realizing that Cinder was absent from the main hold. "Cinder?"

"Ah-aaactually," Orphenn spoke up, "Cinder isn't feeling well, she's resting in her quarters."

"She's not *feeling well?*" Celina voiced. "Since when has that been an excuse?"

"I think she might be really sick."

"But how-"

"I can easily fly to the castle."

"I don't know, Orphenn . . ."

Xeila interrupted, "I can tell you where to go from there, over intercom, Orphenn. It'll be easy. *If* Celina allows it."

Each face turned to their Commander.

Sven laughed. "Maybe this'll be good for the kid. Little Bird's first solo mission."

Jeremiah flicked a switch on the control panel, extending the airship's landing gear, and lowered the Day Star gently to the ground. Hovering was wasting all the fuel.

Celina met her brother's eyes. "Very well." She sighed. "Be careful, Orphenn."

Orphenn folded his golden wings, keeping them partly open, at the ready, as he lightly touched down at the other side of the castle's moat, dew-dropped with rain. "Here." He announced through his shoulder communicator. "What now?"

"There should be a big pipe coming out of the castle wall." Xeila replied. Back at the ship, she had a large map spread across the table in front of her, running her fingers along the hand-drawn lines. "You can get in through there. It leads right to the boiler room with a straight shot shortcut to the dungeon. Freeing the prisoners will be easy. The slaves will be more challenging to free. They're scattered all over the castle. But don't worry about that much just yet. The main point of this mission is to gather any information you can find."

"Gotcha." Orphenn assured, leaping up to flutter along the iron castle wall. He now understood that *that* must have been what Xeila was doing when she had been in Ardara before, when Dacian had poisoned her. She had mapped the entire castle.

His hand found the siding of the massive drainage pipe, and he swung himself inside, feet landing with a splash. A shallow ribbon of water flowed at the bottom of the pipe. It seemed like miles ahead of him, but Orphenn could see a shaft of orange light escape through the top of the pipe, a splash of gold against the darkness. His feet sloshed through the water as he cautiously advanced down the tunnel-like pipe.

"There should be an open hatch some ways down." Xeila added. "Fly up through there into the boiler room. Better get your guns ready just in case."

"Roger." Orphenn pulled his gold pistol from its holster and cocked it, holding up to his ear in waiting, as he waded on, prepared to shoot down any opposition.

He slowly came into the light, gazing upward through the open hatch above his head. The room beyond was filled with steam and pulsed with humidity, gasses fuming down into the pipe below. He could have sworn that he heard someone screaming, sounds of excruciating pain. But he swallowed down his paranoia. He took a deep breath, and leapt up into the steam.

Knock, knock, knock.

Cinder jolted awake. Hurrying to hide her neck under a checkered black scarf, she answered, hitting the release button, and the hydraulic door hissed as it opened.

"Sven." Cinder said, regarding the man that leaned against the metal doorframe with weary surprise.

"Hey there Princess." His muscular arms were folded across his bare chest. "Heard you were sick. You look pale." He stepped inside, his tone more serious. "Your wings aren't even hidden. What's wrong?"

He was right. Her wings sagged, the tips of her straggled feathers sweeping the floor. Her eyes were sunken, darkly circled, and bloodshot, and she shook as she moved, like an elderly woman. She realized now why Ardaran slaves always looked so sickly. "I'm . . . Just really tired." She lied. "Where's Orphenn?"

"He's inside the castle now. Embarked on his first solo mission. Blimey, he's grown fast." Cinder's face merged from droopy exhaustion to wide-eyed panic, but Sven continued obliviously, "Freein' the slaves. Kinda concerned about the kid, but . . ."

"*What?*" Cinder whimpered. Before Sven could stop her, she sped out of the room, wings dragging behind her. He ran after her into the main hold.

"Celina!" Cinder cried, screeching to a halt in front of her sister, who looked abashed and puzzled. "Couldn't you have postponed the mission? It was *my* mission, Orphenn shouldn't be out there!" shouting at Celina took a lot of her diminishing energy, and she began to stumble. She steadied herself against a wall. "He's in danger!"

"We're all in danger, just by being here." Celina reminded. "I was against the idea, but Orphenn insisted."

"He's an idiot! He doesn't know what he's dong!" Cinder wailed. How could he be so rash? He knew the risk of being trapped by the device that enslaved her now, and yet he still insisted? What was he thinking?

"Since when have you been so protective of him?" Xeila put in.

Cinder ignored her. "I can't let him! He can't be hurt for my sake!" she turned around, intending to run for the cargo hold, but Sven was there, catching her as she wavered.

"Cinder, *what* is going on?" he demanded.

"They can't find him, Sven! He's Enma!"

"*And?*" His face was expectant, eyes and clenching hands commanding explanation.

Cinder violently pushed him away and tugged the scarf off her neck, showing them all what was latched at her throat. Her skin was bruised, rashed and bloody where the device clung to her like a starving leech. The veins in her neck bulged blue and purple. "They'll do *this* to him!"

"I'm sorry." Wynne said. He held a slave by the shoulder, an unhinged device prepared in his other hand. "I'm sorry."

The slave could only close his green and brown eyes, knowing inevitably what was in store for him. He screamed when the device attached like a boa constrictor to his already punctured skin-marks from the previous device, being replaced by the shiny new one.

Moments later, he turned on Wynne and hissing, bared his teeth as if to bite him.

"No, stop!" Wynne warned, but in vain.

With another choking scream, the slave's eyes rolled back, and he collapsed in a heap on the floor.

He had tried to use his gift, and the device stopped his heart instantly.

Wynne let out a sorrowful sigh, holding a hand over his face, with nothing but the sounds of steam and forging to clear his head.

Before yesterday, this death wouldn't have bothered him. All his typical Ardaran malice had somehow gone and his fundamental kind and gentle nature had resurfaced. He'd thought about it for hours, but never could he pinpoint the cause. All he knew was that when he looked at the woman in black, memories of his life before the war had all rushed back to him at once. He didn't know why, or what was so significant about this woman. All he could do for now was follow orders, and act like nothing was different.

With a start, his head jerked up. His ears strained to hear the sound of footsteps.

A figure emerged from the veil of steam ahead of him. It held something in its hand.

With another start, Wynne realized it was the boy in white from yesterday. The boy that escaped with the woman in black. That captivating woman that he couldn't wipe from his mind, not for a moment. The instant he had seen her, he remembered his family-sadly, they'd been killed in the war, but he could remember, now. Every memory up until now. Everything Ardara had stolen from him.

The boy stepped forward, then took a startled step back when he saw Wynne, extending his wings partly in case he needed to make a quick flight. A curdling scream emanated from further in the room, likely a slave being punished for misbehaving. So Orphenn hadn't imagined it. *Freaky.*

Wynne held up his hands, calmingly. *The boy must be looking for the dungeon. To free the war prisoners. That's the way it's done, when war is on the horizon . . . What other mission could he have?* Wynne pondered.

"The dungeon is that way." He whispered, tilting his head to the left.

Orphenn nodded gratefully, and rushed into the steam where Wynne had directed him. *I knew I liked him.* Orphenn thought, recalling the day before.

"I might regret that later . . . ." Wynne murmured to himself, watching after the boy until the steam hid him from view. "Can't say I care." He laughed. Ever since his memories returned to him, he remembered how much he hated Ardara and everything that came with that name. He remembered everything the Master had forced him to do under her mind control. He'd hurt so many for her sake. Ruined so much at her will. And now that he could act on his own will and control his own thoughts, he couldn't help but wonder: what was so special about the woman in black, that the mere sight of her would wake him from hypnosis?

As he thought about her, he heaved the corpse of the unfortunate slave up into his arms and threw the body into the kiln.

Evidently, Orphenn never made it as far as the dungeon.

He waded through the steam, down a dimly-lit corridor, firmly grasping his pistol. The steam dispersed, and the temperature dropped significantly the further he strode. When he turned a corner, he was met with the familiar malevolent gaze of Dacian.

Wynne had to double-take, and then blink several times to be sure he wasn't hallucinating, or dreaming.

Just as he had been thinking about her, the raven haired woman rose from a cloud of steam.

But this time, she shook and stumbled as she walked. She looked distressed, and her face held despair. She was bloody and bruised where Ardara's device squeezed around her neck, and her wings' feathers were ruffled and knotted. Wynne would not have dreamt her like that.

He worried for her. "You." He said, and walked toward her, reaching for her.

Before she could react, gunshots sounded from down the corridor.

Was this a set up? Orphenn wondered. Dacian had dodged and deflected each of his bullets, and lunged forward with his lance. *Should I have trusted Wynne?*

"What is your name?" Wynne asked.

The woman looked at him like he'd asked her what her favorite color was. "Cinder." She answered carefully, then pleaded, "Where is my brother? Please! Take me instead! I'll do anything!"

So willing to sacrifice herself for one that she loves . . . . Wynne noted, knowing immediately who it was that she called her brother. *I must help her in any way I can.* "I mean no harm to you or your brother." He explained. "But others do. Come. Run ahead of me. Fast." He gently pushed her forward into the corridor. Judging by the gunshot, he knew ruefully that Nyx or Dacian must have met Orphenn there. He hoped the boy would not resent him, or think wrongly of his intentions. As he chased after her, he knew this was what Cinder desired, but still he hoped he had made the right choice.

Chapter Twelve

~

Capture

Orphenn was pinned. Between the cold metal floor, and the poisonous head of Dacian's lance. In an instant, it would have been lodged in his chest, had it not been for a shout from the other end of the corridor, followed by a cacophony of rapid footfalls.

"Dacian! Intruder!" the voice called. "Catch her!"

Dacian straightened, replacing his lance in the holster on his back.

Orphenn quickly retrieved his pistol from the ground, only for Dacian to again knock it from his grip. He made to dash to the side, but Dacian caught his shoulder in an iron grip and pinned him again, against the wall. "You're not going anywhere." He growled.

"Catch the intruder!" Wynne beckoned.

Cinder shot out of the steam and sped around the corner.

"*You* again?" Dacian mused. He almost let her pass by, but in a blink, he had raised his fist up to meet her. Her head collided with his rock hard knuckles, and she collapsed at his feet. She was still conscious, but only slightly.

Wynne came to a sharp stop at the corner. He was filled with rage at the sight of Cinder writhing on the floor. Yet again, Dacian had overdone it. But he held his calm façade.

"Nicely done." He feigned. His voice was placid, though his teeth were grinding furiously.

Dacian turned his glare to the infuriated Orphenn, pinned like an insect under his arm. Orphenn's breath came as hissing through clenched teeth, like an aggravated snake in a cage. Dacian grabbed a handful of the boy's dark hair and pulled him from the wall. "*You* deal with *this* little angel." He ordered, and shoved Orphenn into Wynne's much gentler grasp. Then he knelt down beside Cinder. "*This* little angel deserves special treatment." He picked Cinder up and flung her over his shoulder, standing and turning toward the dungeon door across the corridor, but then looked back at Wynne to add, "Do with the boy what you will. He is no concern of mine."

Cinder gave Wynne a last beseeching look from her perch in the tall man's lift. Her eyes said *Protect my brother. Please.* Then Dacian proceeded and they disappeared behind the steel-bolted door to the dungeon.

Wynne stared after them for a moment, then remembered the boy in his grasp.

"This way, *vermin*." He instructed, just in case Dacian still listened. He led Orphenn back to the boiler room in soft, but firm hands.

"No! Please, wait-Cinder!" Orphenn struggled. "My sister!"

Wynne admired the love the siblings shared, sad that any similar bond he shared in the past was lost to him now. Despite Orphenn's squirming, he managed to drag the boy back to the large drainage pipe, effortlessly lifting him above the open hatch.

"No! Please!" Orphenn grabbed Wynne's uniform collar in begging fists. "What will he do to Cinder!?"

Wynne looked at him sincerely in the eyes, and spoke with hard certainty. "Young One, I promise you. I won't let anything happen to your sister." He held Orphenn's wrists. "Trust me. I know what I'm doing." He took a deep breath, his face full of sympathy. "Forgive me." He pried Orphenn's fingers from his collar, and let them go. Orphenn lost his balance, catching the hatch lid for support. For a moment he could only stare at Wynne.

"I'm sorry." After one last apologetic gaze, like an expert martial artist Wynne kicked Orphenn's boots out from under him and pushed his shoulders.

The youth fell back, and down into the pipe.

Wynne heard him land with a spatter at the bottom. He closed and locked the hatch, apologizing again.

For a moment he stood there, leaning against the pipe. He knew Orphenn was still in there, the stubborn boy. If he remained much longer, he would be caught, either by obedient slaves or brainwashed guards, and then there would be no hope for him.

Wynne would not let that happen. He knew what he had to do, because he knew Orphenn would not willingly leave with his sister still trapped inside the castle. But he was reluctant. Cinder came to replace her brother, to keep him safe. If Orphenn got hurt, then what would have been the point in trying to protect him? If Wynne opened the spill gate, the water would force Orphenn out the drain, and into the moat. His comrades outside would be sure to notice and come to his aid immediately. And if he didn't open the gate, Orphenn would surely be stuck in prison with his sister.

He took a moment to weigh the options.

"Anything is better than prison . . ." Wynne decided. He flipped up the cap to the bright blue button on the end of the plumbing control panel, and with a deep breath, he pressed it. "I just hope you have the sense to run."

Orphenn stood slowly, surrounded by darkness after hearing the hatch clamped shut, almost in shock. "I can't leave!" he shouted, his voice cracking with the effort. His words traveled down the cavernous pipe and echoed back to him. His throat tightened. "Cinder!"

A rush of damp air blew from deeper down the pipe, and brought with it the cold scent of wet metal.

Orphenn's eyes widened in a jolt of realization. "He's forcing me out . . ." he said with a startled gasp. He spun on his heel and took off at a sprint, desperately attempting to flap his wings and flee faster, but he couldn't seem to catch the air in this tube. He'd have to keep running.

Finally, he could see the opening, a circle of rain, but just as it came into his view, his boots slipped on the slick metal.

The water caught up to him. Soon he was encompassed, and all he could see was foam and bubbles. His throat and lungs were burning.

The water poured into the moat, and Orphenn was dumped into its dark waves, and tossed about underwater like a kite tail in the wind.

Thankfully, he made it to the surface, sucking in a breath of chilly air as he clung to the bank. Coughing violently, he climbed onto the muddy land, raindrops crashing all around him. When he stood, he saw that Cinder's bike was lying on its side among the rubble. Then he spoke as if Wynne would hear him. "If not for you, I would be more persistent." He glanced back at the massive pipe, still sprouting water.

Sopping wet, he lifted the motorcycle onto its wheels and kicked the switch for the wings to snap out. He tried to speak to his squadron through his communicator, but the water had shorted out its circuits. He had no choice but to fly on Cinder's bike and return to the Day Star as quickly as he could. Everything about this was completely against his nature, but what else could he do now?

The instant Wynne had pushed the button, he turned back and dashed for the corridor, intending to make sure Orphenn made it out. Halfway down the hall, a gleam caught his eye. It was Orphenn's gold pistol, shining in the dim lighting. Wynne picked it off the floor and examined it.

There was a bolted window set into the wall beside him. He hastily gazed through the cracked glass into the moat, stories below. With a surge of relief, he watched Orphenn crawl out of the moat and fly away on a sky ride.

And now with a new determination, Wynne held the golden pistol to his chest, as if renewing a silent oath, then slipped it into his belt.

Orphenn tried convincing the others to go back with him and rescue Cinder, to no avail.

"Celina!" he protested. "I watched the traitor Dacian drag her into the dungeon! Who knows what torture she's going through right now! We have to go back, we have to help her!" his voice was raspy from nearly drowning.

"It's not possible, Orphenn." Celina said. "I can feel her through our link. She's not in any real pain. We're not risking the safety of the entire squadron."

"But doesn't it piss you off, that it was *Dacian* who captured her?"

She didn't respond.

Orphenn slumped into a chair and held his face in his hands.

Eynochia came beside him and draped a blanket over his shoulders. "Orphenn." She sympathized. "You're soaked. You should rest."

He shook his head silently.

Sven laid a hand on his arm and said, "We *will* rescue her, Little Bird. Soon. Remember, we love her too."

"There was a man." Orphenn said, looking up at him. "His name was . . . Wynne, I think."

"Wynne . . ." Sven was wide-eyed, as if he'd heard the name before, but couldn't recall where.

"He was there at the warehouse yesterday . . . And he told me where the shortcut to the dungeon was, but Dacian had interfered. When Cinder came, he forced me to escape back through the pipe, like he meant to protect me. And he was apologizing the whole time. He promised me he wouldn't let anything happen to Cinder. I know he's an Ardaran, but I saw his eyes, he's Enma too. And . . . I trust him." He hesitated. "I even avoided shooting him back at the warehouse."

"Well, if he helped you escape safely . . ." Eynochia stated, but Orphenn interrupted:

"You mean *made* me escape, *somewhat* safely. He kind of flushed me out. But even so . . . . I have every reason so far to trust him, and I believe what he promised was honest. I know Cinder isn't in any immediate danger, but . . ." emotion made his voice crack. "But it's my fault . . . I insisted on continuing the mission . . ." his voice lowered to a whisper, "And now she's trapped and she's defenseless . . ."

Xeila looked up from her map to gawk at him. "Orphenn. What Cinder did was her own choice. It was her own decision to go after you, and the stubborn ass wouldn't have taken 'no' for an answer! She took your place to save you. And, if anything, she felt the blame was on her for being hindered by that freaky device and forcing you to go in her stead in the first place. So really, the blame should be put on Ardara. Again. Don't blame yourself. She'll be okay. Especially if what you tell us about this Wynne is true."

Orphenn managed a teary smile.

"That name sounds so familiar, doesn't it Dad?" Eynochia queried. "Wynne . . . ."

"Yeah," Xeila concurred, "Wynne, Wynne . . . ."

"Criminey, girls!" Sven remarked. "You're memory's just as bad as your daddy's! Can't even remember what I had for breakfast this mornin'. Did I even have breakfast? Cripes I'm hungry again."

Orphenn could feel the love between this family, however broken they were by loss. He could take comfort, at least, in that.

Chapter Thirteen

~

Ruse

Cinder awoke to the sound of someone singing. She felt miserable. Her arms were shackled and chained behind her back, her legs to the metal floor. Her wings folded awkwardly around her arms. Her skin was slicked with sweat, and her favorite jacket and boots had been removed, as well as her and communicator. She could feel the device on her neck like it weighed a thousand pounds, and her wings felt like they were nailed to her back. She was sore and famished.

She was surprised to see a man in the cell ahead of her. But she could only see the back of him-his head and arms were restrained by an iron stockade, which was melded into the metal floor. She couldn't see his face, but she heard his voice, carrying an upbeat tune. It started to give her a headache. It wasn't that the singing was bad. Even the flickering electric light was searing into her retinas-each sense was oversensitive and painful.

"Ugh . . . Hey." Cinder groaned. "Hey, *Music Man*. Can you tone it down a bit?"

"*Songs to ease my weariness*," he sang, ringing around the metallic prison, and continued the melody.

"Gah!" She seethed. "Can you at least sing something more . . . Mellow?"

At this, Music Man ceased. Then his voice carried into a song that dripped with emotion, and secret meaning, the words holding the air around them and remaining. The sorrow in it brought tears to Cinder's eyes.

> "*I never saw the light*
> *I never saw the sun*
> *Knowing you has changed me*
> *When loving you begun*

No tale can be told
Without a word from you
No question can be answered
Without telling what to do

But when all seems lost
I'll hold you to the sky
No matter what the cost
There will always be you and I."

His voice caught in his throat, and Cinder got the feeling that he'd started to cry. She was confirmed when she heard his sobs reverberating around the cell. The song must have meant something more than Cinder heard.

Suddenly, the cell door creaked open, completely on its own.

It hung there, waiting for something.

Music Man went uncharacteristically silent.

Ardara appeared in the entry.

"Cinder." said she, in her light, feathery voice. "I knew this day would come."

"And what day is that?" Cinder asked wistfully. The sight of her sister, deranged and so changed from old self, made Cinder's heart heavy with regret and grief. Her green and blue eyes were mourning.

Ardara's red and blue were hard merciless. She lifted Cinder with her mind, until she levitated at eye level, no slack in the chains. She grasped Cinder's chin, and raised her head to stare in her eyes. "This day," she whispered, her voice growing louder with each word, "is the day I look my sister in the face and say . . ." she brought her face closer, "*I hate you!*" she squealed, and dropped Cinder. She tumbled to the metal, grunting painfully. "What about *you?*" Ardara questioned, full of rage. "What will *you* do today?"

Cinder's hair covered her face and clung to the sweat on her skin. "Today is when I realize," she replied breathily, "how crazy my sister really is. How lost she's become. How sick she is." She looked up at Ardara with sadness in her features. "How badly she needs to come home."

Ardara screamed in a fit of anger. With a swish of her arm, the device around Cinder's neck surged with small bolts of electricity that grew larger the longer they crackled around her. Cinder painfully convulsed, and then abruptly, stopped moving at all. She went limp, collapsed onto her side, and the blue bolts died and receded, as did her heartbeat.

"I have no home." said Ardara, when she halted the shock. "And neither do you, little drifter."

But Cinder wasn't as lifeless as she had thought. "You're wrong." said the Drifter.

Ardara gasped. That should have killed her. It should have stopped her heart. And yet she lay there still breathing, even speaking.

Ardara didn't hear what Cinder said next, nor did she want to, for she had run away from the dungeon in a huff. The cell door slammed and locked on its own behind her.

Music Man released an audible sigh of uneasiness.

"I'm sorry, Music Man . . ." Cinder said. "Hey . . ." she heaved herself into a sitting position. "What's your real name?"

"*My name is unimportant to the tale,*" he sang.

"Hm. Alright, then, Music Man it is. Think you can sing me a song?" she fell back to her side again. "How 'bout a lullaby? I'm feeling sleepy."

Cinder couldn't see his face, but he smiled. He sang the meaningful song he had sung before. His even voice put her to sleep almost instantly.

The Day Star was hidden in the lee of a forest, its crew waiting, for lack of anything else to do. This forest was the only sign of vegetation anywhere near the Ardaran wastelands, though still it was dry and free of any wildlife.

Orphenn looked out the window, up over the trees, where he knew Ardara's castle was just beyond those mountains, easily within flying distance.

"We can't sit here forever." Sven told Jeremiah. "A war's about to begin."

"I know . . ." he responded, tying back his blonde dread locks. "It's like water coming to a boil in a stew pot . . . . You can feel it in the air . . . ." He shook his head. "Should we go to Plenthin for fuel?"

"That might be best. Let's take off."

Orphenn gave Sven a look of disbelief. "But . . ." He objected.

"I swear we'll come back, Little Bird. We just need to resupply."

The orphan nodded, and trumped to his quarters. Eynochia noticed his head hanging in disappointment as the Day Star took flight. She caught up to him and touched his shoulder. She was alarmed at her own audacity, whenever she was near Orphenn. With any other boy, she might have been too shy to offer him comfort, and too indecisive to choose to do so in the first place. Orphenn made her feel at ease, she realized. Calm. She never worried what he would think of her, or cared anyway. She felt comfortable, safe, by him.

The two walked into Orphenn's quarters and sat across from each other at the tea table. In an attempt to peel his mind from Cinder's well being, he started the conversation.

"So, you're a Sergeant?" He inquired with a tired curiosity.

Eynochia chuckled. "The ranks are just for fun, really. The Enma never had a really *organized* army. But Celina made it work. That's what makes her a leader. And an amazing one at that."

"I think I want to speak with her later . . . Ask some questions . . ." Orphenn pondered.

"What for?"

"I want to know more about Dacian. Why he is how he is now."

Eynochia's face darkened. "From what she tells me, he used to be a really sweet guy. He just . . . . Decided to kill everybody one day . . ."

"That's just not possible." Orphenn's voice was skeptical. "How? How do you just get up one morning and say to yourself, 'Well, I feel like a murderer today.' Sven was in his squadron too, wasn't he? How did you and Xeila survive?"

"Dad made us stay with Mom, and her squadron. It was too bad they had to be separated most of the time. Children didn't really count as members of the squad, but if you had them, they fought with you."

"Who was in your squadron?"

"We were called the Condors and our ship was the Phoenix. There was my mother-she was the only one we really knew at the time. We kept to ourselves most of the time. Jeremiah was there. And he was always with me and Xeila, since we were more his age. And his mother and sister. I can't remember their names. Oh . . . And my uncle, Ira. My dad's brother." *Sven has a brother?* Orphenn marveled. "He was with us. I can barely remember him. There was a boy that he had taken under his wing, and cared for him like a son after Ardarans killed his family. A blondie. He was older than us, probably seventeen or eighteen. Dad was really fond of him. The one thing I remember about him was his eyes. They were both the same color and they were *pink*. Can you believe that? Pink! But he was quite handsome and he totally pulled it off-"

"Wait, wait, wait . . . Pink eyes, like . . . Like an albino rabbit?" Orphenn recalled Wynne, staring at him kindly with his pink eyes.

"Yeah, exactly. But he and Ira both went missing in the middle of battle. Dad said they both died. 'Ardara killed them herself' is what he believes. And I think it was that next year that Dacian turned against us."

"It must be terrible to lose a brother." Orphenn tapped his lip in thought.

"Yeah. I don't think Dad ever recovered. To lose your brother and your wife in one war . . . And so many friends besides."

"I think I'll go talk to Celina. I'm feeling curious now."

"Can I tell you something first?" Eynochia touched his hand.

"Of course." He twined his fingers with hers. She blushed at the gesture, though her skin tone didn't show it.

"I never thanked you. For bringing me home, a while ago. I was so lucky that you were there in the forest. I don't think I would've made it any further."

"I *know* you wouldn't have made it. You were so bloody . . ." he remembered. "You're welcome."

"You know what Xeila said? 'I really like that Orphenn,' she says. 'You were carried to safety in the arms of a golden angel!'"

It was Orphenn's turn to blush. "Angel?" he repeated. He'd never seen himself as an angel. His sisters had always been the angels.

"I think she was right." Eynochia stated. She stood up to touch Orphenn's shoulder and kiss his cheek. "You are my angel." She walked to the door and pressed the release button. "I'll fetch Celina for you." Then she left and the door hissed shut behind her.

Orphenn could feel the heat in his face, incredulously touching his cheek where Eynochia had kissed him.

At length, there was a knock at the door.

"Come in."

The doors spread open for Celina to step inside. "You wanted to speak with me?" she asked. Orphenn noticed the dark circles under her eyes, bloodshot and pearly from lack of sleep. He guessed he wasn't the only one worried about Cinder. *Celina must be scared to the point of puking*, Orphenn realized. She did look a bit peeked. *She does a great job of hiding it.*

"Yes . . ." Orphenn met her with a warm hug. "Just out of curiosity, I . . . Wanted to know more about Dacian? I was wondering if you would tell me about him? If it's not too sensitive a subject . . ."

"Dacian?" she reiterated, taking a seat. "Of course, Little Brother. What do you want to know?"

"What was he like before?" he sat beside her. "Why did he change?"

"He used to be very kind, though he had quite a temper."

"He seems to have kept the temper part." Orphenn noted.

"Yes." Celina agreed. "As for his sudden change of heart . . . I don't know. But it broke mine.

"He was the White Herons' sharpshooter. He never missed. But after his family was taken from him . . . Executed by rapid-fire . . . he never touched a gun again. Sven loved him like a son."

"Did *you* love him?" Orphenn inquired.

She looked at him with solemn blue and brown eyes. "Yes." She breathed, almost like she too was still coming to terms with the matter. "I'm still . . . In love with him. I thought he loved me . . ." she reached out and took Orphenn's hand.

The room around them disappeared, like the parlor had, back at the palace. Celina showed him a memory. He looked around, and instead of seeing his quarters aboard the Day Star, he saw a balcony outside another airship. The Avian, he realized. The two floated in the air ahead of it, the wind twisting their hair as they watched.

A much younger Celina leaned on the balcony's railing, looking out into the twilight sky, clouds lined with orange and vermillion.

Dacian had crept up and hugged her from behind, presenting her with a bouquet of violet lilies, and slipping one colorful bloom into her hair.

He looked different in Aleidian white, as opposed to Ardaran black and burgundy. His face was bright and free of malice, and he had no smug grin, or sharply groomed sideburns. Only a genuine, joyful smile. An entirely different man.

Celina kissed him and held his hand.

"Lilies were my favorite. Especially the purple ones." She informed.

Sven had come between them, holding their heads back playfully. His smiling face had no scars or worry lines. "Alright you two love birds. Time to get while the gettin's good! We have a lot a work to do!"

And then the memory faded, and they were in Orphenn's carpeted room again.

Celina released his hand and sat back. "I guess it was all just a ruse."

Orphenn shook his head vigorously. "What if it wasn't?" he reasoned. "What if it was something bigger than that?"

Orphenn's words stayed in Celina's head the entire day, and long after, becoming engraved in her mind.

Something bigger?

Chapter Fourteen

~

Uncovering

Cinder woke again to the creak of the cell door and the smell of food.

She opened her eyes. She saw that a black tarp had been thrown across Music Man's stockade, covering his head. Though she could still hear his muffled humming.

Wynne was standing in the entry holding a trey.

Cinder struggled to sit up. Wynne came closer, set down the trey and helped Cinder into a sitting position. "You're very weak." He said. "I brought you some food." He slid the trey in front of him. It had a bowl of stew, a hunk of bread, and a cup of water.

Cinder's throat burned from thirst and her stomach ached from hunger, but she paid no heed. It wasn't important to her right now.

"Where is my brother?" She coughed. "What did you do with Orphenn?"

He gave her a comforting smile. "Orphenn is safe. I watched him fly away on your motorcycle." He pulled Orphenn's gold pistol from his belt and held it out to her. "Sadly, he left this behind. You should return it to him."

"How can I, when I'm chained up here?" Cinder protested, as Wynne subtly slipped the gun into her shirt.

"You won't be for long." He assured, holding the rim of the cup to her lips. He tipped it up to help her drink the water. He was surprised at how quickly she gulped it down. He set the empty cup on the trey and began to feed her spoonfuls of soup. "Your mission," he said, "to free the prisoners of war. I'm going to help you."

When the soup was gone, Cinder said, "Why? Why are you helping me?"

"Because . . ." he began, searching for words. "You are the one that opened my eyes. You brought me . . . Back to the light."

His answer confused her. Perhaps he didn't understand the exact meaning of it either.

After a pause he added, "And besides, I wasn't always Ardaran. I know who you are now, Lady Cinder. You looked so different back then, when I was a Condor. I guess that's why it took me some time to realize your name was no coincidence."

"What is *your* name?" she asked.

"Wynne." He answered. He plucked the bread from the trey and tore off a piece for Cinder to chew more easily.

"Thank you, Wynne." She said.

The bread was halfway gone when a smug voice sounded from behind Wynne's back.

"What's Wynnie doing here?"

Wynne tensed in surprise, before cleverly coating his lip with excess soup from the bottom of the bowl. He stuffed his mouth with bread. He casually cleared his throat, stood, and turned to face Dacian with an emotionless stare, chewing nonchalantly.

Dacian cackled. "Eating your lunch in front of hungry prisoners? How *wicked* of you." He sauntered over to Music Man's stockade, and flicked the tarp that hid his face. "I covered this guy so he'd stop singing. Not very effective. Sure shut him up though.

"Anyway, I came to speak with the *angel*. Master Ardara is incredibly glad to have you with us," he announced as though he should have been wearing a tux rather than a uniform and headgear, and carrying an informational brochure instead of a lance. "She's been waiting so long. In fact, she *commanded* that you be kept in *this* cell. Reserved for 'offenders of the highest threat.'" He quoted. "As in, the most powerful Enma prisoners."

Cinder couldn't wrap her brain around the idea of mellow Music Man being a threat to anyone. "You came down here just to tell me that?"

"Well, that, and that we're tracking your airship and are preparing to ambush. Ta-ta!" he waved, and left the cell, leaving Wynne and Cinder in a state of shock.

After a moment f grave silence, Wynne gulped, and spun around to pick up the food trey. "I can only give you this much food a day, I apologize. I'll be back, same time tomorrow."

"Wynne, wait!" Cinder pleaded mutedly. "What will happen to my squadron? My family!"

Wynne set the trey aside and kneeled closely in front of her. "Who is in your squadron?"

"My sister Celina and brother Orphenn. Jeremiah, and Sven, and Sven's two daughters, Xeila and Eynochia." Wynne's face brightened at the mention of Jeremiah and Sven, and his daughters-names he recognized. "And me."

"Oh, Cinder." Wynne smiled reassuringly. "No matter what happens, nothing can defeat that squadron. I've known each of them in the past. They're amazingly strong, probably stronger now that years have passed and their mutations have matured. They're almost unbeatable, that group. You know it. My Lady Celina is yet another assurance of success. There are countless that would give their lives for her and her squadron."

"Thank you, Wynne." She smiled and rested her head on his shoulder. He patted her back, then grabbed the empty food trey and walked out of the cell, locking the bars behind him.

Dacian stood in the throne room, sitting on the arm of Ardara's plush throne. He twirled a golden feather between his thumb and forefinger.

Nyx came through the wide double doors at the end of the room and walked down the black carpet toward him.

"Where is Master Ardara?" asked Dacian as Nyx came to meet him.

"Taking her nap." Nyx replied, giving Dacian an expectant look. He took the hint, noticing that one of her eyes was bright and golden, and her pupils had changed.

"She made you Enma." He concluded.

"She told me how to use my gift."

"She foresaw the gift you would have." He deduced, nodding.

"I was against becoming a filthy mutant . . . But she told me that I would be better than the rest of them, our enemies. She told me to forget what my parents taught me, that prejudice against mutants would get us nowhere. So now I'm just like her, and you, and Wynne."

"And you can track someone quite easily, I hear?"

"If I touch an object that belonged to someone, I will know exactly where they are and who is with them."

"Perfect." He grinned, and gave Nyx the golden feather.

"Should be an hour or so before we get to Plenthin." Jeremiah informed, setting the Day Star on auto pilot.

"Good." Said Xeila, giving her fiancé a kiss. "We need more food, I'm starving."

"You said it." Sven concurred. "My big ones are eatin' my little ones."

Orphenn sulked at the table across from Sven, tired from a sleepless night.

"Little Bird," Sven advised, "you're exhausted. Go to bed."

"Eh . . . ?" He droned, eyelids fluttering. "Oh. Yeah." He rose drowsily and slumped to his room.

But once he was in his quarters, he found himself unable to sleep. He mumbled, sleepily, "I have to find a way to get to Cinder . . ." he thought harder and harder about her, and Dacian, and Wynne's promise, chanting. "I have to . . ."

His eyelids drooped when tears came to his eyes. His throat tightened, but he took a deep breath and swallowed. His eyes closed. But instead of sleep, a pulling feeling came over him. His head rolled to the side, and his body went limp as his spirit was torn from his body.

When he opened his eyes, he was staring down at his dormant form. His mouth gaped in disbelief. He looked at his hands, and down at himself, floating above the floor. He appeared to be made of golden stars that matched the golden feathers of his wings, which fanned out around him, also threaded with stars, like he was sculpted from glitter. With every movement, sparkling particles trailed after, as if he'd been bathed in pixie dust. On top of that, he levitated in mid air without the effort of his wings.

When he looked at himself, he was transparent and twinkling, but when he turned to look in the mirror, nothing reflected back to him. He was outside his body, in spirit form.

With a gasp, he looked back to his body. It lay there on the bed, motionless except for the rise and fall of its chest as it breathed.

Breathing . . . Not dead. Could he be dreaming?

He flowed gracefully to the door, and went to touch it, when his hand went all the way through it, as though it wasn't there. Astounded, he stepped through to the other side of the door, out into the hallway.

"*Weird . . .*" he tried to say, but his mouth and face seemed to move in slow motion, and his voice came out as if he heard from miles away, coming *to* him rather than *from* him.

He drifted to the main hold.

No one noticed him. He gravitated curiously toward Sven, who was gazing out the window again, with his back to the rest of the room. Warily, Sven turned his head to slowly look over his shoulder, as if he felt a presence behind him. Finding nothing, he turned back to the window.

They can't see me. Orphenn reveled. *This must be a new gift! To walk in soul instead of in body.* He fluidly paced around the room, right in front of their faces, and no one reacted to him. He was invisible.

There was a sudden startled squeal from behind him, and everyone gazed toward it in concern. Orphenn attempted to swiftly spin around to face the noise, but ended up performing a graceful twirl. This form brought to him an almost timeless elegance.

The scream was Eynochia's. A hairbrush had fallen from her hand, onto the floor. She was staring right at him.

"*You can see me.*" Orphenn enthused, in his far away voice, with many echoes. He kindly picked up the brush and handed it back to her. "*You dropped this.*" She took it, wide eyed, clueless as to why Orphenn was floating there like a magical fairy ghost. A magical fairy ghost with manners.

Abruptly realizing that what the other members saw was a hairbrush floating from the floor to Eynochia's hand of its own accord, Orphenn dashed back to his room, straight through the closed door, stopping at his bed. Quickly, he lowered, and lay down into the fitted mold of his own body.

He snapped awake with a gasp, hopping up so quickly that he fell off the bed, disoriented. He rushed to the door, ramming into it and falling to the floor again, forgetting he could not go through a closed door with his body. He laughed at his own foolishness and pressed the release button.

"It was Orphenn!" Eynochia wailed. "It was, I swear! He was right there!" she waved the hair brush where Orphenn's spirit had been.

The others looked at her like she was talking to them with a finger in her nose. Until Orphenn came shouting into the main hold.

"Guys!" was the first comprehendible word they heard as he stomped to a halt. "I know how to save Cinder."

Chapter Fifteen

~

Branding

The dungeon was dank and filthy, and its prisoners were restless, until they froze, motionless, as if time had stopped in its tracks. The only one that freely moved was Wynne, strolling down the hallway, taking his own sweet time, gazing into each cell. He examined droplets of water that had spilled from an upturned pail, stilled in place, congealed in mid air. He smiled. "It's working."

He opened a random cell and stepped inside, keys jingling. The prisoners in that cell were engaged in a suspended card game. He closed the door again and turned to a slave that was serving another guard in pause. The guard had been scolding the slave for some unknown reason, spit flung from his mouth, floating like the water droplets. Wynne looked at the slave, who looked irritated. His eyes were yellow and hazel, like two different snakes.

"I have to take a chance . . ." Wynne said. "This could end badly . . ." he predicted. He reached out to touch the device at the slave's neck.

He was sick of death. But he had to find a way to help the White Herons' mission.

He unlatched the device. It opened, and he gingerly tugged the spines out of the base of the slave's neck, where three deep gauges were left.

Wynne grimaced and clicked the device shut again, careful to hold it on the edges, so to avoid touching the blood and puss that coated the inside. He hid behind a wall. With a snap of his fingers, time started again, the water drops splashed to the metal floor, and he watched the outcome of the slave and the guard.

The dungeon burst to life again, and the guard's upraised hand dove to slap the slave across the face. The slave turned right back with a snarl. Needle like points came to each of his teeth. Scales rose from his skin, green and reptilian, and razor spines lifted from his back and his bald head. His long forked tongue slid out of his mouth with a menacing hiss.

"It worked!" Wynne whispered excitedly. Then he became serious. He had to intervene when the slave spit toxic venom into the guard's face with no warning, like a threatened cobra.

Wynne sped to the slave from behind and swiftly slammed the device back onto his neck. Without hesitation, he blew a peculiar white dust from the palm of his hand. The dust was like diamond sand, but it floated onto the slave like snowflakes. Like a sleeping spell, the dust made the slave faint and topple to the floor in involuntary slumber. His fangs, spines, and scales receded and disappeared.

Wynne then tended to the guard, whose stinging eyes were streaming with tears and swelling shut. But instead of worry painting his face, Wynne brandished a triumphant smile.

Now he knew how to help the Enma.

Wynne slipped silently into Cinder's cell with another trey of food. Cinder noted that there was much more food there than on his last visit.

"I thought this fellow would like to eat." He explained, motioning to the stockade, where Music Man's face was still covered.

He kneeled closely in front of Cinder once again, and held out a jingling key ring with an excited smile. "I have *keys* this time!" He whispered.

Cinder smiled at his enthusiasm.

He reached behind her and unlocked the padlock that bound her arm chains. The chains fell to the floor at her sides, and moaning, she gave her arms a good stretch.

"Wynne. Thank you." She said, beginning to devour the food on the trey. He nodded, tucking her hair behind her ear. She flushed at the affectionate gesture, but continued to eat.

Wynne took a hunk of bread and a glass of water from the trey and stepped over to Music Man. He pulled and let the black tarp flow to the metal floor, and took the bag from his trapped head. At the sight of his face, Wynne's rosy eyes went wide as saucers. The glass cup broke as it hit the floor, bread crumbs scattering at his feet.

Cinder still couldn't see Music Man's face, but Wynne could, and he had never looked so shocked.

"I thought you were dead." He said, staring at Music Man.

Then, for the first time since Cinder was imprisoned, Music Man spoke without a melody. "Have some faith in me, Wynnie. Did you really think I would die so easily?"

"But I saw! I saw you fall off the tower! In fact, that was exactly before Ardara . . ."

"Took your memory. I know. I remember."

Before the reunion could continue, Cinder's chains came to life, and rebound her, painfully tight around her wrists. And before any of them could wonder what happened, a device was chucked at Wynne, and it latched around his neck. The spikes shot into his skin and he collapsed to the metal, chest heaving.

Ardara emerged in the doorway for the second time. "Dacian was right to be suspicious of you, Wynne." She said quickly. "I read the memory of the cell guard you helped assault last night. Very clever, using your hourglass gift to safely remove that serpent mutant's restraint.

Your little experiment went according to plan, but nothing else of yours will be so fortunate." She lifted Wynne telekinetically, and as he hovered in the air, Ardara tore the uniform from his body, including belt and headgear. His hair string snapped, and his long blonde locks fell into his face and across his bare shoulders. She used her mind to disconnect the chains at Cinder's ankles, and used them to bind Wynne's hands. She let him plummet again to the floor beside Cinder. "I don't know how you broke my power over you, Wynne. But you both will be punished." Nyx and Dacian, now the two remaining favorites, came to her side, ready for any command. "How would you like to teach these miscreants a little lesson before embarking on your ambush mission?" she offered.

"We'd be delighted." said Dacian, with his signature smug grin.

Cinder and Wynne both had their faces pressed to a wall. They were on their knees, with their backs to the rest of the boiler room, and their hands were tied behind them. Nyx had Cinder firmly held against the rusted, steam-warmed metal, and Dacian restrained Wynne in the same way.

Wynne knew exactly what these viscous Ardarans had in store for them. He'd executed this same punishment on several slaves when he was a guard. And he knew by experience that Ardara dirtying her own hands to do it would make it all the more excruciating.

"Cinder . . . I'm sorry. So sorry." Was all he could say. *I broke my promise.*

Ardara was behind them, her high heels clicking the floor as she paced. "You brought this on yourselves." She said.

Cinder craned her neck to look at her, Wynne's apology elevating her anxiety. Ardara held two long iron rods in either hand. Cinder was terrified to realize they were branding irons. Wynne looked away, and clamped his eyes shut.

Ardara tightened her grip on the irons. They were cold to the touch. There were forges behind her where she could heat them, but she decided to display some power. The crown of both irons went scolding red and began to emit sparks.

Cinder saw that the iron in her right hand was a red hot T. The one in her left was shaped like the letter E.

"*E* for *Enemy*." Ardara muttered to Cinder before viciously pressing the E iron to her sister's shoulder blade. Cinder shouted in agony, her skin smoking where the metal scorched her. Ardara commenced, "And *T* for *Traitor!*" she ravenously branded Wynne's shoulder as well, listening to his pained shouting.

Ardara tossed the irons aside, admiring her handiwork. The letters were burned black onto their skin, still smoking like a roast left too long in the oven.

"Throw them back in their cell." Ardara ordered. "Now they are forever marked by their mistakes."

Plenthin was just as Cinder had described. For miles, all that could be seen out the Day Star's windows were dunes of rolling sand, as far as the eye could see. Only when the radar detected a water source could they find the oasis. It was gargantuan, like a palm tree jungle the size of a city. There were white buildings and runways for airships to land.

Jeremiah flew the Day Star onto a fueling dock, where a team was waiting to assist. "As soon as we're done here," he said to Orphenn, "we'll go full speed back to the wastelands. Then you can save Cinder."

"Gotcha." Orphenn replied. He gazed out the pilot's window at the dock. There were workers below like a racecar pit team, ready to fix any of the airship's errors. There were food and necessity markets along the edge of the dock. There were other airships too, landing, fueling, resupplying.

"Alright, men." Jeremiah announced through an intercom that sounded outside the ship to alert the workers. "This squad's in a hurry. We need three loads' replenishment while you're filling the tank. And you. Yeah, you-I see you doing nothing over there. Considering our Supreme Commander is on board, I suggest you haul ass to that gas cap before Lady Celina revokes your fueling license. Yep, there 'ya go. Tha-ank you!"

The men below got to work immediately and efficiently.

"She wouldn't really revoke his license . . . ?" Orphenn worried.

"Nah." Xeila snickered. "Just a motivation technique." Then, "Gah! Dad! I'm so hungry!" she said for the tenth time.

"You're tellin' me!" He countered. "Now my big ones are eatin' each other!"

Orphenn turned to Celina. "So, this is like a giant gas station?"

"Pretty much." Celina laughed. She still had Orphenn's words stuck in her head, making her rethink her ideas of Dacian. *What if it wasn't? What if it's something bigger than that?* Could there have been a hidden reason for his betrayal? She couldn't stop wondering, acting out scenarios in her head.

But her train of thought was interrupted by the resonant thud in her chest and eardrums, the kind one feels when watching large fireworks. The blast could be heard from inside the ship.

The White Herons rushed outside onto the deck, and saw that the airship at the pump ahead of the Day Star had burst into flames.

Orphenn looked above and saw a massive, dark airship drifting across the sky, closing in on the loading dock. It had a long rope ladder hanging down, and dozens of Ardaran soldiers cascaded down it and onto the dock.

A squad was evacuating the blazing vessel ahead of the Day Star, only to be met with another disaster outside. The Ardarans opened fire on anyone standing on the dock.

Jeremiah was off the deck in a flash of speed. He created a colossal force field around the burning airship and shrank it until every flame was suffocated, the fire snuffed out. As the force field evaporated, Jeremiah sped like lightening into the crowd of Ardaran soldiers, who were attacking innocent passerby. He raised his fist, then sent it smashing into the metal of the dock.

His squadron watched in awe as it sent a wave through the structure, until it was torn apart by the seems, iron bolts flying. It broke apart, leaving an incredible crevice. Many Ardarans fell into it, screaming their last breaths as they plunged toward the forest floor, miles below.

Sven came right behind Jeremiah, wielding a summoned crossbow in one hand and a spear in the other. He fiercely attacked, and his daughters barreled behind him, lunging and slashing with claws and fangs. The other squadron came to their aid, fighting with their gifts just as fiercely.

Orphenn looked at Celina. The two nodded at each other and made synchronized leaps into the air, their wings outspread. Celina soared up with an arsenal of Sven's summoned weapons at her heels. They sliced through the air and into the bodies of Ardaran soldiers with razor sharp frigidity. Orphenn flew above, firing his silver pistol, after having finally realized his gold one was missing. He swooped down to knock a few soldiers off their feet, and rose up again to shoot them down. Each one of the silver bullets hit their targets without fail.

Cannons began blasting from the Ardaran ship's hull. Jeremiah was quick to spring into the air. He vaulted with immense strength, at least as high as Orphenn was gliding, and he landed on the wide barrel of one of the cannons. He twisted the cannon off its gears, the metal crinkling beneath his might as if it were aluminum foil. He threw the cannon's barrel into the Ardaran ship's windshield with the power and force of a two-ton elephant. He dispatched the second cannon by crushing it inside a constricting force field. Sven took out third cannon with a bigger cannon he had summoned on the spot. Any remaining cannons were dealt with by the other squadron-melted down and torn apart with their powerful gifts.

Jeremiah leapt down from the ship and landed beside Xeila, where he held her taloned hand.

"Damnit!" Dacian yelled. Nyx had nearly been pulverized by the cannon that crashed through the windshield. The two of them had only just escaped a painful death. Then the other cannons were destroyed, obliterated, eliminated, and demolished. Dacian was having a bad day.

"Dacian, we need to retreat! All our men are dead already!" Nyx insisted.

"*Hmph.*" He defied, scowling as he pulled himself up, shattered glass sprinkling off his shoulders. "They still have *me* to deal with."

Orphenn's feet landed with a clang on the metal dock, when he had shot down the last Ardaran soldier. Celina touched down close beside him, signaling to Sven that he could send his weapons away. Then she stared up at the dark Ardaran vessel, realization struck into her features. She had seen Dacian at the wheel. "He's about to drop a bomb!" she screamed.

Jeremiah took note of this. He held up his arms, and a diamond barrier surrounded the entire dock, monstrously large and strong, protecting them all.

Dacian fully expected the bomb to break through the barricade, but it was steadfast. The bomb hit and exploded on the crystal surface—dangerously close to the ship, Dacian saw. The blast blew the ship across the sky, and it was engulfed in the orange cloud.

Those beneath Jeremiah's barrier were untouched, though Celina's heart grew heavy at the sight of Dacian's peril. When it was safe, Jeremiah let the barrier evaporate, and watched as the Ardaran airship turned and retreated.

"Your ship is ready, My Lady." A worker bowed to Celina.

"Good!" Sven shouted immediately. "Now let's get our asses out of here before something else blows up!"

"Prepare to evacuate if necessary." Celina advised the worker, and those standing around him. They all nodded, bowed, and rushed inside the building.

Chapter Sixteen

~

Halo

The White Herons gathered at their airship's lounge, discussing their imprisoned comrade.

"Can't you find her on the radar?" Xeila asked Jeremiah.

Orphenn answered for him. "Her crest was most likely stolen when they shoved her in the cell. We can't trust the tracker. There's no way to exactly locate her unless I go and find her myself. I know she's in the dungeon, at least."

"Alright then, Orphenn." Sven patted his shoulder. "Show us how it's done. Let's bring our Little Drifter back home."

Orphenn nodded. He took a deep breath and closed his eyes. He opened them again slowly. Then they rolled back, and his head lolled when his knees gave, and he collapsed onto the lounge's cushioned sofa.

Orphenn watched from afar as the others swarmed around his body. In this form, which he had decided to name *Halo*, he discovered that he could choose whether he would really touch something, or go straight through it like a hologram. He needed only to wish it.

To hint to the others that Orphenn had left his body safely, Eynochia, who miraculously had the eyes to see him in the Halo form, smiled and said, "Hurry back, Angel Face." She stared at his sparkling apparition, his eyes like molten gold, and her smile widened.

Orphenn smiled back at her, his face an odd panorama of happiness that no one else could see.

"*I will.*" Came his distant echo. Then he turned slowly, his wings twirling behind him as glistening veils, toward the wide, bolted picture window.

"You look like a pixie." Eynochia threw the comment at him in the last moment.

Orphenn laughed, a sound that pervaded like honey in water.

"*Jerk.*" His voice faded into the air almost as soon as he spoke, but still Eynochia heard him.

Orphenn jumped, and flew his pixie self out of the Day Star's hull and across the wastelands, into the castle of Ardara.

This time when Cinder woke in the cell, after passing out from the pain, Wynne was chained beside her. If their backs were visible, one could've seen that Cinder's brand had already healed, leaving an E shaped pink scar, while Wynne's was still crusted and blistering. Wynne was speaking with Music Man.

". . . What will happen now? What are we going to do?" He distressed. Cinder stared at him, at the metal ring clamped to his neck. His neck looked like hers now, bloodied, yellowing with bruises, veins protruding.

"I don't know." Music Man said, still with his back to them, always hindered by the stockade that trapped his head and arms. It also constantly scraped against the device where it came around his neck, causing even more discomfort, if imaginable. "But at least neither of us is alone anymore. We'll figure it out together."

"*Ehey* . . . Music Man . . ." Cinder beckoned drowsily.

"*Music Man?*" Laughed Wynne. "You're notorious, Old Man!"

"Yeah, well . . . ."

"Ugh . . . . What happened?" Cinder asked, feeling her lip split.

Wynne drooped in his binds. "We were branded." He said sadly. "I'm to blame. I should have thought ahead. I'm so sor-"

"Don't apologize. I don't want to hear it." Cinder ordered.

His mouth clicked closed.

After an interval, Cinder spoke. "Wynne . . . What was she talking about? Before?"

"Ardara?"

"Yes. You . . . Helped to assault a cell guard?"

"Oh . . . That . . ." he looked down bashfully.

"What did you do?"

"Nothing really, I-it was just an experiment."

"*Curiosity branded the cat and locked it in a cell,*" sang Music Man in a mocking melody.

"*No,*" Wynne corrected lengthily, "*Ardara* branded the cat-I mean me-and branded-I mean-oh, damn. You always jumble me up!"

Music Man let out a triumphant "Ha!" and Cinder giggled. Then she frowned in the realization that not only was she *laughing* in the midst of one of her most dangerous predicaments, but she saw that Wynne and Music Man seemed to share a filial bond-similar to that of Sven and Orphenn.

"But what *happened?*" she said finally.

Wynne relented. "I used my gift, and tried something, merely out of curiosity. It worked, and I would have been able to help you escape if it hadn't been for . . ."

"My sister."

He nodded.

"What is your gift?" Questioned Cinder.

"My gifts . . ." he contemplated, ". . . For lack of a better word, are *moody*."

"Moody?" She chuckled. Again . . . Laughing? What was it about these two that she found so amusing? Well, she was glad at least that they lifted her spirits a bit.

"Unpredictable." Wynne clarified. "Sometimes they work, sometimes they don't. Sometimes they backfire, sometimes they cooperate. At times I might as well be rendered human."

"That's very odd. Well . . . What can you do?"

"I can . . ." he paused, searching his mind for words. "*Manipulate* time. And impose slumber on another."

"You can go back in time? And into the future?"

"No, my friend. No one has that power."

"Oh . . . So you can *stop* time?"

"Sometimes."

"And you can make someone sleep?"

"On occasion."

"Well what's the catch then?"

"I can't say why, but there comes a time when my powers just *stop*. With no explanation, sometimes for months on end. That's the reason Ardara favored Dacian over me. His gifts were more reliable I suppose."

"So . . ."

"My eyes stay the same, but I'm left inept and defenseless."

"I see. It's not all that bad, is it?"

"Not to me. But in Dacian's eyes, it's weakness."

"What about that purple girl? The one that was there at the warehouse? And pinned me to the wall in the boiler room?"

"Oh . . . Nyx. I really have no idea why she's here to tell you the truth. But Ardara seems to have a soft spot for her."

When Orphenn reached the dungeon, there was no sound but for the echoed dripping of a leaky pipe. But then he heard the clinking of chains and happy laughter from deep within. He followed the euphoria, such a strange sound to hit the ears in a place like this, and he found the source rather quickly.

As he neared the correct cell, he recognized the voice he had longed to hear.

"She's not even Enma." Cinder assumed.

"Actually, I've discovered she was recently mutated. Her gift is quite unique. She helped in the ambush at Plenthin."

Orphenn started. *Wynne?* He couldn't imagine what the pink-eyed man had done to deserve an Ardaran dungeon sentence. He listened.

"Ambush. Were there any fatalities?" Cinder queried anxiously.

"Only Ardaran casualties, rest assured. There was an airship bombed, but no one was hurt. The White Herons were spared from harm. And I bet they fought violently. There were no soldiers left when Dacian and Nyx returned."

Orphenn recalled Dacian and the Ardaran soldiers at the Plenthin fueling dock. He was now even more thankful that Jeremiah had been able to thwart that second bomb.

He gracefully moved to the iron bars, invisible. This cell was entirely of metal, instead of inlaid sandstone like the others, and thoroughly reinforced. It was apparently meant for more threatening prisoners. Inside this metal cell, there was a man in a stockade, who looked surprisingly at ease, despite how ill and weak he must have been.

Orphenn sighed. Already, he could feel the Halo's energy waning.

Unseen, Orphenn flowed through the bars, a glistening phantom. He knelt as close to Cinder as he could without touching her. Though he wanted to let her know he was there, somehow.

Cinder turned to speak to Wynne, but stiffened with a gasp as goose bumps rose on her skin. Orphenn saw his wing had brushed against hers, and jumped back. Then he spotted a glint of gold at Cinder's belt. Feeling suddenly stingy, as if it were a squabble between siblings over who's playing with whose special toy, Orphenn tugged his pistol from her belt. Wynne was wide-eyed and open-mouthed. Incidentally, this gave Cinder the clue she needed.

"Orphenn." She smirked, gazing at the levitating firearm.

Perfect, thought Orphenn. *Now it's time to put my* new *trick to use.*

He stuffed the pistol back into Cinder's belt, stinginess vanished. Then he grasped her chains. His fingers tightened vigorously on the iron. They began to glow-not with red heat, but with warm light. The links seemed to vibrate, until they vanished in bright, firefly-like particles, that circled and faded as they floated to the ceiling; freeing Cinder from her binds.

She stretched, and laughed. "Orphenn, you clever dog!"

Wynne remained awestruck, even as his own restraints were erased in gold light. And even still, when Music Man's stockade began to glow, and finally disappear.

Orphenn thought of erasing Ardara's devices from their necks as well, but knew, regrettably, that he wouldn't have enough energy, and feared that it would kill them besides. So he made a hole in the iron bars for them to escape through, as there was no key.

A fear rose in his stomach. He felt, like a rope at his spine, a force pulling him back to his body.

Back at the ship, his body's eyes and mouth had opened wide. The shell breathed deeply, its back arching, and with every one of its breaths, Orphenn felt another tug. The body was greedily, urgently calling back to the soul-for it couldn't go too long without a spirit or it would die; leaving the soul to wander.

So he turned and left the castle, faster than he expected he could.

Eynochia watched in amazement as Orphenn's glittering spirit fell back into his body's shell, like two pieces to a puzzle. He gasped, and full consciousness came to his eyes. He sat up shakily, leaning into Eynochia to catch his breath.

"Did you do it?" She asked eagerly.

He smiled.

Chapter Seventeen

~

The Grace of Eagles

Cinder nearly shook with suspense. Music Man began to rise to his knees, and slowly stand, his amber-colored hair waving down his lean shoulders.

Wynne cautioned, "Don't be hasty." He stood as well, and supported the weight of the older man.

Music Man waved dismissal and turned to face Cinder. He looked so familiar that she slightly jumped. His right eye was hazel-brown, his left a pumpkin orange.

"*You*, little lady," he addressed Cinder, "must leave now. You have friends to get back to."

"But-" she objected.

"Not a word, little missy. Wynnie and I will free the others-don't worry that pretty little head of yours, Puddin' Pie." Even the way he spoke oddly struck her memory.

"What if something happens . . . ?"

Wynne reached for her, and held her hands in his. The look in his rose-petal eyes warmed her to the bone. "It will be alright. We will come to find the Day Star and join you when all is done."

Music Man sighed, gratefully. "Ah, won't *that* be a sweet reunion?"

She hesitated, confused by his words, but gave in. "Okay."

"Now go." Music Man said almost excitedly. "Get goin' little jackrabbit!"

She complied. With one last look at Wynne's gentle face, she turned and ran from the cell. When she finally reached a way outside, after what seemed like a lifetime of wandering aimlessly through the castle-a massive crack torn through the castle's siding-sirens were wailing and people were shouting, red lights flashing. From another hole in the decaying castle wall, far below, she saw prisoners upon prisoners, some still with shackles and chains, escaping, flooding out of the opening and running out of sight beyond the rubble.

Wynne had done his part. But they were only from the dungeon . . . How would the remaining slaves be freed?

This thought was wiped from her mind in an instant, when from behind her came the clack of heeled footsteps, and she jerked around. Ardara was there, frozen in disbelief.

Cinder wasted no time. She leapt out of the gaping hole, knowing she couldn't use her wings-even previous mutations were stunted by the device. She made her way down to the ground by jumping from jagged protrusions of metal that stuck out from the wall. When she reached the bottom, Orphenn was there to meet her, revving the engine of her motorcycle.

Wynne and Music Man swiftly made their way out of the cell and ran down the corridor.

"What now, Old Man?" Wynne inquired between breaths. The devices made breathing more difficult, especially with arduous activity.

"You free all the prisoners in this here dungeon. I'll haul ass upstairs and free all her little 'favorites.' Wish me luck."

Wynne momentarily jogged in place, then stopped, breathing deeply. "You're off your rocker, Old Man."

Music Man halted. He hugged his ward close to him. Wynne leaned on him. "But that's just how I like you." He said. "Good luck!" he called when Music Man started again to dash down the corridor. Wynne hoped against hope that his end of the mission would succeed.

Now it was time for his own.

Music Man rushed through the steam and sped out the boiler room door, into the chill of a dark hall. He veered left, only to be stopped short by the stone cold hands of Ardara. Her eyes were unforgiving.

Wynne hastily scanned the cell block, the prisoners wailing at him through the bars. "You're free! You're free!"

"Not yet." He said, and when his eyes found the red-painted lever geared into the wall, he ran to it. With a grunt of effort, he pulled it and immediately, every cell in the dungeon opened wide in synchrony, while sirens howled and all the lights flashed red.

The Enma flooded the dungeon, with a cacophony of cheering and rejoicing. They swarmed out of a hole in the castle wall, in rusty disrepair as much of the castle was. They ran out across the waste, and finally, to freedom.

Amidst the chaos, Wynne enthusiastically kicked the lever several times, until it bent, and broke right off its gears, preventing any future use. The bar clattered to the floor.

Then someone picked it up.

Only seeing their shoes, Wynne assumed it was an ex-prisoner and stepped forward. When he looked the other in the face, he was met with a strike across the jaw with the detached lever bar. He fell to his knees. The blood at his lip glinted in the flashing red light when he turned up his face to glare at Dacian, who stood menacingly over him.

"Dacian." Wynne seethed through clenched and bloody teeth. He suffered another blow to the head from Ardara's favorite, and was knocked on his side.

Dacian flung away the bar, landing with a *clang* down the corridor. He furiously kicked Wynne in the ribs and stomped on his stomach.

"I don't know how you got out of that cell," Dacian snarled, when his temper slightly regressed, "but your punishment will rival Hellfire."

"Dacian." Wynne coughed. "You haunt my every step."

"It's my job, Wynnie." He pulled Wynne ruthlessly to his feet, and turned him forcefully to face the other way, hands clamped on his shoulders.

Wynne's breath caught in his throat. Before him stood Ardara, and in her clutches, Music Man stood, head low, and eyes wiped of any consciousness.

Dacian leaned forward to whisper in Wynne's ear, "Enjoy your madness." And he shoved Wynne into the arms of the megalomaniac that would lead the planet into a war to end all wars.

Wynne was almost paralyzed at the mere touch of her fingertips, and a rush of fear came to him when he understood: Ardara now had yet another new gift. Not only could she control an unprotected mind, but now she could manipulate another's physical body even further than levitating it in mid air. Now, like a puppet master, she held Music Man and Wynne in a shadow hold. They could not move of their own accord. They could not speak. Now, they could only watch as Dacian had an angry fit.

"Damnit!" he stomped. "What will we do now?! Those Enma prisoners will go to join their cause, and we'll be slaughtered! I told you about the butchery of our soldiers at Plenthin! We outnumbered them, and still I was forced to retreat!"

"All will be well, Dacian. We haven't lost any strength." Ardara assured lightly.

"But what about the strength our opposition has just *gained?* All those mutants at Denoras will render the city impenetrable!"

What Ardara said next put Music Man and Wynne in a state of terror.

She was half crazed as she predicted, "It'll give me more of a challenge. More of an accomplishment afterwards-when they all go back to their precious capital, our men will have someone to fight. Soon. When I lay siege over Denoras."

"How are we to 'lay siege'?" Dacian muttered to himself irritably, after half an hour or so of solitary concocting. "Anything, for my Master . . . But this is *ridiculous,* we'll be butchered! *Again.*" He paced, beginning to monologue. "How to please her? I need a strategy . . ." he ceased, un-strapping his dark uniform and slipping out of his top. He lay it across the back of a chair, looking over his bare shoulder at his wound. Four wide gashes ran across his back and his upper arm, given to him by the mutant Eynochia when she had escaped the castle in a rage. "*Disgusting dog.*" He mumbled, remembering. It was healing quite slowly. Probably much slower than it would, had he not been picking off the scabs, as he was now, growing angrier by the second.

He leaned on the side of a wooden table, his other hand clenching the edge of it. Without realizing, his temper igniting his poisonous tendencies, the wood where he clenched the table started to rapidly erode away, an acidic toxin that began to suffuse from Dacian's palm eating away at it like salt on a snail. It fizzed and sizzled, and began to drip away, unbeknownst to him, grumbling and scratching angrily at his scarring wound.

It was this that eventually gave him new confidence in his own strength, and the motivation to lead a battalion: abruptly, he fell onto his back, for the table that supported him had disappeared. Not into thin air, no. He was lying puzzled in a puddle of table-colored liquid. Brow furrowed, he examined droplets of it on his fingers, knots of wood liquefied inside them.

Had he done what he thought he had done?

Curiously, he wrapped his fingers around the leg of the chair. It seem to burst at his touch from its very molecules, like wood-toned fireworks, and the particles fell back to the floor as a liquid, his uniform top splashing into the puddle.

He had changed its entire composition. He had made a solid into a liquid.

Now he stood, a smile slowly growing at his lips. He bent over to touch the liquid in the puddle. It solidified again, only he shaped it into a wooden pole. He twirled it around and lunged in mock attack. He unsheathed its spear and performed the same twirl.

Apprehensively, he held up the wooden pole, palm faced up. The pole turned to liquid, and in the next second, to gas, and immediately evaporated, leaving no trace of the wooden table and chair.

Using this process more slowly, he was able-without the use of his hands—to change the shape of his lance head to different points and sharpen the blade as if it was made of clay, and hardened when he was satisfied with his alterations. Then he dropped it and walked.

Still in a bit of a daze of puzzlement, and still bare-chested, he sauntered through the metallic corridors in the direction of the guard's retreat. Once there, he trod into the doorway to meet the reverence of his inferiors. It was a dark lounge, complete in its repair-concessions, seating, and even an enormous hot tub in the center, its water heated by the forges of the boiler room, conveniently one story below. The bustling gossip and small talk disappeared to oblivion, and not a move was made.

After a moment of pause for vain dramatic effect, he stepped forward theatrically, his mood shockingly elated.

"Squadron Nine." He addressed the ten or so soldiers gazing at him in deference. "Proceed."

At this they seemed to melt in relief, and un-froze, relaxing somewhat, though no one yet said a word.

He cantered his way to the steel-rimmed hot tub, bubbling and steaming. As he spoke he paced around the edge like a cat on a fence.

"Shall I join you?" He asked, and without waiting for an answer, he stepped down into the luxurious foam, letting a smile feign across his face and he settled in comfortably. Knowing not his intent, Squad Nine smiled too.

"The castle," he said, nonchalantly, "has been infiltrated."

All was silent. All smiles left.

Dacian stood in the water, looming above the others like a tyrant.

"And while my best squadron has been *dallying* in the *lounge*, the *Enma* have freed more than half of our prisoners of war!" His scream seemed even to silence the bubbles. "Now *THEY* have all the advantage! What will we DO *NOW*, do you *suppose!?*" *Wait* . . .

He stopped abruptly. He looked down, and tapped the solid surface of the water. He *had* stopped the bubbles. They topped the solidified water like glass domes. Seven members of Squadron Nine squirmed in an attempt to escape, trapped like popsicle sticks in flavored ice.

Dacian realized then, his new gift, as the hot tubes, jets and turbines, backed up from the solid change in state, crashed and broke down, echoing downward with a tinny wail.

And then came his trademark.

A smug grin colored his face.

"This will come in handy."

The Day Star retrieved the rescued prisoners, and set a course for Denoras. They were all fed and bathed on the ship, and grateful for it. They slept on fleece in the cargo hold until the destination was reached, after a day and a half of travel. Each of them, all eighty-seven of them, took an oath. They vowed to their Supreme Commander that they would risk their lives for Aleida, and swore to her their loyalty, just as they had in the First War.

As they landed at the Denoras air dock, Orphenn hugged to Celina's side, and lay his head on her shoulder. Celina was surprised at how affectionate he was. It was like he was still only a young ten-year-old. She looped her arms protectively around his neck. They both smiled, recalling the numerous times they had held each other this way: when their family had moved to New York from Delaware, leaving all their friends behind-when they had lost their grandmother-even when a boyfriend of Celina's had broken up with her. And even in the lee of a battlefield, at the River, just before Cinder was forced to take Orphenn back to Earth. Not always though, did they embrace this way in times of grief, but also in joy: when Orphenn had returned from his first day of school, and when he had graduated from kindergarten-the day their parents renewed their vows; and now, as they returned home from their perilous first mission.

Celina kissed his forehead. "I'm so proud of you, Little Brother."

"I'm proud to *be* your little brother." He responded.

As they broke their embrace, Cinder emerged at Orphenn's side. The look in her eyes could only be described as paranoia, as if she waited for anything to jump around every corner, every flickering shadow. She made no attempt to hide the device now, her neck bare apart from it.

She had just finished assisting the ex-prisoners into the capital, where they would be readied for war.

"Cinder, are you okay? Is there something wrong with the others?" Celina worried, referring to the rescued Enma.

"No, they're fine." Cinder assured. "It's just . . . . After all this, I don't feel . . . . safe. Not even here." She gave Celina a meaningful look. Celina was compelled to console her, but she could not, knowing that her sister's fear wasn't just a result of paranoia. She herself felt an ominous pressure-an almost instinctive aura, foreshadowing the worst. She bit her lip.

Though, Orphenn's mind was not so psychic as his sisters'. He felt no oncoming threat, and he made sure to convey that. "Cinder." His voice held an intone of encouragement. "Everything is fine." He said these words crisply, and clearly, as he pressed his forehead to Cinder's, their secret embrace, similar to the one he shared moment ago with Celina.

Cinder greatly appreciated the comfort, however faulty.

"Now," Said Orphenn, "let's get off this ship. I need a picnic or something."

And it was a picnic he got. After loading, and taking naps, the White Herons strolled outside the palace walls, the sun only just coming to rise. They chose a grassy spot near the meadowed edge of a cliff (a kind of landmark that seemed to be plentiful on this planet). They ate, and they enjoyed each other's company.

Jeremiah was the first to speak. "So, you two." He turned his face to Orphenn and Cinder. "What was this *Wynne* fellow like? I can't deny how familiar you make him sound. Perhaps I can remember if you describe him."

Sven jabbed his temple with a forefinger. "I got the worst memory . . . Who was Wynne again? Sounds so deadly familiar I can't stand it."

"Doesn't it though?" Eynochia agreed. "I swear I knew someone." She sat behind Orphenn, picking bits of grass off his back.

Orphenn began, "Well he had really long blonde hair and weird pink eyes, like a white rabbit." Cinder chuckled at his comparison. He continued, "He was in the cell with Cinder and another guy when I freed them all. I don't know where they ended up though."

"Wynne was a guard." Cinder informed. "Ardaran uniform and everything. But he was very kind. Because of him, I was able to escape unscathed. But not before he was thrown in jail too. Ardara found out he had been helping me and we both were punished."

"He was kind to me, too." Orphenn added. "Like I told you." He craned his neck backward to look up at Eynochia behind him. "Eynochia, didn't you tell me once about someone in your old squadron?"

"Oh, lordie." Grumbled Sven, who by this point was bopping his head and furrowing his brow trying fruitlessly to search his memory.

Eynochia hesitated, toying with something behind Orphenn's back. "Well, yeah, but I only remember the pink eyes. I can't recall much else."

"It must be the same guy, then!"

"How do you know?" She never broke her focus from her moving fingers.

"Hey, do you know anyone else with pink-oy! What the-are you *braiding* my *rattail?!*"

"It looks good!"

"Cut it out!" He fidgeted, though he was smiling.

Xeila, who uncharacteristically hadn't made a sound the whole afternoon, suddenly exploded, slamming her beverage to the ground. "Would you stop *screwing around?!*" she screamed. The group froze, staring at her. "I can't stand this!" she rose to her feet angrily. "Why in the hell are all you just sitting here, jolly lolly-gagging, when there's work to be done!? *War* is on our doorstep! But we're having a *picnic!*"

Sven looked up at her, and tapped her hand. "You'll give yourself an ulcer. Sit down, Poppet."

Though perhaps Xeila was right to be impatient. How could the others have known they were in the wrong? How could they have known who lurked in the trees behind them?

Just as the sun set, a flash of black-red uniform darted between them, colliding with Cinder-an Ardaran soldier. The man tackled her to the ground as other soldiers stamped out of the forest and began to attack. Their airships loomed overhead, dark clouds trailing after them.

With a shout, Orphenn rose to his feet, as did the others, taking offensive stances, all but Cinder, who in her weakened state was overpowered. Orphenn called her name as she was thrown over the edge of the cliff, at this time when her wings were no help to her.

With intent precision, he fired his silver pistol. The Ardaran that attacked his sister collapsed over the side as well.

"Nice shot, now go!" Sven commanded, engaged in a grapple of his own.

Orphenn dove. He shot like a bullet, his golden wings held close. There was nothing he wished for more at this moment than Cinder's survival. He could still catch her before she hit the bottom-or so he hoped.

By the time her dark attire came into his sight, she was splayed unnaturally across the dirt, motionless.

Tears blinded him. He fell clumsily to the earth and rolled, staying in a prone position. He kept his head down, not daring to open his eyes. After a moment, he lifted his heavy head.

Ardara's device had shattered to pieces from the impact of the fall. Her neck was free of it, though her skin was still reddened and bruised where it had been latched. Orphenn dared not observe anything else. Even the idea of her still, lifeless body, and sightless, blank stare shook him with sobs. He was too late.

A mournful cry escaped him as he turned his face away from what he thought to be the empty body of his sister.

But a frightening noise made his tears come silent. It forced him to look back.

The noise came from her throat like a choke or a gag. It disturbed him, and scared him to the bone. Was something taking over her?

Orphenn looked on in shock, tears freely spilling.

One more spine-chilling choke, and then the noise stopped.

Then she took in a breath.

Loud, and desperate.

Orphenn gasped as she did.

Cinder blinked as she returned to consciousness.

Blinked, and breathed, blinked, and breathed. She shot upright, dazed, as if woken from a nightmare.

She had come back to life.

When she finally calmed, her eyes found Orphenn. His breath was shallow, and his hand clutched his jumpsuit at his heart, still sobbing.

Cinder stood slowly and spread her wings.

"Orphenn . . . Was I . . . ?" she shook the words out.

Orphenn could only shake himself, until finally, he rose to his feet as well, cautious, timid. "You were dead." He whispered, unable to raise his voice any louder.

"We can't tell anyone about this . . . . Not anyone, Orphenn. If the wrong person found out . . ."

"I understand."

When they both had regained their senses, the two spread their wings wide, abyssal black against glistening gold. With faces turned skyward, they ascended with the grace of eagles.

The battle above did not look promising.

Chapter Eighteen

~

The Clock Tower

Suspense ate at Sven's stomach as well as the others', impatient in the back of their minds to know what became of Cinder-if she lived, dreading the future if she didn't-all the while, fighting against the followers of Ardara.

This time, the opposition did not falter. No, this time, the Enma were the outmatched ones.

It was just as Orphenn and Cinder flew up over the cliffside that the White Herons began to realize this.

Sven's summoned wooden mallet dispatched two soldiers in succession as he spun around to face them. "I knew you'd make it, Princess!" he called to Cinder.

The fight did not go well.

"Herons!" Celina cried. "To the Day Star!" After a slight scuffle, she shouted, "Jeremiah! Can you barricade the city?"

"I can try!" he loyally complied. His diamond armor crackled as it formed around his body.

"Jay, no!" Xeila snarled, her claw stopping him before he could rush away.

"I must."

His determination enchanted her.

"Don't die. I'll kill you if you die."

"You have my word." He smiled. He kissed her, and with that, he dutifully ran toward the heart of Denoras. As the others retreated to the airship, he reached the palace at twice the speed of any other. By the time the Herons had taken shelter inside the Day Star, they witnessed through the windshield when Jeremiah took a mighty bound, soaring into the air, landing perched on the palace's highest clock tower. His crystal armor gleamed in the moonlight. He held his arms out, palms turned up.

"Will he be able to sustain a barrier of this size?" Orphenn motioned around them to the city of Denoras as Xeila took the Day Star in to the city, extending the landing gear inside a courtyard, just beside the palace.

No one replied, for no one had the answer.

Jeremiah took one deep breath, just as Ardaran airships surrounded the capital. As he exhaled, a shell of crystal began to form, high above his head.

An awe-inspiring sight, to witness Ardara's bombs crashing against his barrier, exploding upon it only just as it was formed, red clouds against the stars, warped through the sheen of the crystal.

"Yeah! That's my macho man!" Xeila cheered.

Jeremiah stood tall, and mighty atop the clock tower, his strength never wavered. He held his position. Ardarans were being beaten against the barrier's walls when they attempted futilely to escape. Those trapped inside the barrier were quickly eliminated and taken care of. They stood no chance alone against these mutants. Those who waited outside the indestructible force field could only stare at the slaughter.

"Celina." Sven said with a serious tone. But she had already seen it.

"I know." She said.

A brawl was playing out beside the Day Star, on the tiled roof of a palace gondola, just above the vessel's deck. A clash, between a swift and talented Enma, and a deathly determined Dacian. The mutant had likely stopped him on his way to harm Jeremiah, steadfast on the clock tower.

"You forget," Dacian grumbled, "look at my eyes." He grabbed the other's face and glared him straight in his green and brown eyes, brandishing his one red iris with contempt. "I'm just like you." He parted his lips and allowed a black poison to mist out of his mouth. The toxin invaded the other mutant's lungs. It stained his mouth and lips like tar. To seal the deal, Dacian twirled his toxic lance before stabbing it deep into his enemy's abdomen. The Enma collapsed, and slipped off the roof to descend lifelessly to the cobblestones far below. Dacian sheathed his lance, looking down on his fallen enemy. "Just like you." He repeated.

"You're wrong, Dacian." Came the call of brave Orphenn. He stood on deck, staring fixedly at the traitor on the roof.

"Is that a challenge I'm hearing, boy?" Dacian mused.

As response, Orphenn spread his wings big and wide, a heroic span of fifteen feet across. His gaze narrowed. "You tell me."

Dacian leapt from the gondola and onto the deck, landing at a kneel beside Orphenn.

The boy backed away and took his guns from their holsters, aiming both barrels at the Ardaran as he rose, giving barely a sideways glance to the teenager.

"You are not just like us." Orphenn said. "It takes someone very different to follow in the shadow of Ardara."

Dacian struck, but using the long gleaming barrels, Orphenn blocked the lance's blow with his pistols and kicked Dacian to the side, his boot against his ribs. The man hunched over, but lashed out, the rod of his lance knocking Orphenn's heels out from under him. Orphenn fell back, thankful that only his gold pistol flew from his grip and slid across the deck when his back hit the metal.

Dacian, with cruel precision, jammed the altered blade of his lance into Orphenn's wing with the strength of both hands, pinning him like a pathetic Biology butterfly.

Orphenn reacted with a cry of pain, and two shots from his silver pistol.

Celina gasped and whimpered from the helm.

Dacian's eyes went wide, and his heart thumped in his ears, as if it were a siren sounding at the bullets lodged in his chest.

That second, Sven was there, with a steel broadsword sparkling in dust, and in one swipe, sliced Dacian's lance in two, tearing his red-black uniform open shoulder-to-shoulder. A wide gash corresponded with the ripped leather, a red crack across his chest.

Dacian toppled, ebbed against the deck rail. Sven met him there, leaning into him with the tip of his sword at his throat.

"Give me one good reason not to make you the world's fastest sword swallower."

Dacian gulped. His life was slipping. Red colored the corners of his mouth.

Orphenn painfully pulled the severed lance blade from his wing, blood staining his golden feathers. In his prone position he saw Jeremiah standing high above. The super-human's resolve was beginning to wane, his strong stature wavering. The weight of the bombs bursting against his barrier was becoming cumbersome.

"Sven, no." Orphenn stood, lopsided, his wounded wing drooping low.

Sven raised an arched eyebrow.

Orphenn gestured above to the clock tower. Sven's eyes followed his pointed finger. Then he looked to the helm. Celina was frozen there.

He released the traitor. The scene unfolding before her eyes must have been traumatizing for the Supreme Commander.

Orphenn also realized this, and made a choice to make it easier on Celina. Someone his dear sister loved so deeply would not die on his watch, no matter which uniform he wore.

He limped to the deck rail, and with a scowl of disgust, Orphenn slapped his palm to Dacian's chest, wet and sticky with blood.

Dacian grimaced, drained of the energy to do anything else.

"Don't make me regret this." Orphenn threatened, though he knew he would probably rue this day, regardless. He then exhaled, and a white glow shone beneath his palm. It spread up Dacian's chest, illuminating the space between them. When Orphenn lifted his hand, the light was gone, and so were Dacian's wounds. The silver bullets plopped into his palm. Then Orphenn spotted the slash on Dacian's upper arm. He remembered Eynochia's words. *I slashed the traitor and jumped out the window.* "I think I'll leave this one." He decided. "Just to remind you of the wolf that bested you."

"Why?" Dacian growled. "Why did you heal me?"

He felt a push in his mind, someone trying to reach him. Master.

Before Orphenn could give an answer, Dacian had back flipped off the rail to flee, heeding Ardara's call. It took him a while of running across the white cobbles to notice that he still grasped the useless blunt end of his lance before he discarded it.

In that moment, Cinder and Celina ran side by side onto the deck, Just as Jeremiah's barrier shattered and evaporated. The exhausted man wavered, eyes half lidded in weariness. His legs gave out, and he slipped dizzily from the clock tower, fainted. The two sisters unfurled their feathers and soared to him in haste. They caught him in air before he could plunge, and carried him back to the ship, where Xeila waited anxiously.

When Jeremiah woke, it was still dark. He lay in his quarters aboard the Day Star. Judging by the surrounding drone, he could tell they were in flight.

He shot upright.

He was pilot. Who was flying this thing?

"Whoa there, Sonner Boy." Came Sven's calming voice. "Not so fast, you'll give yourself whiplash."

"Where is my Xeila?"

"Poppet's flyin' us outta here. Don't worry, Celina's watching her close. She's actually pretty good for a first-time flyer. Er . . . second-time." Sven sat in an arm chair beside Jeremiah's bed.

"What happened, Pops?"

"We had to evacuate the city."

"Because my barrier failed . . ."

"Don't you say that. Failure had no part in that battle for us. You saved many lives with that barricade.

"Now we're leading a few other squadrons to an encampment site."

"Where?"

"It's close to an Ardaran camp, just off the capital province border. We may be able to send in a spy."

"Hopefully more successful then our last undercover venture, eh?"

"Hopefully."

The two gazed out the porthole at the passing stars.

The same stars that Cinder gazed at from the balcony. She leaned her elbows on the railing, the wind tousling her hair.

Celina stepped out to join her.

"Cinder?"

"Hey, sis."

"Are you alright?"

Cinder wasn't certain of the answer. It showed clearly on her features.

Celina came to lean close beside her.

"Something on your mind?"

Cinder hesitated, but replied, "I never thought I'd live to fight *one* war, let alone two. The world is nothing but a big stupid quarrel anymore. I look around, but nothing holds beauty anymore. Not that I can see."

Celina gave an understanding nod. "Do you remember Mother Sun?" she reflected. "Do you remember how beautiful she was?"

Cinder's fists clenched. "All of this is *her* fault. If she hadn't 'gifted' us, we would be on Earth right now. Living out our lives like humans. She could have chosen some other poor children to *mutate*, and save the planet. If it weren't for her, Cira never would have gone insane! We would still have a sister! Mom and Dad would still be alive! If we would've just gone home earlier, that day at the park . . . We would be *normal!* There would be no *Enma*, no war, no *Ardara! None* of this would have happened if it weren't for *Mother Sun*."

"If you think a little further . . ." Celina spoke slowly, "It was the Day Star's fault. The *supernova*. She was the one that put Earth in danger. And if you think even further . . . It was Earth's gravity that pulled her close. We can hardly blame this on anyone. Besides, Cinder. If it hadn't been for Mother Sun, there would *be* no Earth. We would be dead. Blown into oblivion by an angry supernova."

Cinder sighed. "Why must you always make so much sense?" After a pause, she added, "That's why you are Supreme Commander, Celina. And not me."

And with that, she retreated inside, just as the dawn began to lighten the sky.

Night had fallen once again by the time they found the camp. They were welcomed warmly, and hospitably.

"Where is Eynochia?" Orphenn wondered.

When the only answer he received was a shrug, he set out to search for her. He didn't enjoy the knowledge that an Ardaran camp was close by, and worried for her safety.

He found her, just outside of camp, sitting in the grass, staring off absently.

"I'm sorry, Orphenn." She said, immediately upon seeing him.

He came closer. "For what?"

"I'm sorry I wasn't out there. On deck with you when you fought Dacian. He hurt your wing, and-"

"It's fine now. I healed it. Everything's okay. Don't apologize." Orphenn pulled her close and hugged her.

Eynochia hugged him back. "I'm glad you saved his life."

He pulled away to give her a quizzical look.

"Celina would have been more hurt than you know, had he died." She clarified.

He nodded. "I'm just surprised he didn't kill me as soon as I healed him. It must have been powerful, whatever urge compelled him to run away like that."

"Cowardice, my best bet."

"No . . . No, I don't think it's quite so shallow as that. He was a wonderful man once, you said so yourself."

"True. But people change. And not always for the better."

Orphenn brushed hair from her gentle face with the back of his hand. "I feel bad for Jeremiah."

They both looked over the wide expanse of lake water at the city of Denoras, shining white in the distance. The tallest tower was clearly visible against the night sky.

"It must have been like holding the world on his shoulders when he stood on that clock tower."

"I envy him." Eynochia confessed. "I've always dreamt of standing on top of that highest clock tower, even as a little girl. But now I'm scared that I'll never have the chance."

"Why's that?"

"I just know that tower will fall. Before I ever get to stand on it."

"You think it's going to fall?"

"With my luck, yes."

"'With your luck'?" He mocked.

"Well," she considered, "I guess I'm not *that* unlucky. I mean . . . I have you, don't I?" Her black and green irises eyed him adoringly.

Orphenn's red and blue eyes seemed to glow more than usual at her words. He thought nothing could be any more beautiful than this moment.

"You sure do."

There by the lakeside, where the moonlight poured down in shafts and glistened on the water; *would* have been the place of a brilliant first kiss, had Jeremiah not appeared from the camp before their lips ever touched.

"Eynochia." He beckoned. "Xeila needs you at the ship."

And so, they bid their farewells and good-nights, clueless as to what the morning would bring.

Chapter Nineteen

~

Light and Darkness

When dawn came to light the smoky sky, Orphenn started to wonder if the fighting would ever stop.

He was washing his face in the lake water, knelt before the bank, thinking about the previous night at this very spot. So close . . . But his thoughts were broken by a series of shouts from a ways behind him. He stood and spun on his heel to cast toward the camp. Several of the tents had been set on fire.

"What the-" His interjection was cut off when he felt a sudden warmth around him, as if he'd walked out from the shade and into the sun. He looked from side to side indecisively as he saw that the trees near him had all caught aflame, as though every leaf and pine needle had ignited itself.

"Orphenn." A wispy voice came from behind him. It was only a hushed whisper, but he heard it clear as day, despite the growing mayhem filling the air. More shouts came from the camp as he spun around again.

Ardara was there, floating above the lake like a dark spirit. She splayed her black feathered wings behind her ominously. "Orphenn." Her voice came again, though her lips had not moved. He looked down, letting his eyes rest on her reflection in the lake water, intimidated like one look could turn him to stone.

He took a step back as if to turn and run, but a ring of fire had been drawn around him at that second.

Orphenn couldn't help but marvel at her power. Trapped in a cage of flames, he felt like a hoodwinked lab rat under the gaze of a cruel scientist. He could only stare as Ardara flowed through the wall of fire to hover before Orphenn within the circle.

"Wherever will you run?" she echoed, smoke curling around her, her voice as hushed as the flames.

She had a point, for there wasn't room enough for Orphenn's outspread wings, let alone to take flight, and the flames licked too high to pounce over.

"How did you find us?" Orphenn demanded.

She gave no answer but a smile and a flicker of her glowing red and blue eyes, so alike his own, though they held a unique madness, gazing from the shadow that her hood cast over her face.

Orphenn couldn't recall seeing any other enemies, and there were none of her soldiers in sight. "Why did you come alone?"

This time she opened her mouth to reply. "Oh, but I didn't." A blink of her ravenous eyes, and the loop of fire was snuffed to a ring of twisting smoke whirling around them.

A pair of hands came to clamp Orphenn's arms behind his back, and an arm came around his neck in a chokehold.

Dacian, who had jumped into the circle from outside the plume, greeted Orphenn lowly. "Hello again."

Before Orphenn could growl a sarcastic remark, a squall of darkness whirled at Dacian's back, and the shadow changed to reveal three figures, one of which came behind Dacian to stay a dagger at his throat and point a revolver at his head.

"Hey there Sunshine." greeted Sven.

The remaining two figures un-shrouded were Cinder and Celina, Cinder creating a dark spear of shade, holding at the ready, and Celina came forward to bravely stand between Ardara and Orphenn.

Orphenn admired Celina's courage as she stood tall before her powerfully maniacal sister, orange embers from the blazing trees dancing in the air between them.

Unarmed, Dacian chose to avoid a clash with Sven, who was equipped with an expansive armory at his beck and call; and so cautiously released Orphenn, hands in the air, eyebrow arched expectantly.

Orphenn fell forward, steadied by Jeremiah, who appeared in a flash at his side, Xeila and Eynochia coming up behind him at a more human pace.

Sven mercifully released Dacian in return, dismissing his blade and firearm in shining dust in the knowledge that Dacian was at the moment weaponless. Despite the injustice the traitor had done Sven in the past, he remained fair.

Cinder was not so compassionate. With her shadow spear she attacked Dacian, swiping quickly and numerously. He only just avoided each blow, before another that wore the red and black uniform came between them in a blur of violet.

Cinder pulled back her spear's blade in haste, slightly snipping stray threads of purple hair.

"Nyx." Cinder seethed.

"Have we met?" Said Nyx, blue and gold eyes blank and unfeeling, twirling a golden feather in her fingers.

"Yes," Cinder griped, the words in her next statement molding together in her fury. "I seem to recall a branding iron being burnt to my shoulder while you held me down in the boiler room ring a bell yet?"

"Ah, yes. E for Enemy. I remember."

Cinder slapped her, then again, then punched her. She fell to the grass.

Dacian made an attempt to back away, but was met with a wall of diamond.

Jeremiah, of course, was there when the traitor turned, armor crystallizing. He made no attempt to attack. He only held his fist at eye level, the diamond at his knuckles crackling as it grew to a frightening point, nearly pricking Dacian's nose.

His brows came together in puzzlement when Dacian cooed, "Ooh . . ." gazing admiringly at the reflecting sunlight upon the adamant armor. "This will do nicely." He grasped Jeremiah's arm, and at his touch, the armor there slid off as a glittering liquid. Dacian caught it and solidified it before it splashed to the ground, molding it into his ideal lance-just as Xeila and Eynochia caught up, consoling Orphenn.

Jeremiah held up his other arm to combat Dacian's new lance, and the two continued to spar, as Nyx did with Cinder.

"Never fought someone your own size, have 'ya?" Cinder taunted, easily overpowering the violet-haired twenty-year-old.

Jeremiah's success was similar. Though Dacian now had a way to fight back, Jeremiah was still faster, and stronger by far. He had torn through Dacian's jumpsuit faster than he had made his new lance.

Eynochia stared knowingly at the scar on Dacian's newly revealed skin, the scar she knew was made by her own claw.

Dacian took note of her eyes on him, and slyly molded his lance blade into a four-pronged fork. He made as if to attack Jeremiah, but instead he lunged oppositely, fooling everyone, and giving Eynochia a slash that matched his own.

She flailed to the ground with the pain, but Orphenn was quick to heal her, just as Jeremiah was quick to knock Dacian to the ground with the force of an airship collision.

Orphenn's light warmed the air, but he was unaware of the poison that had infused the wound from the toxic lance.

Dacian glared up smugly from his prone position in the smoky grass where Jeremiah held him down with a foot as if he were a hickory stump.

The poison etched a scar across Eynochia's shoulder as Orphenn healed the wound, four wide marks.

Orphenn shot a glare of absolute abhorrence at the tyrant who was once his sister. Ardara smiled back at him.

"Cira . . ." Celina beseeched, inching closer. "Cira, please stop this." Her typical, confident, arm-folded-behind-her-back posture had slumped into a more desperate pose, drooped shoulders, hands clasped before her. ". . . Cira . . ."

Ardara's eyes seemed to glow with an extra flash of rage. She said her next words with clenched and shaking fists.

"My name . . ." she lifted her arm, flames licking her fingers, "is *Ardara!*" she shrieked. A burst of fire shot from her palm and barreled outward.

"No!" Orphenn wailed, but his cry was lost in the blaze's loud crackle.

The burst torched Celina's side in her effort to evade. She fell to the singed grass.

"No!" Orphenn cried again and stumbled to Celina's side. No other had his strength to move, seemingly frozen by shock.

Even Ardara was still, staring astounded at the smoke rolling off her fingers, as if she had subconsciously realized that she'd fatally injured her own sister. Then, as she witnessed Orphenn's healing light illuminate Celina's burns and erase them, her personality switched again to a state of wrath. She looked at him. Almost instinctively, she felt the bonds of the people around him, connected to him. Like threads running through each of their hearts in a web.

Ardara looked harder. All of the threads were impossibly strong, she could see, but there was a special one that seemed to emanate a silver hue, and it looked absolutely unbreakable. Upon further observation, she realized that this invisible thread connected Orphenn's heart to Eynochia's.

Orphenn saw the look in Ardara's eyes. He knew what she was thinking in a split second when her eyes traveled from him to Eynochia. The desperation on Eynochia's face showed she knew it too.

Ardara smiled.

She aimed her palm at Eynochia.

In an instant, that seemed to take eons, almost like slow motion, Orphenn yelled once again, "No!" his hand pleadingly reaching out to Ardara. A heavy, dreadful fear weighed on him as he realized what Ardara would do, and that he was already too late to stop her, all in less than a second.

Ardara's hand fumed, the precursor to a rapid fiery end to anyone at the other end of her palm, too quickly to prevent, when just as rapidly, erupted from Orphenn's outstretched hand a shaft of golden light, burning their eyes and somehow putting out any remaining flames.

Orphenn's light bombarded Ardara's pale frame before she could cover Eynochia in flame. Fearful, he strained to clench his fingers and held his arm to his chest, cutting off the flow of light.

"Master!" exclaimed Nyx and Dacian in unison as Ardara toppled to the burnt ground, bleached-out grass flying.

With a painful squeal, she looked at Orphenn, face twisted in rage. Her skin was singed in patches, bloody and steaming, tears falling. The strange light had scalded her skin. She hadn't believed it possible, but it was so. This light wasn't the same as the elemental fire she manipulated. It was purer, and white hot.

Orphenn was just as surprised. He glanced at his palm in disbelief.

At Ardara's command, Nyx rushed to her Master's aid, Dacian following suit when Jeremiah hesitantly relented to release the traitor from under his foot. The two readied to carry her to a cruiser and flee-but not before Ardara furiously produced one of her favorite instruments from the folds of her cloak-a syringe—and quick as lightning, thrust the needle straight into Orphenn's abdomen as he stood.

He lurched at the assault, and the black liquid was quickly injected into his body. When the syringe was retracted, Orphenn clambered back down to the grass in agony. The substance was like molten tar in his bloodstream, burning every vein.

The cruiser flew Ardara and her two favored henchmen across the lake and away, without even a scornful threat as farewell. She sat backwards on the cruiser's platform and leaned her head back against the motor, watching the White Herons shrink in the distance. She twiddled the syringe in her fingers, then let it plunge into the lake.

"Let that be a lesson to you, my brother." She aimed her thoughts, and they vibrated loudly in Orphenn's head. "Even the brightest soul has his own darkness."

Orphenn writhed on the scorched earth as the cruiser sped out of sight, blackened soil and soot smearing his skin, wailing painfully and muttering unintelligibly. His one arm clenched around the painful injection point around his stomach, the other hand pulling and ripping at the charred grass.

Eynochia screamed a demand twice, the second time even more imploring than the first. "What did she do to him, *what did she do?!*"

She crawled as close as she dared to Orphenn's seizing and snarling body, the others only staring, frozen, horrified, stricken.

He looked as though he were being possessed, eyes brightening, mouth foaming. He didn't look conscious of anyone or anything, only of the pain. He bellowed.

"What did she put inside him?!" Eynochia cried with a banshee-worthy shriek, terror twisting her face.

Then there was a darkness, similar to Cinder's traveling shadows, but unmistakably more menacing. This darkness swirled about his eyes, his face, tendrils whipping about his body, dark appendages pulling him deeper. Soon he would no longer be Keiran, nor Orphenn Avari, but a winged creature of nothingness, a harbinger of destruction.

Sven took action, clamping his hands on either side of Orphenn's face to look him straight in his clouded eyes. The deep tentacles of malicious nothing whisked at Sven's wrists and forearms as he reached into Orphenn's mind.

It was almost like Déjà vu for the boy. Just like Sven's power had opened the flood gate of Orphenn's trapped memories before, he closed a protective drawbridge, complete with portcullis, temporarily sealing Orphenn's darkness, though as only a hindrance to the creature that was now inside him. Nonetheless, he managed to bring Orphenn back and the angry tendrils subsided.

"Little Bird." Sven beckoned as Orphenn's eyes cleared and his writhing ceased.

Eynochia scurried closer and held him as he heavily exhaled, and lost consciousness.

"He's fainted . . . What was in that syringe?" she asked, the question directed at no one in particular.

Celina and the others moved closer.

"Likely a tainted essence." Said the Supreme Commander. "There's no telling what it's done to him." She fondly stroked her brother's face. "I suppose we'll find out sooner or later." Her eyes closed, then harshly opened.

"Cinder. Port us to the ship. We're leaving."

Cinder eagerly complied.

Chapter Twenty

~

Weaver

"Is it safe to return to the capital?" Jeremiah chided his Supreme Commander at the helm, testing the wheel.

"What else is there to do?" she countered.

"Can we not invade the enemy camp? It's so nearby. We'd have the advantage."

"You know we can't risk that. Especially given the state of my brother. He needs the stability of the palace."

"How can you be so sure that it *is* stable? We could be heading straight for ambush."

"I assure you, Jeremiah. Denoras is the safest place to be now. So let's not dawdle. Lift off, full speed."

"Aye aye, Commander."

Before Celina could exit the main hold, Cinder appeared to block her path in a dark shroud, the portal revealing with her a strange young boy clung to her side.

"Celina." Her voice was infinitely serious. "This is Sparrow. He needs our help."

When Orphenn came to, Eynochia's face greeted him, eyes glowing in the dim light. There was another pair of eyes, but they did not glow.

The distasteful gaze of Sparrow caught him off guard.

"Sparrow!" Orphenn exclaimed, sitting up in his bed. "What are you doing here?"

Sparrow sat back in the beside chair, arms folded.

"Why don't you ask your psycho sister? The one that's trying to rule the world? And willing to kill anyone to achieve it?"

Eynochia's eyes fell, and she shook her head ruefully.

Orphenn frowned. "What? Ardara?"

"*Bingo.*" Sparrow's head tilted, hair beads clicking.

"Oh, no . . . Sparrow . . ." Empathized Orphenn in realization. His mouth didn't want to say the words, and they came out as a slur. ". . . Your gang?"

"*Dead.*" The younger boy stood, and pressed the hydraulic release button. Cinder stood on the other side of the door. "Your favorite's awake." He sneered at her as he left the room.

Cinder stepped into Orphenn's quarters, the door hissing shut after her.

"Cinder!" Orphenn worried. "What happened to Sparrow? What's he here for?"

She swallowed the lump in her throat. "The gang . . . Gryphon, Ibis . . . All of them . . . Ardarans killed them. Only Sparrow escaped." Her voice wavered, mismatched eyes bright with tears and red with grief.

"I'm so sorry . . ." he said, recalling in a moment how they had all been so friendly to him. "What did they do?" he asked, suddenly malicious. "What did they do to deserve death?"

Cinder took a deep breath, brows furrowed with her own distaste. "They were in the way. I don't know how it happened. He won't talk to me." Her face was downcast and sorrowful.

After an interval, Eynochia asked Orphenn, "Do you remember anything from earlier?"

"Earlier . . ." Orphenn looked back. "Yes . . . I remember the weird light from my hand . . . But after that it goes black."

"Oh, damn." Cinder cursed. She held her face in her black-nailed hands.

Eynochia tried to ignore her. "Something *happened* to you, Orphenn. Ardara put something inside you. Something . . . was taking you over."

Orphenn thought it over, scared out of his mind, and dreading anything that may happen next.

Just then, Sven came through the hissing door.

"Ship's about to land. We're home."

The Denoras Air Dock looked somehow smaller than before, compared to all the danger Orphenn had seen.

The people welcomed the White Herons home with enthusiasm and vigor.

There was no news of Ardara planning once again to attack the capital, so the city had no reason to fear; but other sites *had* been attacked, and the air still smelled of war. It was as if the people were releasing their strife and worry with every outward breath.

Cinder advised Sparrow to remain in the palace, and he did so, however reluctantly, and with a facetious attitude.

Orphenn found him in the main hall at sundown, gazing out to the bustling plaza.

"Sparrow?" He slowly approached the young biker.

"What do you want, Angel Boy?" Sparrow leered, never taking his eyes from the angel monument ahead.

"I want to tell you that I'm sorry."

Something suddenly changed in Sparrow, something almost invisible.

"You don't need to be . . ." He whispered, so that Orphenn had to lean closer to hear what he said next. "Looking at that statue now," he confided mutedly, "now I know that I've been wrong."

"What do you mean to say?" Orphenn intoned, as if speaking to a younger sibling and trying not to upset him.

"There's only two angels in that monument. The third is missing. I should not have blamed you and your sisters for what Ardara has done. And I . . ." He turned, but still avoided Orphenn's intense eyes, preferring to stare at the crest on his uniform. "I should not have been jealous of Raven's . . . . Cinder's . . . Real brother. I'm happy for her . . . For all of you." Orphenn patted his shoulder. "Heh. I'll stop running now. Cinder's not a drifter anymore. So why should I be? I don't even have a gang anymore. Hell, I don't even have a *bike* anymore."

"Sparrow . . . Why did you survive? How did you escape?"

"Hmph. That's a dang good question. I don't remember much, just . . . Fire, and explosions . . . All the bikes blew up. Finch had been shot . . . I saw Ardaran soldiers, but Gryphon told me to run away, so I did, and somehow Cinder was there, and she ported me to your ship. I really don't know."

Orphenn thought for a moment. "The Flock was just at the wrong place at the wrong time. Don't worry yourself about the how and the why. Just look at the ways you have grown, and be grateful for them."

Sparrow nodded once, finally looking the other in the eye.

Orphenn leaned against a great column. "So you're an orphan?"

Again, he nodded. "Just like you."

"What were you called before you joined the Flock?"

The question surprised him. "M-my . . . Real name? Before I was Sparrow?"

"Yes."

"My real name was . . ."

There was a pause.

Orphenn asked, "Would you like to know mine?"

"You mean you weren't always Orphenn?"

The older boy shook his head. "My name is Keiran."

"Keiran . . . Huh. My true name . . ." Another pause, ". . . Nero. My name is Nero."

After a moment, Orphenn asked another question that took the other completely off guard.

"Would you like to be Nero again?"

Sparrow gasped. For the second time, he looked Orphenn in the eye. After a deep breath, he gave one wordless nod.

Orphenn smiled, then suddenly spotted Eynochia at the foot of the palace steps. His smile widened. "Talk to you later Nero." He said, and began to descend the steps.

Nero chuckled. "Go get 'em Tiger."

"Well," Eynochia said as Orphenn came down the steps at a trot to meet her, "I'm glad to see that you and Sparrow are getting along."

"Nero." He corrected. "Call him Nero now."

"Oh." She said, puzzled.

"That's his real name."

"I see." She seemed to be thinking of somewhere else, mind and eyes wandering.

Orphenn followed her skyward gaze. Naturally, she was staring longingly at the highest clock tower.

Orphenn looked back at her with a foxy smirk.

Before she knew it, Eynochia was in the air. She shouted once in bewilderment, clinging for dear life to Orphenn, who carried her ever higher on his golden wings. Her fear vanished the moment he flew her toward the palace's towers. She couldn't help the wide, beaming smile at her mouth when the two landed on the tip of the highest clock tower.

She was absolutely speechless. She held her arms open wide, feeling the wind.

"Do you still believe this tower will fall?" Yelled Orphenn above the gale.

"Ha! I don't care! I'm *standing* on it!" She laughed in triumph.

He steadied her, holding her waist for fear she would lose her balance. Then he feared to lose his own balance when she turned and jumped into his arms, and they twirled happily.

With a grateful squeal and a smile of delight, Eynochia said, "Thank you, Orphenn!" And then again as a whisper in his ear when they'd stopped twirling. "Thank you."

Wind blowing their hair and clothes all about, they held each other close.

Orphenn brought his wings to surround them both and shield them from the wind.

And then-that moment they'd both imagined, that marvelous first kiss-happened and it seemed to be the happiest they've felt in forever, and they were oblivious to their audience.

Sven and Jeremiah stood smiling at the balcony, snickering and wondering where the popcorn was.

"Whataya know." Sven laughed. "Lovebirds."

Jeremiah's smile was solemn and his hand touched his heart. "They are able to find happiness in a time of such war. Now I know what I've been missing."

Without another thought, Jeremiah rushed to his Xeila in the gazebo with a flower in his hand.

Weeks went by with no news, and soon, regrettably, the city's guard was let down. So evidently, no one expected what would come one day at sunset.

They came in airships and they came in hovering cruisers, on foot and on jets. Though the most fearsome mode of newly acquired Ardaran transport were colossal, komodo-like lizards with scales black as the coming night, slithering tongues, and were saddled and bridled, with breath that would ignite and combust like sparks on a fuse. They bore down on the glorious capital city with intent and determination, airships looming, cruisers advancing, serpents creeping and scuttling up every building and statue. Denoras was under siege.

The White Herons had been reminiscing in the Commander's study when the sirens began to wail.

"What is it, Orphenn?" cried Jeremiah to the boy at the window.

"Ardara!" Came Orphenn's quick reply. "Looks like an air raid! And a cruiser . . . Raid . . . And there's-what the-lizards?"

"Lizards?" The others repeated in unison.

"They *must* be desperate, they're riding giant lizards! And they-whoa! Oh yeah, they breathe fire, just sayin'."

Celina rushed to her panicky brother's side to peer out across the plaza. "Creatures from Plenthin. You're right Orphenn. They're becoming desperate." She wailed, "There's no time to evacuate! We must move the city to the bomb shelter! Hurry, before-"

The earth shook, and the air outside brightened with shrapnel.

"They're already dropping bombs!" Shouted Sven, picking himself from the floor.

"Crap!" Orphenn interjected. "Guys! Where is Nero?"

Cinder, with a start, immediately ported from the room in a whirl of black smoke.

Nero had only just escaped the explosion. He seemed to have a knack for *only just* escaping.

The beads had fallen out of his hair, his cornrows falling loose, face bloodied, with scrapes all over his skin.

He ran the perimeter of the palace, heading for the plaza. *I have to get to the shelter.* He realized.

But Nero was stopped on his way when he reached the angel monument, the one he had admired only short weeks ago, as a large reptilian head crept over the side of Cinder's replica, its claws scratching the marble. Sparks flew from its mouth when it clicked its tongue.

From over the lizard's shoulder, Dacian appeared at the saddle, lance unsheathed, tightening the monster's reins.

"*You.*" Nero grimaced, frozen in his tracks.

"A pity," Dacian sneered, "that our next meeting is on such . . . *Shaky* terms." He twirled his lance as another bomb rumbled the ground, causing Nero to fall backward onto the pavement.

The lizard came upon him, mouth sizzling in his face.

"Wow," came Cinder's voice out of the abyss, "you've been around a bit, haven't 'ya? It seems everyone has vowed some sort of vendetta against you."

And then came the whirlpool of darkness that engulfed Nero's body and swept him away before Dacian could end his life.

When Nero again came into the light, he was beside Cinder inside the underground bomb shelter, where Orphenn and the other White Herons were guiding, directing and comforting civilians.

"Nero, stay here, where it's safe." She instructed. Then she ran to Orphenn. "Come with me." She told him.

Nero watched as Cinder and Orphenn disappeared through a dark portal. Then he wondered, *Is anywhere safe?*

The Palace of Denoras was falling, covered in red flame and smoke, much like the rest of the city.

Orphenn rushed with Cinder down the corridors of the crumbling palace, shielding their heads with their arms from the falling ceilings and trying not to breathe in the smoke.

"There are still people here!" Cinder informed. "We have to find them and get them out!"

The two scampered about the palace halls, kicking the doors down and searching thoroughly. Cinder sent any distressing remainders through portals to the bomb shelter (as she was now able to port others without touching them) and away from the burning palace where they would be safe from Ardaran attacks.

Orphenn followed Cinder into a dead end corridor, where she abruptly stopped at the last door, and stayed paused there for a moment.

"Cinder, come on! The palace is crumbling all around us!" He urged her, evading dislodged ceiling bricks. "We have to hurry! What are you waiting for?"

Cinder placed her palm on the door, as if searching inside the room beyond. She yelled over the rumble of battle outside with a serious glance at Orphenn, anticipation in her blue and green eyes.

"That's no damsel in distress beyond this door." She said, one hand pressing her abdomen as if a sense had risen there.

"What do you mean?"

But Cinder had already ported herself to the other side of the door, neglecting to use the doorknob.

The moment she materialized inside the room, an invisible force gripped her body, and held her in the air, boots lifted above the tile. It forced her eyes to look down at the grinning countenance of Ardara.

"I saw you coming." said the psychic, whose telekinesis pressed painfully on Cinder's torso.

She had also foreseen that Orphenn would come through the door, and when he did, Ardara said, "Ah, just as I suspected. The poisoned Enma essence has weakened you. Sven's shield can no longer protect you."

As though an invisible tranquilizing dart had hit his neck, Ardara forced him into unconsciousness by only a look in his eyes and he collapsed, head hitting hard on the tile.

"What did you do?!" Cinder writhed in midair. "Don't touch him!"

Ardara arrogantly traipsed to Orphenn's side, and lifted him from the floor to float before her, his body limply hanging on her telekinesis.

"He's my brother too, Cinder."

Cinder growled. "You lost the right to call him brother long ago! Get your psycho hands off him!"

Ardara ignored her command, stroking Orphenn's face.

"How like Father he looks. Though he has *my eyes.*"

Ardara's last two words seemed to send a shudder of pain through Cinder, although it was her eyes that signaled the electricity to shoot through the Drifter's frame.

Orphenn's body hung motionlessly in the air like a dormant string puppet.

"What did you do?! You took something from him!" Cinder shouted, but her voice seemed to become muffled by a phantom hand.

"Only his consciousness." Said Ardara. "Sadly," she sighed, "I will need my full focus to continue, therefore I haven't the energy to restrain you, Cinder.

"Good night."

As Cinder's mind had not been weakened as Orphenn's had, and was still fully protected my Sven's shield, Ardara resorted to a simpler method of debilitating her. Without the use of her hands, she hurled a white wall stone at Cinder's head.

The Drifter fell to the floor, silent.

Cinder would not succumb easily.

A splitting headache pulled her eyelids open, awoken to the sight of Ardara knelt lethargically over Orphenn, hands circling over his forehead, as if she weaved a dream into his skull.

Cinder heaved herself onto her elbows, and picked up the brick that had left a lump on the side of her head.

Just as Ardara brushed stray hair from Orphenn's brow, saying, "Ah, it is complete. Sleep, Little Brother. Sleep into eternity." Stone scraped her face, thrown by Cinder's accurate arm. A pen-stroke of blood underlined her eye, and a nick at the bridge of her nose when the brick swiped her face. It landed with a rocky clatter on the white tile, and Ardara snarled with rage. She stood, an ominous aura surrounding her.

Out of the blue, the wall behind her was ripped from its foundation, fallen due to another shudder that shook the earth by a bomb's chaotic explosion. Like a new picture window it revealed the state of Denoras outside as the brick and mortar fell away. Every building was on fire, among the rubble of other structures that had already fallen, vagrant smoke and flames still coloring the debris.

The sight filled Cinder's heart with sorrow. Though she could not help thinking, that even the dying capital city was beautiful, if not more so that the living one.

The high buttressed ceiling above began to crumble and fall, wreckage from the higher stories toppling through, and crashing down, nearly crushing Cinder. Looking back up from her crouched position after covering her head with her arms, she saw that another portion of the ceiling was teetering and ready to collapse, directly over the spot where Orphenn lay inert.

In desperation, Cinder let fly a portal in his direction.

He evanesced with the darkness before his body was pounded, the ceiling crunching down onto vacant tile.

Ardara screamed, frenzied and anxious, "Where did you send him?!"

Cinder shook her head, for she did not now. In the next second, she hurled another portal at Ardara, this time knowing exactly where she wanted to send it.

Ardara shrieked as the dark maelstrom enveloped her and she vanished from the burning palace.

Cinder herself ported away moments before the entire palace fell in on itself.

The sun had set hours before, so now the only light came from the flames that riddled Denoras's ruins, the stars wiped out by the constant smoke.

She materialized inside the bomb shelter, guilt-ridden and defeated.

Sven and Celina gazed her down when she appeared, shortly before Xeila, Eynochia and Jeremiah did the same, terror plain on all their faces. They knew by the look in Cinder's eyes that something horrible had happened.

As for Orphenn, the next time he opened his eyes, he could not grasp what he saw.

Chapter Twenty-one

~

Deception

Orphenn was in an alley. A dog barked down the street. Police sirens wailed. The sky was gray and polluted over the roofs.

The familiar smell of cat and garbage surrounded him. He sat erect in one fluid movement, eyes wide and unbelieving, mind blazing. He jerked around, suddenly on his feet, looking all around him almost frantically.

"What . . ." he could barely speak above a hush. "M-my alley?"

He looked down at himself. He saw worn boots, ragged clothing, a filthy trench coat and long greasy hair falling into his face.

Incredulously, he patted himself, touched his face and tugged his unruly hair, as if he was unable to believe he was truly there.

In his fit, he noticed an important looking man in a black suit at the end of the alley. He jumped in fright when Orphenn ran toward him.

"Hey! Hey wait! Have you ever wondered about other worlds?" He pleaded, for he thought perhaps, maybe he had been somehow sent back to Earth by mistake and that Cinder would return to retrieve him.

But how? Orphenn thought at the same time, *How is it that I'm the same as I was before? I'm just a hobo again, my old hair, my old clothes, everything. Why?*

He needed some kind of confirmation or he was sure he would go insane.

When the suited man grimaced, Orphenn said, "No, no I meant . . . Like different planets-solar systems-galaxies . . . Oh, I don't know! Somewhere different! Do you know anything about someplace else?"

The man scowled. "Are you hung over or something? Get the Hell off me before I whack you with my briefcase."

Orphenn hadn't realized he'd been clutching the man's lapel, and slowly released him.

After several similar encounters, begging for knowledge or ridiculous advice, and being pushed away, Orphenn began to panic.

What if . . . . There was no Aleida?

He looked all around him. This Earth seemed so dull and devoid compared to his Aleida. Although . . . Dreams always seem a bit brighter than what's right in front of one's eyes, don't they? The sky almost seemed to fall. Or was that his imagination too?

"No . . . Aleida?"

Orphenn stumbled dizzily back into the alley, like he really had been hung over. Who's to say he hadn't been?

Finally, it set in. He stared at his dirty hands, grime in the lines of his palms and under his fingernails. No longer strong enough to stay upright, he frailly fell to his knees, eyes still glued to his palms, feeling that he could erode away at and second.

He heard a constant rush in his ears, as if a waterfall crashed incessantly inside his head. Nothing but that sound seemed at all real to him, and yet he came to the realization that, maybe . . . The river in his head was the only thing that wasn't real.

At length, he fell back against the wet brick of the alley wall. His hands fell weakly to his lap and he looked up at the gray sky that seemed to reflect back to him his own despair, his stare blank and desolate. He was numb, his body seeming to float away. His utter heartbreak was staggering.

"All of it . . . Was only . . ." Tears filled his eyes and fell, smearing the dust on his cheeks. His own words seemed as unreal as the world he had woken from.

"Only a dream?" It made sense. He woke up back in New York with an intense head ache as if he had fallen asleep on a chunk of asphalt. Then he dared to turn his head slightly, to see that homely bottle of vodka resting innocently on its side beside the trash can. Right where he had left it. Had he even dreamt seeing Sam again and apprehending a criminal? It seemed like so long ago.

He turned away, lip trembling.

Then his eyes no longer saw the gray sky above him, but instead the memories he thought had been so real, every face he had come to know flashed before him; his family, Celina, Cinder, even Cira. All those he met and grew to love . . . Sven, Eynochia, Xeila, Jeremiah, even Nero and his gang . . . Imaginary?

His voice was hindered by the lump of sorrow in the back of his throat, his words choppy and quivering.

". . . They weren't real?"

He saw his adventures, every single danger he had faced, all that had been made up . . . His mind's own invention.

Had he been so desperate for company, for family and friends that loved him that he would conjure his own world in a drunken stupor? An entirely fictional venture that seemed to explain every question he'd ever had in his life? His family, his real name, his "oddities?" What were the odds of any of that being true?

How completely pathetic he felt.

"My name is Orphenn."

This lament brought the images of his old parents and his sisters-the ones he had created-and dissipated them, as if in finality to say back to him,

Yes, that is your name. You were never 'Keiran.' How foolish.

"And I am an orphan."

Sven, Eynochia, Xeila. He remembered the photo of Oriana. They had been a family too. And Jeremiah was to become a part of it . . .

Their image was swiped from him just as the last had been.

Then a vision of Wynne, the kind guard who had sacrificed so much. Nero's gang that had been murdered . . . They had been kind too.

Kindness isn't real.

Love is a myth.

Happiness . . . Isn't real.

They aren't real either.

"And I am . . . I am an orphan . . ."

Very good. Reality said.

Now repeat after me: 'And that's all I will ever be.'

"I am an orphan and . . ." He took a deep, desperate breath, a precursor, ". . . And that's all I will ever be!" He sobbed enormously, body quivering, chest heaving.

He had devised a make-believe illusion to compensate for everything that was missing in his life. Every bit of it had been fake.

Orphenn's heart broke then. He felt it so truly that he thought his own soul had clutched it and crushed it in its hands in mourning.

He continued to grieve, rolling over on the concrete, grasping at his chest.

It must have been hours that he lay there after his sobs subsided, hearing nothing, feeling nothing, barely seeing his own hand splayed on the pavement before his face. There was only one thing that seemed to come to his thoughts when he tried to tell himself to rise. Like a stern hail it beat him down, and he remained.

Not real.

~~~~~

When Cinder emerged from the bomb shelter, where they all had been confined for days, she felt much like her brother did. Something other than her free will seemed to be moving her legs, shoving her forward. She could no longer stand the miserable sanctity of the shelter, where the guilt pressed on her like all the gazes of those surrounding her. Still, she had not told them what had happened to Orphenn.

All was ash and ruin, and deathly silent like snow freshly fallen. Cinder was helpless to the thought that the scene was subtly beautiful, despite the death that lay beneath the ashes.

She continued to trod through the ashes, entering the remains of the city plaza. Only one structure still stood tall against the sky, all others a mound of rubble.

She glared hurtfully upward at the angel monument that depicted her image and the likeness of her sister so perfectly, the marble dusted with ash. She could almost see another face there, floating between the two sculpted heads like a lost specter. A face she knew was supposed to be there, and touchable as the other two, though it wasn't. The face of Cira. The one that belonged there just as much, but couldn't be there.

Celina came to stand beside her, wordlessly. She wore her imperial robes of white, rather than the Heron's jumpsuit, truly a regal vision of elegance amidst the remnants of Denoras, unlike the other, who stood out like the contrast of a single black bead on a porcelain tray.

"Why is it that *this* is the only infernal thing left standing?" Seethed Cinder.

"Don't be that way." Was Celina's calm reply. "We can't grovel in the ashes. We'll stand tall like our statues. We can find the answer to this."

"So positive." Cinder shook her head. "Always, when you try to be uplifting, why does it seems to make everything worse?"

"Cinder." The other insisted, forcibly turning her sister to look her in the face. "What happened to Orphenn."

It was not a question.

Cinder's eyes were morose and sullen, and shone with wet sadness.

"I don't know where he is. I tried to save him. I didn't know what else to do. The portal acted of its own. He could be anywhere now. If I hadn't done it Celina, he would be dead for sure. He's only missing. We only have to find him."

Celina's eyes glimmered with understanding. She released her hold on Cinder's shoulders.

Only then did they simultaneously realize the presence of a silenced airship, dormant and swathed in ash, only a short distance from the palace remains. Its dark metal and clumsy welding indicated Ardaran manufacture.

"An Ardaran airship . . ." Murmured Cinder.

There was the gradual tick of expanding metal, heating up.

"It's about to lift off . . ." Celina noted, mouth gaping. Then, an idea. Crazy, but an idea nonetheless. "Cinder!" she exclaimed, "Port me inside that ship!"

"What? Why?" After a moment, Cinder added with severity, "Cira's on board that craft."

They both could sense that fact, in their cores.

"I know."

"You're planning to stow away? What will you accomplish?"

"Maybe I could discover something to give us the advantage in this war we're fighting. Anything, *anything* could help."

"But-"

"*Please*, Cinder. Let me do this."

Greatly reluctant, Cinder touched Celina's face. Celina returned the gesture.

"Celina, if anything happens . . . I'll be to blame for Orphenn, and for you."

"We will find him." She assured.

A deep, revealing look passed between them, and Cinder was suddenly even more unwilling to let her go, like trying to pry apart the links of a chain.

Then from Cinder's palm, against Celina's cheek blossomed the blackness that would port her inside a deep hidden corner in the Ardaran ship's cargo hold.

When Celina disappeared, and Cinder's upraised hand touched nothing but open space, the rush of air came from the airship's liftoff, and she watched it ascend and fly out of sight with a heavy heart.

Her worries ate at her. Her upraised hand clenched into a fist, trembling with her strife as she glared again at her own face carved in marble above her head.

Without warning, a tremendous crack sounded across the expanse of ash, almost like gunfire. It was as though the noise had emanated from all around her with the way it echoed, but in truth, it was the result of a fracture, plated diagonally through the body of Celina's statue. The marble body collapsed in a cloud of dust and ash, leaving only the tall depiction of herself standing alone in the rubble, all but a mirror image, albeit a blurry one. Cinder had no room left to think of the cause of the sudden rapture, or what it might foretell. Only her own self hatred was allowed to her.

Cinder plunged to her knees. Her cry of anguish could be heard faintly in the confines of the bomb shelter. She wept for the city. For her home.

Not long after, Cinder elected to teleport back to the bomb shelter, though she didn't port inside-only to the threshold of the large, inclined, double trap doors. She dreaded to go inside; knowing what glances and stares would meet her upon entry. Nonetheless, she ported to the other side.

As she had predicted, thousands of eyes immediately fell on her, Sven's being one of the first heads to turn. His face was puzzled when Celina did not appear at Cinder's side.

Cinder swiftly made her way toward him, the crowd spreading apart to allow her path, each face full of a reverence that she felt she did not deserve.

As "Lady Cinder" was many times more infamous than the true Supreme Commander due to her mysterious reputation, the vast sea of citizens-though significantly not so vast as before-screamed her name and cheered at her presence, as if she was a pop star.

"Sven," she whispered when she was close enough, "can you shut them up for me?"

He nodded once, instantly summoning a very loud-looking revolver. The dust glittered like the tail on a comet as he aimed the barrel upward and fired three times at the ceiling, miles above their heads.

Cinder ascended a platform and spoke.

"It is now safe to leave the shelter, but, people, I warn you. What's outside is not a sight for the weak of heart.

"All of our homes are destroyed. And I know we have all lost. There have been deaths . . ." She looked down at young Nero, who gazed painfully back up at her from the first row. Pliley and his young partner Hollei stood in that front line as well, the officials who once worked in the plaza. Cinder felt it had been like years since she had last seen them both. She continued.

"There are only remnants, but anything you may find among the ash I guarantee is unsalvageable. It is my strongest advice that you all take refuge at Verlassen." She glared at Nero as if to say, *That goes for you too.* The look on his face indicated he got the message. "I've sent for a zeppelin to transport the lot of you." Already, solitary sobs were escaping the crowd, and many were dripping with tears. "As for my valiant sister . . . . I think it best that you all remain ignorant as to the whereabouts of our Supreme Commander." Several protests followed this statement. "But I assure you, most emphatically, that she is acting with the courage that I feel many of us have lacked."

The other White Herons each took on features glazed with horror, especially Sven, who glared straight at Cinder with a desperation that could have stopped a stampede in its tracks. They longed to know what Cinder knew.

"Jeremiah, if you would kindly open the doors." She requested.

Jeremiah gave a low bow, trying to hide his anxiety, and obeyed.

Light flooded in, and Xeila and Eynochia professionally led the people up and out, like officers directing traffic. Nero gave one last glance at Cinder before he sullenly followed suit.

Sven grasped her shoulder as Cinder descended the platform.

"Spoken like a leader, Cinderella."

She looked over her shoulder at the man who seemed to emanate understanding.

"Sven . . ." she found herself unable to speak above a whisper, eyes wet with emotion. "She made me do it. She's stowed away inside an enemy airship. She made me, I swear."

"I trust her." Was all he said, but his eyes said, *So should you.*

After an interval, Cinder asked, "Are we off to Verlassen as well, Marshall?" Playfully yet wearily using his rank, the White Herons' inside joke.

"I've decided against that, Little Princess. We're making camp outside the capital." He replied with a look of knowing. She took the hint.

To Cinder's squadron, "outside the capital" nearly always meant "on the banks of the River."

"I'll meet you there."

Without another word, Cinder was gone, the darkness sifting between Sven's fingers. He let his hand fall to his side.

"What are we gonna do with you, Cinderella?"

Chapter Twenty-two

~

On the Banks of the River

Night had passed, and the sun rose bleakly on New York City.

"Wow." Orphenn chastised himself. "I sat here, all night, *pitying* myself." He shook his head, gazing at the vodka bottle, and realizing its contents weren't so appealing anymore. He clicked his tongue in disdain. "Time for a little walk." He decided, and heaved himself up.

He couldn't say how long he'd walked, but after only a few minutes, he'd gone back to pitying himself.

Everything he saw, everything he heard, reminded him of all that he'd lost. It weighed him down, but he kept walking, with a limp, as if each thought was an anvil carried on his shoulders.

He passed a white cat on the street that looked at him with curious mismatched eyes. Blue and brown like Celina's had been. He walked through a public planetarium with an exhibit on supernovas, like the one the Day Star had been named after. He hobbled by a pawn shop with large selections of blades and firearms, like Sven's armory. Each flickering shadow reminded him of Cinder, every motorcycle that went growling by.

Every little reminder broke off a little bit more of him, until, much like the night before-or a few nights before, he couldn't be sure-he felt utterly hollow.

He walked on, for days, or for weeks, he couldn't tell, as the sky was infinitely gray, and he couldn't differentiate day from night.

He fell into a fathomless depression.

Only boredom kept his legs moving, though he didn't really see the things he walked past anymore, his eyes sightless, body purposeless.

The days blurred together and time meant nothing.

Though he did at one moment come across an electronics shop, a dozen televisions of different sizes showing the same news cast.

"*. . . Entire Earth's water supply has become polluted . . .*" Said the monotone anchorman, as a side screen displayed film images of rivers and lakes all over the world, the Amazon, the Mississippi, the Great Lakes, the English Channel, the Dead Sea, the Gulf of Mexico, all gone soupy brown, every ocean gone completely black.

"*. . . All beaches and national parks closed down . . .*"

Orphenn realized curiously that no one was on the streets. No traffic, no voices, no aircraft overhead, not even birds.

New York City was silent.

Or it might have been New York City, or somewhere else. He had no idea where he really was.

His body felt weak.

Little did he know, his true body lay right under his sister's nose.

Cinder was aghast to realize the state of the River, though she made no shout to release her dismay, for fear of being heard by the others. She didn't want to worry them even more.

Anxiously she glanced over her shoulder at the White Heron's camp to ensure no one was watching her. When she was confirmed she squirmed closer to the water until the tips of her long black hair almost kissed the surface.

The water was a sickly gray, and no longer sparkled with secret warmth, no natural luster-it looked cloudy, stormy, ill.

Cinder reached her hand into the water and held it there in sympathy, as if reaching into a baby's cradle, like the River's pain was her own.

Her fingers curled in the diseased water, tightened into a fist. She could feel Aleida was close to dying. Her fist shook.

She leapt up and ran to the camp.

"The River is tainted." She announced as she broke into the tent.

"*What?*" Came the unanimous reply.

Jeremiah reasoned, "That could mean anything. It could be the omen that predicts the Apocalypse. Or it could be a simple pollution problem."

"Has it ever turned black before?" Cinder countered.

"We're all gonna die." Xeila said plainly.

Sven scolded her for her skepticism. "Poppet, you don't know that."

"We're part of a *war*. Odds are, we're gonna die."

"Oh, shut up Xeila. Don't you think we know that?" Cinder snapped, tensions rising. "Aleida . . . . She could be trying to tell us something. What if . . . She's warning us?"

No answer. Even Sven was skeptical now.

"We all know this planet is alive. We *know* it's more than just a hunk of rock. What if her essence is tainted because of something that we . . . Aren't seeing?"

All of them in their anxiety were oblivious to the fact that Orphenn's body lay only a few yards downriver, hidden by undergrowth, twitching at intervals as if he walked through a convincing nightmare.

Hours passed and no answers came. The River's sickness, Orphenn's well-being, Celina's whereabouts; all remained a mystery.

Celina regretted wearing her formal robes, but was unwilling to discard them.

She slipped in and out of the shadows, a stow away in the almost pitch dark of the Ardaran ship's cargo hold.

Like an instinct arisen in her chest, she knew her sister was close. She hoped against all hope that Ardara's own end of the triplets' link was clouded. If she sensed Celina or saw her coming, it was all over. She could only pray that Ardara was too absorbed in her own disastrous plotting to make room for anything else.

So as the engine roared, and the craft lifted off, she swiftly made for the door to the main hold. Her coronet glinting and eyes luminous in the dismal light, she wished her heartbeat would calm.

Not knowing who or what would be waiting on the other side, she firmly pressed the release key.

It was maddening, to sit there, *not knowing*. Clueless, they sat around the campfire, hoping the blaze could clear their heads. They each felt it like an agonizing itch at the back of their skulls, excruciatingly out of reach. Nothing passed between them but the crackle of the flames.

Attempting to lighten the atmosphere, Eynochia suggested, "Why don't we tell stories?"

Xeila gazed doubtfully at her sister. "Like what?" She mocked. "Like the time Eynochia fell on her face in front of a cute guy?"

"Hey!" she defended. "You're just as clumsy! Or need we be reminded of the day Xeila 'accidentally' spilled custard all over her ex-best friend?"

Xeila smiled. "I was framed!"

Laughter erupted from the group, apart from Cinder, who only smiled wearily.

More bouts of laughter, and then Xeila turned to Jeremiah and bumped his shoulder. "Maybe you should tell them what happened after."

"Oh, but you tell it so much better." He declined.

"Sure, sure enough." She agreed, eager to share.

She told a tale of heartbreaking split-up, and how Jeremiah helped her recover.

"I was all bawlin' and cryin' and feeling bad for myself, when *this* big lurpy oaf comes up to me-and he was a skinny little thing back then before that First War-and," she gesticulated, imitating a low bow, and holding out her hand, "he says, 'excuse me Miss, I believe you dropped this.' And he had a flower in his hand, and he stuck it in my hair." She grinned, remembering, settling back in her chair around the fire. "How old were we then, like ten or eleven? I don't know. Well, years later, he proposed to me with that same line. But with our pendant instead of a flower."

Jeremiah twined his fingers in hers and for the first time Cinder noticed the matching pendants around their necks.

Oh yes, she recalled, Aleidian courtship differed slightly from Earth traditions. Instead of purchased rings, couples showed engagement with pendants, inlaid with the birthstones of both, in Jeremiah and Xeila's case a topaz and an emerald. In a wedding ceremony, the counterparts are exchanged for pendants of pure and glistening white crystal, or diamond for the more wealthy, white being the color of eternity. The pendants are presented by the father of the groom. The original pendants were always kept safe and cherished.

At length, Sven asked, "Have I ever told you about my brother?"

Xeila and Eynochia both straightened subconsciously, keen to hear of the mysterious uncle they knew so little about.

"I never knew you had a brother." Cinder confessed sullenly.

"He died before you could ever meet him."

"What gifts did he have?"

"My only brother, Ira, was much more powerful than me. Think of it kinda like Cira and Celina. Celina is somewhat telepathic-psychic, but not nearly as powerful as Cira. That's a lot like me compared to my brother.

"I can summon weapons, and I'm able to reach into other's memories, and even shield their minds. In exchange, I can't remember jack squat. I swear I have the worst memory on the planet.

"Anyhow. Ira was much stronger. He'd always loved music, he was always singin.' But when he was mutated, he was able to *control* others with his voice. Make them walk for him. Do his will. Just by singin' a song." The others were amazed by this, and their eyes widened as they listened even more attentively to the best story teller Aleida ever knew. "And not only that. He could protect the minds of others, like I can. The thing is though, *my* Mind Shield is only as strong as the mind it protects." He jabbed his finger at them all around the circle, narrowing his eyes. "Which is why all of *you* better keep your heads screwed on right. I can't protect you if you lose your marbles.

"Back to the point. Ira had the same ability. But his Mind Shield *always* stays strong, impenetrable. Even after *death*. Thanks to him, no one can read my mind, not even if I go 'round the bend, not even from the grave."

"Remarkable." Breathed Jeremiah, awestruck, hazel and lavender eyes gleaming.

"And even more remarkable," Sven added, far from finished, "he had the memory of a Goddang elephant!"

"Heh, you *would* find that remarkable," Xeila teased.

"I'm not even jokin'! There he was like twenty-five, and he's ranting about how he hated the way his diaper used to rash! *I* remembered it, bein' I was probably nine or ten, but he'd only been a baby!

"And he could always prove me wrong that way too, when we would argue. Even before the First War, he was special. He remembered *everything*. He could tell you what color socks Mama wore at her wedding."

"Why is *that* so important?" Eynochia queried.

Sven then produced from his white trench coat pocket a small tome, held together with ribbon. It was a photo book. To make his point he flipped to a certain photo and held it up for them to see. It was old and faded, wrinkled at the edges.

In the picture was a couple, obviously a wedding photo. Eight-year-old Sven stood at his father's knee. The mother's socks were green. But her belly was bulbous. Pregnant.

The group was struck to silence, all their pairs of eyes sending to him a glowing spectrum of amazement.

Satisfied, Sven replaced the photo book and continued. "Uh-huh," he sighed, "he could tell you what the air smelled like on a Saturday morning when he walked one-hundred-seventy-five steps to his friend Mallabella's house that looked like a gingerbread house from a certain angle and if the grass was cut and how green it was and if it was cloudy and what position the sun was at in the sky and what he ate that day even though that day was five years ago and he was two years old at the time."

He took a deep recovery breath.

". . . . Wow." Was the only response.

He chuckled. "Tell me about it." Then a quiet moment passed and he added, "Oriana just loved him. After the war started, he had taken on a young ward. Little blondie. I was quite fond of the kid, but he was so withdrawn . . . I never learned his name. The boy's family had been killed in an Ardaran attack, and my brother took him in. I never got to see either of them, since we were in separate squadrons. I never saw him after he was mutated so I don't know what gifts he has. I know his eyes had been green. I don't reckon you two remember much of them, bein' so young as you were." He looked to his daughters, who both shook their heads. "It was Orio that told me Ira had been killed. She was there. Cira had confronted your squad herself. Your mother had told you to go to the main chambers to hide.

"Cira wanted Ira's power. She'd given my brother a choice. To join her or die. You can guess which one he chose." Sven looked into the fire, reminiscently. "Then his boy went missing. I expect he died too. It was a year after that that my wife died.

"So . . . Now it's just me and my girls."

He gave a sad smile to his daughters.

"That's not true." Countered Jeremiah, as certain as if it were set in stone. "You will *always* have us."

Cinder nodded her approval, and the night was ended in smiles.

Just before dawn, Eynochia stirred.

She tossed and turned on her cot, and finally she elected to visit the River.

She perhaps was the one who felt Orphenn's absence the most. She could no longer deny her feelings for him as she exited the tent and trod across the grass in the dying moonlight.

She felt no resentment towards Cinder, she knew she had only wished to save her brother from Ardara. Still, she couldn't help but feel cheated somehow. Like he was stolen from her.

Now Eynochia remembered the campfire hours earlier, and thought of Ira, and his ward. How she wished she could have known them. Then she thought of her mother.

Sven had once told her that Oriana was . . . *pure.* In heart, in soul, in everything. He said that was probably why her hair had gone white when she mutated, and why Xeila's and her own locks were the same.

You're like her, her father always said. *You're like her.*

To Eynochia's surprise, Cinder had beaten her to the River, sitting solemnly on the banks. "Is it . . . Really tainted?" The canine Enma asked feebly.

Cinder looked back, her eyes luminous in the pre-dawn light, and then turned away. "See for yourself."

Eynochia stepped timidly closer, and what she saw made her heart hurt, more than it already ached.

The very essence of this same River flowed through her veins, the veins of every Enma. It was part of her, and she was part of it, as were them all. It hurt her to see the River's pain.

Now she kneeled in the grass and did as Cinder had done before, curling her fingers in the raw, gray water, feeling its exhausted current, her throat tightening with its anguish, the misery she felt for it.

I really am pure, aren't I? She thought. *To feel this way about something so predictable as a river. I am pure.*

As soon as she realized this, she also realized that this River was anything but predictable.

Chapter Twenty-three

~

Smile and Sacrifice

The hydraulic door came open with a snake-like hiss. To her relief, no one waited on the other side.

Still not at ease, Celina cautiously came forward, making her way slowly through the labyrinthine metal hallways.

Ardara rubbed her temples, trying in vain to soothe her headache.

"Wynne . . . ?" She requested, also in vain.

"Wynne awaits our return to the castle." Dacian provided. "Your lesson made him into quite the humble servant. Loyal. He's learned much of allegiance."

"Ah . . . Yes . . . He's . . . At the castle . . ." She muttered through the pain, heedless to Dacian's praise toward the degraded henchman. "Nyx?"

"Yes, My Liege?" Answered the young violet-haired Enma.

"Do you have any herbal tea?"

"M-Master?" She questioned, exchanging a confused glance with Dacian.

"It would certainly help with this headache." She elaborated. "My senses are so jumbled . . . What with maintaining the Dream Hold and so many other things . . . . My psychic ability seems to be backing up. I need . . . some calming herbal tea."

"Regrettably, this ship doesn't happen to carry any, Master . . ."

"*Well*, stop in Plenthin for herbs then."

Without another word, she retired to the lounge.

Dacian sighed wearily. "This means we'll have to *turn around*. What a drag."

"She scares me when she's somewhat amiable." Nyx admitted.

"Better get used to the mood swings." Dacian motioned to the helmsman. "You heard the Master. Turn the ship around."

"We're really changing course? Why can't we just pick up some tea on the way to the castle?"

"Judging from past experience, she'd instantly know it wasn't from *Plenthin*. And putting into account her recent irritability, she'd probably throw the box at my head. She does that. So only Plenthinian herbs will do." Dacian, normally cold and merciless in demeanor, seemed to be warming up to violet woman. It could be said, he was becoming attached. "You'll definitely have to get used to it, Nyx. Ardara will rule this world and we will stay beside her until death comes between us. Definitely. Better. Get used to it."

"Ah, I see . . . But why did she ask for Wynne?"

"That . . . I don't know."

Evidently, they never flew all the way to Plenthin.

Ardara and Dacian stood side by side, gazing through a porthole as the ship passed over a forest, and Celina hid silently beneath the main hold entrance, making not a sound.

"Master." Dacian alerted, pointing. "Below. The White Herons."

Celina started, mouth dropping open.

Ardara peered down. As he said, the tents of the White Herons' camp lay far below, the Day Star at rest beside it.

"Initiate Stealth." Ardara ordered.

The helmsman was quick to comply, and soon the ship was invisible as it flowed through open sky.

The sun rose.

Its light kissed every surface as it shone through the portholes.

Ardara spat, "Attack."

As the sun began to rise, the water that swirled around Eynochia's fingers began to clear. She gasped. A circle of revitalized, glittering water twirled about wherever she touched, growing larger, until she could see to the Riverbed like a single shaft of light through the darkness.

Cinder gasped, and instantly rose to her feet. Eynochia squealed, a grin slowly spreading on her face.

"Daddy!" She shouted. "Daddy!"

Cinder joined her calling. "Sven!"

When he arrived, Xeila and Jeremiah curiously accompanying him, Eynochia jumped into the water, spinning and twirling, a widening spiral of warmth, not caring how dripping wet she was. She was purifying the water, with only the touch of her skin, the gloomy gray disappearing faster with the more excited she became.

By the time the sun rose, its light glittered over the entirety of the rejuvenated River, flowing strong and gallant, as if showing gratitude.

"Dad, look!" Eynochia yelled emphatically, dancing and splashing, in the vitalized, glistening, breathtaking water. "I-I fixed it! I healed the River!"

And then those words came, the ones she'd heard in her head only moments before.

Sven said, "You're like her."

Eynochia smiled, looking to Cinder. "You were right, Cinder. Aleida *was* trying to tell us something. I know what she wants.

"Cira isn't evil, Cinder. She's like the River. We just have to give her light back."

Tears fell down their faces.

Then Sven leapt, splashing into the water, followed soon by the bride-and-groom-to-be.

Cinder watched while they soaked each other, laughing, jumping, dunking, brilliant water droplets flying.

"Take this!"

"Back at 'ya!"

"Ha-ha! En guard!"

"Oops, betchya didn't see that one comin'!"

"Have at thee, demon! Ha!"

They're to be a family, Cinder thought. *As soon as this wretched war is over. They'll be happy forever.*

At first she felt slightly jealous of them, the absolute promise of happiness they all possessed, but then she felt something else.

The dreadfully familiar sense rose in her abdomen, the one that told her that her one of her sisters were close.

Then the pain came.

Their link had acted too late.

"No." Celina whispered. Without thinking, she ran for the nearest exit, down the hallway, and her footsteps echoed.

"Please, let's not be hasty, Master." Said Dacian, ever the perceptive henchman. "I beseech you, don't start without me. One matter of business. I'll be right back."

"Very well." Ardara relented, rolling her eyes. "Abort. Wait for Dacian's word to drop the missile."

The helmsman saluted obedience.

Dacian turned and ran, crossed the main hold, and dashed down the hallway.

Celina ran faster, knowing she'd made a mistake. But she had to warn them. She would jump out of the ship and fly down to her squadron. She had to.

When she saw a door, she slammed into it, hitting her body against it until it broke open. She had no time to be considerate.

Again, without thinking, she ran out. When she saw nothing but open air and the green earth below, her stomach lurched. She drew in a terrified breath, thinking she would fall, but she stood solidly. Then she recalled that the craft was in stealth mode. It looked as if she floated on nothing in the middle of the sky, but in actuality she was standing on the deck of an invisible airship.

A voice made her turn, robes and hair flailing in the free wind.

"Ah. A stow away."

Dacian was there, stepping out from a door that appeared to come from nowhere, the red insides a drastic contrast with the brightening stark blue of the sky all around them.

He stepped out onto nothing. The wind tousled his hair.

She should have jumped then. She should have flown. But the sight of him froze her body, tightened her heart.

They stood together in the unobstructed sky, in silence.

She stared at him, the face she knew so well. But his eyes were different. They were not his eyes. Emotionless black and sacrificial red. They were glazed over with malice. He didn't see, not truly. He saw through another's eyes now.

Ardara's eyes. She thought. And then it came to her, the meaning of Orphenn's words. Something bigger.

Now she knew what must be done.

So she made no move to fly.

She only looked at him, and she wept.

She knew what he would do.

And he did.

Without preamble, Dacian closed the distance between them, unsheathing his lance. He thrust it into her core.

As all light left her eyes, it all came back to his.

The only woman he had ever loved fell to her death.

He watched her fall.

He fell to his knees, in the sky.

And the sky was the only one that heard his mournful cry, lost on the wind.

As the news had broadcasted, the park at Niagara Falls was closed.

Orphenn, feeling nothing, let alone any obligation to honor the law, stepped right over the webs of yellow tape and jumped the gate.

He suddenly wondered what had led him to this abandoned tourist destination. Equally suddenly, he realized, *Niagara Falls? That's on the other side of the state. I must have been walking for weeks.*

The place was utterly empty, save for the constant roar of the falls that seemed to harmonize with the river in his head.

He ambled up the solitary pavement and let his sullen fingers curl around the aluminum railing, looking out unseeingly, unfeelingly over the enormity of the sullied water. He drowsily eyed the other side, far across Canada's border, and then back down at the river below.

The River . . . Of course. That's what brought him here.

Orphenn paled, and became almost numb with his shocking thought, a desperation blooming deep within him.

Could it be?

Orphenn's true body slid down the bank precariously.

Senseless with hope, he didn't feel the dew-dropped aluminum under his hands, didn't feel his lank hair cling to his neck as he dizzily swiveled to look around, abruptly light-headed. And as a public restroom rolled into his view, built of hazy gray brick, he didn't feel his legs vault him toward the unhinged door.

As he rushed inside, he clumsily grasped the steel sink plumbed into the wall to slow himself down, his boots thudding the cement floor of the humid, revolting lavatory.

His both hands steadied him, leaning fearfully on the sink for support.

When he finally gathered the courage, he looked up, into his own face, upon the mirror.

Like he had always done since his first days at the Kinder Rose Orphanage, the first thing he thought was, *My eyes.*

He began to shake, his eyes widening in realization.

Eyes that were both the same, uniform, icy, blue.

Then his trembling ceased and he was filled with such a strong certainty that his body seemed to grow in stature, his timid depression now replaced by stagnant determination.

His fingers dipped into the River, followed by a hand, a wrist, a forearm, sliding slowly down.

"This is a lie . . ." He said lowly at first, but then his confidence launched and he screamed, "*This is all a lie!*"

His wrath burned him, and he sent his fist with all his might into the mirror's reflective glass.

It shattered, and fell all around him, crashing on the cement, and as if his epiphany initiated it, every pipe fissured, all the sinks and all the toilets began to spout water as if rebelling against him.

The water sprayed angrily, and yet, not one drop of it was murky or tainted. In fact, it glimmered.

The structure around him began to collapse, and he sped outside before he was crushed beneath it. As it was reduced to a hump of debris, he spun around to again look at the falls.

It too had been purified, its waters shining clearly and free of muck, and it too surged across the horizon as if Orphenn's truth had sent it into a rage.

He sprinted across the path, and flung himself over the rail, his cry becoming one with the roar of the falls, the River in his head joined with it in concrete harmony.

His body slipped the final few inches, and submerged, billowing with the current beneath the surface of the River.

When he hit the water, the harmony was quieted. The anger dispersed.
Then his world went black.

What if there was never another world?

What if it's just . . . A different dream?

Orphenn emerged, gasping, from the River, clutching the mossy banks. Climbing up onto them, he took reprieve to take back his breath. Anxiously, and still breathing loud and heavy, he turned to see his reflection in the pure, sun-sparkling water of the River.

One red eye, one blue. Choppy haircut. White uniform.

Yes. He was finally free of Ardara's Dream Hold.

And yet . . .

He noticed the knuckles on his muddy hand were cut and bleeding.

Almost all was well, until the next moment when everything went bad.

The almost-family horrifyingly silenced. Stiff and fearful, still dripping water, when Cinder's agony cut the air with a blood-chilling shriek.

Sven ran to her writhing body, splaying water drops about him as he rushed.

Dacian's lance hadn't just run Celina through; unsuspecting, Cinder and Cira felt the same pain, the same sensation of falling through the air.

Cinder wailed, face and body contorted in pain. "No! *Celina!*"

Her Sense remained acute, pulling through the miserable spasm. Crippled in the grass, her wings unfurled. She looked up, neck craning. "No!" She screamed, and then she was gone.

"No way . . ." Sven denied, as he saw Celina's body tumult from the sky, and Cinder port to catch her. The others were speechless, torment clear on their faces.

When Cinder ported back down, she had miscalculated, reappearing waist-deep in the River.

She tried to haul Celina out of the water, but her sister held her so that when Cinder ascended the low bank, she remained in the water.

"Cinder . . ." her voice was hardly a whisper.

"Celina, come on!" Cinder sobbed. She could feel everything Celina felt. The heartbreak, the burn in her abdomen, weakening bones, slowing heartbeat. "Come on."

"No . . ." Celina could no longer stand, and Cinder propped her up and held her tight. "No, Cinder." She hushed. "I . . . I must stay with the River."

"Celina . . ." Cinder shook her head, desperate.

"Listen . . . It may look like I've made a mistake, but . . . I'm satisfied."

Cinder couldn't speak.

"Trust me, Cinder." She reached up a frail hand to slip the coronet from her forehead. She tucked it into Cinder's layered jacket, knowing she wasn't yet ready to wear it.

"He's back." She gasped suddenly.

Cinder turned her head. Tears fell from her lashes when she saw Orphenn standing there, sopping wet, eyes fixed on Celina, features twisted in grief and surprise.

He watched as Celina brought Cinder's face back to look at her.

"Just remember to trust me." She whispered. "Trust me."

Cinder knew she was dead because the pain went away.

It was then that the River took her.

She slipped out of Cinder's arms, fell away from the banks, and like a mother and child the warm, dazzling water cradled her, and then she was gone.

Oriana now shared with her that resting place.

Chapter Twenty-four

~

Succession

Dacian was a shell of a man when he returned to the main hold.

Cira was crumpled on the ground, reeling and raging, not just from the pan, but from the loss of her grip over Orphenn. "Dacian . . ." she said, quaking, herbal tea forgotten. "You . . ." Her voice wavered, vacillating. "You killed her . . . My sister is dead . . ." She looked to be in genuine pain at the loss of her own sister, but then Ardara came pouring back into her face.

"My sister is dead!" She stood, arms in the air, glowing with enthusiasm. "The Enma are without a Supreme Commander!"

Dacian was a severe opposite to her. Eyes rimmed in red, peeked, gaze downcast. She paid him no attention.

"Now . . . I only have to be rid of my remaining siblings . . . And . . . Aleida will be mine!" Then she changed slightly. "Wait . . ." She reconsidered, recalling the two instances that Cinder had escaped death. Once by her own hands. "She can't die, can she?" After a moment of wicked contemplation, she called, "Dacian!"

"What do you wish, my liege?" He replied robotically.

"Nyx will keep a trail on the White Herons. We follow them until the time is right. Then I have a mission for you."

Orphenn found himself unable to do anything. He couldn't move, couldn't feel, couldn't think.

Most of all, he couldn't believe what he was seeing.

He stood there frozen. He was still in a state of shock from his painful liberation from Ardara's illusion, still denying the real world around him.

And he returned to *this*.

He couldn't even notice the astounded regard he received when he numbly approached his squadron, dripping wet, shivering.

All he could see was Celina.

All he could do was stare at her, limp in Cinder's arms. Dread overwhelmed him. *No.* Was the only thought he could manage. *Not her. Not her.*

"He's back." She had whispered, though he never heard her.

The River took her.

It took her, like it had taken Oriana.

The gleaming, twinkling water enveloped her.

She became the River.

And then she was gone.

Orphenn felt a part of himself fall away with her. With no sign that she ever existed, but for the tears on all their faces, the voids dug into their chests.

As if a load about his shoulders had been lightened, he did the only thing he believed himself able to do.

He ran.

Eynochia fell shakily to her knees, staring after him. So crippled she felt, after only seeing his face. Now after witnessing him turn and run away after weeks of fearing for his life, she felt utterly barren.

The others couldn't so much as twitch.

Cinder was the only one with the strength to run after him, though she couldn't think of where it had come from. She could hardly think at all, her head like a numb block of ice. When she saw him, the ice seemed to melt, and came dripping down in the form of tears.

He'd already reached the edge of the forest by the time Cinder caught sight of him, a white phantom against the tree line, stumbling aimlessly through the brush. His sobs echoed.

"Orphenn!" she called. Now that she could see him, she knew where to go. In a swathe of black, she ported, reappearing to block his path.

He'd been running too fast, and could not avoid her. His speed sent him straight into her grasp.

"Orphenn!" She scolded, angered by her own tears.

"Let me go!" He struggled. "Let me go or I *swear*, Cinder! Get *off!*" Several times his voice cracked, his objections continually interrupted by staccato sobs and cries.

"*Orphenn!*" She demanded harshly. Something in her voice made him stop dead. He went still in her hands. The look that masked his face tugged Cinder's heart. Lost, like he didn't know what to do next, couldn't see any future.

"What would you have done?" She whispered.

He felt weak, and his head lolled. He quietly said in a voice dripping with sorrow, "I-I could have helped . . . . I could have healed her!"

"It wasn't your fault, Orphenn, it was mine!" She shook him, his eyes growing confused. "It was my darkness that took you." She explained. "I was careless."

"How does that have anything to do with Celina?" He snapped sourly.

"Orphenn, just listen! If I hadn't thoughtlessly ported you, we never would have lost you, we never-"

Amazed, Orphenn stopped her. "Cinder, I'd be *dead* if not for you. You know that."

Cinder could not speak for the lump in her throat. She let her head lean lightly on his shoulder. The only word that escaped her was a hushed ". . . Sorry . . ." Followed by a long sob.

Now Orphenn finally saw his sister's position in all this, how confused she must be. Then he felt incredibly selfish-he had been so absorbed in his own grief-and now he felt horribly guilty.

Soon they were bawling for the tenth time in less than an hour, and Cinder released her brother, relenting.

"Go ahead and run if you want." She sniffed bitterly. "Doesn't matter."

Orphenn shook his head fervently. "I don't want to run anymore." His voice wavered with emotion. Being a few inches taller, he bent slightly to press his forehead to Cinder's, as she had when she found him as a drunken hobo. They stayed that way for several minutes, letting the tears come silently.

"Let's go."

They walked back to camp together, and the squadron remained in mourning for the rest of daylight and on into the next night. From there they traveled to the Denoras refuge camp, the new home for citizens whose capital had been reduced to dust. Once there, a service was held for their beloved Commander.

All seven squadrons had come to attend, their airships at rest at points outside the camp. A great bonfire was erected in the center of the camp, and thousands of Denorasians gathered as Sven came to stand in its light. In his scarred hands, he delicately held a grand paper lantern. A pair of angelic wings folded from parchment decorated the sides.

Silence filled the air, but for the crackling of the massive fire.

Sven spoke in a voice that boomed across the plain. "Lady Celina . . . Was this world's finest ruler. Many of us recall the days before the First War, the times of the Verlassen Empire. Generations of Emperors and Empresses have come and gone, and not one of them compare to our Supreme Commander. I can still hardly believe she ain't here . . ."

He looked down. Sobs escaped the crowd.

"What will happen now, Marshall?" A voice called out. Sven was aghast to see that it was the young Nero, standing in front, as always. "Who will take Lady Celina's place?"

Sven looked off to where Cinder was trudging away on her own toward an abandoned tent. He knew she hated it when strangers saw her cry. He forgave her.

"There are . . . Complications by way of succession. A highly trusted delegate shall stand in for her until the capital is rebuilt. But for right now . . . Let's honor the woman who brought this world to peace in its darkest hour."

He lit a long wooden match with a lick of flame from the bonfire. As he did so, he raised the lantern, and his voice.

As he lit the wick inside the lantern, a song waved from his chest softly at first, and rose in crescendo as the lantern began to lift from his hand. As he shook the flame from the match, others had started to join in, and when he discarded it into the bonfire, the entire plain had illuminated in song.

The lantern floated higher and higher, the light inside it turning the folded paper into a set of golden, shining wings.

The song seemed to lift it higher, to usher it across the sky, a hymn to comfort an angel.

Soon, it was so small that it mingled with the stars against the sky, and no one could tell the difference.

Orphenn sat, head drooped in his place around the small fire which popped in front of the tent the White Herons shared. All others had retired to their own tents, only a few other fires burning, scattered apart, the colossal bonfire extinguished.

Sven gave him a look of deepest empathy. It was as if he knew the boy's every thought.

"Orphenn." He said, his rumbling voice kind. "Let me tell you something." He stood and moved to take a seat beside him, resting a scarred hand on his shoulder. "I've been shot in the head so many times I can't even count. And yet here I am. Speaking to you."

Orphenn looked up at him expectantly, still blood-shot from fresh tears, not yet understanding the other's meaning.

Sven went on. "How many injuries did Celina sustain? Next to none. And my wife? She never had more than a bad scrape.

"Oriana taught me a long while ago, that there is nothing more *unpredictable* than who will die in a war and who will survive. Get it?"

The boy nodded.

Cinder's head rested on the fold-out table, inside the lonely candle-lit tent. The song had stopped long ago, and now she could hear the voices of her squadron outside the tent. She could hear Sven's voice mingled with the popping of flaming firewood, in his typical storytelling tone. That was the thing-people like him always had lots of stories to tell. Sven was probably Aleida's finest re-enactor, apart from Celina of course who only needed to touch someone to show them her history-

Cinder let out a sigh and lifted her head. No matter how she tried to resist, her thoughts always led back to Celina. Reaching into her jacket, she pulled out Celina's coronet, the silver-white circlet with a single modest gem at the crest.

"You left too soon . . . Celina . . ." She whispered. "I need you now . . . More than ever." She felt again the heat behind her eyes that melted the ice of her numbness, threatening tears.

Desperate to hold them back, she grabbed for the photo book that Sven had left in the corner of the table and flipped it open; anything to distract her from the grief.

It worked well, scanning through faded pictures of Sven's family, most of them deceased. She paused on a picture of Xeila and Jeremiah, teenagers. She laughed at how little they'd changed.

It was the next picture that stunned her into silence.

Her eyes darted up and down it, disbelieving, attempting to right her vision, had it somehow malfunctioned.

It was a photo of Sven, but there were two others on either side of him that Cinder recognized all too well from her time in prison.

Wynne and Music Man.

"What . . . ?" She could not make sense of it, until she saw scrawled along the margin:

Left to Right—Wynne, Sven, Ira.

"No way . . ." She breathed. "Music Man is . . ." Her astonishment broke her sentence. "Wynne is his . . ."

The photo book fell from her tingling fingers.

She turned to dash outside. She needed, *needed,* to tell Sven, to scream it into the night. Finally, a discovery that may lead to something of happiness! *Ira is alive.*

A shame, she never made it out of her own will. Before she could take the first step toward the flapping tent exit, a pair of eyes froze her in her tracks, red-rimmed and bloodshot. They were confused, hurt, desperate-uncharacteristic to the face they belonged to. Dacian had never looked so frail.

"You . . ." Cinder exhaled. She stared at him, making no move, and realizing she didn't want to. She knew he was different somehow.

"Cinder . . . Please understand." He was no longer smug and arrogant, but genuine, and solemn.

"I *do* understand!" She realized suddenly, eyes widening. "It was you . . . You-"

"Please, I beg you!" He winced, interrupting her. He did not want to hear the words. "I know, and . . . . I know . . . . I . . ." He seemed to crumble before her.

Cinder softened. For the first time since the beginning of the First War, she saw clearly the man that was Dacian, and not Ardara's creation. He looked like a man that was burning at the stake. His words hissed with his own pain.

"I've made the greatest mistake . . ." He said, body lurching in anguish.

Cinder couldn't help but sympathize. Tears dripped freely from her lashes, as she waited for him to act. Like Celina had when she stood with this same man in the sky, Cinder knew what Dacian had been ordered to do.

"Dacian." She said, a low murmur. Her eyes met his with compassion, each of their irises like colored fireflies in the candlelight. "I forgive you." He was only able to look at her, puzzlement plain on his features. "For what you've done. For what you're about to do."

At length, with a deep, wounded breath, he straightened.

So did Cinder.

In the next moment, poison vapor leapt from his mouth to hers. Gagging, she fell into his chokehold, though it was mercifully gentle, and he dragged her outside.

Sven was quick to act, summoning on the spot a high caliber shotgun, but Cinder shook her head at him violently. *Please,* her eyes said. *Trust me.*

The Field Marshall lowered his weapon, his hurt, worried, betrayed expression backlit by the campfire.

At the sight of him she'd longed to shout at the top of her lungs, *Your brother is alive! Ira is alive!* Sadly, the lance head at her throat and the sedating effects of the poison had made that impossible.

Dacian held his façade admirably.

"Nobody move." He demanded.

The look in Cinder's green and blue eyes told them to listen.

Orphenn had shot upright when Sven had, and now objected, "Cinder, no!"

"Listen to him, Orphenn." Cinder slurred with great effort. "All of you, just . . . Stay . . . Just trust me." Dacian's tranquilizer began to kick start, her eyes rolling back, lids fluttering.

Dacian held her tighter. "Take us to the ship." He said softly, and soon there was nothing left of the two of them, Cinder teleporting as she was ordered.

The darkness left swiftly, too fast for Orphenn, who had tried to jump for her, and landed prone in the grass with an *oof.*

The drone of an airship could be heard as it readied and soared away.

Orphenn writhed and let out a frightening cry, emitting a low, eerie harmony, and his squadron was reminded of the tainted serum in his veins. All at once they feared it would take him again, as it had when Ardara first injected it.

Fortunately, he managed to overcome it, the brief outbreak silenced.

He stood, lopsided and weak.

Sven saw the determination there, despite the weakness of the boy's stance. The words he couldn't say were opening up on his face. *I'm not running.*

Without another word, Orphenn took a deep shaky breath, and took flight.

Sven turned to his family, the remainder of the squadron. "To the Day Star. Now. There's no time to wait anymore."

He looked to the sky.

"We're right behind 'ya, Little Bird."

Chapter Twenty-five

~

Flight

Dacian was appalled.

"Take the ship to Ardara." The master had ordered Cinder, still restrained in his arms. "Port us, now."

How could she demand so much of her, weakened as she was?

He was partly surprised that she was able to do it so effortlessly. Without a single indication, the airship was being pattered by rain in Ardara's wasteland, far from the White Heron's camp. Four days flight at least. He was especially amazed that she was able to teleport such a large craft so far, even when she was under the effects of his toxin.

Soon though, it grew too much, and her vision left, falling unconscious in Dacian's arms.

"Perfect." Ardara said, after a long interval, grinning ear-to-ear.

"What did you see?" Dacian queried, knowing without a doubt that she had seen something, in premonition.

"The White Herons come. But worry not, Dacian. We have time. In Orphenn's weakened state, it will be simple to reclaim him. Then, everything will be easy."

Jeremiah pondered at the helm, softly steering the Day Star's path.

"Sven, are you sure that was wise?" He fretted.

Sven stood stoically beside him. "Little Bird has to blow off some steam. I hope he kicks that traitor's ass."

"Are we going after him?" Eynochia put in hopefully.

"Damn straight!"

With a sudden burst of ambition, Sven shoved Jeremiah and took the wheel, sending the Day Star flashing across the dawn-lightening sky at a dangerous speed.

Jeremiah stumbled, Xeila and Eynochia thrown back in inertia. "Pops, I'm pretty sure we can't go this fast!"

"The *Hell* we can't!"

Vroom.

The instant Ardara clambered into the castle, she began to badger the slaves. The ones who came to her call were scolded.

"Wynne!" She rebuked. "Where is Wynne?"

"Here, Master." The lanky blonde limped as close as he dared, disturbed at her utterance of his name. His pink eyes glowed through the shadows of the tremendous entrance hall, but the rest of him was not so shining. He leaned against a great metal column for support. Being now degraded to a slave, he was treated as one; dressed in rags, fed little, his energy drained from labor and from the parasitic device at his neck. "I'm here." He said thinly, as if speaking to a frightened child.

Ardara turned. "Wynne . . ." She whispered.

Wynne was astonished. Ardara never remembered any of her prisoners' names, or ever cared. Since he'd been branded, he'd been nothing more than a slave, yet still more or less the favorite one.

"Yes, Master?"

"Wynne . . ." She spoke in an injured tone that she was not known for. ". . . My sister is dead . . ." She sounded honestly hurt, forgetting that she'd already realized this fact back on the ship.

Then her face went blank.

"My . . . Sister . . . She's . . . My sister . . ."

And then she smiled.

"My sister is dead." This statement had a frightening twinge of joy. The next time she spoke, she stood herself up straight and laughed with scary, yet true fulfillment and raised her hands. Then she began to repeat anew her theatrics from before, as if stricken with Alzheimer's. "The Enma are . . . Without a Supreme C-Commander, they have no one to lead them!" She danced, reenacting her prior enthusiasm. "My job is halfway done! My-"

Dacian stumbled into the hall, and Ardara became instantly sobered. She lowered her arms to her sides and spun to look at Dacian, blue and red eyes unreadable. He had just returned from imprisoning Cinder in the containment unit. She glared at him.

She hated him. She was proud of him. She wanted to hurt him. She imagined killing him-no. She wanted to kiss him.

All these feelings flashed across her face like freeze frames.

She was in love with him, but no-he killed her sister. Wait . . . How did she know? She felt Celina's death, as if she herself had been run through. She wanted to cry . . . Tears of joy. Then she wanted to inflict the worst pain, and then: "Dacian." Her voice was calm and light again.

"Retire with me to the lounge . . . Feed me wine. Slave," She ordered Wynne, any fondness or favoritism discarded, "fetch my munchies."

The two disappeared through the columned hall, into a wide, double-door entrance to the throne room, and off to the left of that where a wall section of gossamer curtains led to the lounge.

Wynne followed, feeling more afraid of what was to come than he had ever feared anything in his life.

Now midday, though in Ardara it was always dark and gloomy, Dacian and the Master lay together in the lounge, taking reprieve before the White Herons arrived. Ardara cleaved to him like she was draining his life force. He fed her grapes and sips of wine, all with a false, weary smile.

"Dacian. Do you know how proud I am of you?" She said, twisting his dark hair adoringly in her fingers.

"You neglected to mention it." He replied. His smile began to fade, like lapsing into a trance. Playing pretend was beginning to wear on him.

Ardara caressed his face, but then her smile also faded. In the next second her hands clenched in his hair, and snarling, she sent him flipping off the sofa and rolling into the hard tile. She stood slowly and ominously, rage burning in her face.

Then she changed again.

"My darling . . ." She rushed to kneel at his side, robes billowing. "I apologize . . . I don't know what came over me, I-"

"Sssh." Dacian placed a finger to her lips. "I do."

He never told her, though. Instead, he kissed her, to take her unstable mind from the matter. He didn't know how much longer he could endure her sudden personality changes.

"I will try again," she said finally, standing, not bothering to help Dacian back to his feet, "to take Orphenn's dreams. When I have him, we must act."

With that, she exited through the gossamer, mounting her dark, magnificent throne.

She tried again and again to gain full submission over Orphenn's mind. When she at last succeeded, she fell into a hypnotic niche, and Dacian was able to escape, at least for a little while. He took advantage of the momentary freedom to take refuge at the peak of the castle's monolithic tower, climbing every stair to the top and standing high above the land. The rain had finally subsided, but the air was still damp, and wind lashed about him in gales. He couldn't help thinking how opposite, and yet how similar this monument was to the fallen clock tower at Denoras-the capital, now only a pile of rubble. He stood there, letting the cold gusts push at him.

Though he had been followed.

Wynne appeared at his side, the wind sending his platinum hair whirling around his face. He was about to protest, but Wynne spoke before he could, his rodent-pink eyes penetrating.

"Dacian. Why are you still here?"

Dacian only stared.

"I saw what you did."

"What are you talking about, Slave?"

"*Cut the act*!" Wynne roared, giving Dacian a start. His tone became angry and facetious. "I was on the ship the whole time, though the three of you took no notice of a *worthless slave*, being so high class. Dacian, I saw what happened! I *know* Ardara no longer has any power over you!"

"And how are you so sure?" Dacian hissed.

"Because I know! I saw the light return to your face when you cut her through! I saw your pain as you watched the only woman you ever loved fall to her death!"

Dacian's heart throbbed at the truth of Wynne's words, like decisive grenades in his chest, exploding at just the right points. He clutched his chest, sobbing and heaving, as if the pain could make him regurgitate. He wanted nothing more now than to leap from the tower, fall into nothing, just so the pain would stop.

When he could breath calmly, he growled, "And since when have *you* been free of Ardara's mind?" He looked at Wynne, who watched him with uncanny intensity.

Wynne hesitated. Looking down into Dacian's peeked face, his red-veined eyes, he answered, "Since before I was stripped of my rank, and branded . . ." He turned away bashfully, looking out across the wastes almost nostalgically, and as the gale puffed and whipped around his loose brown rag-tunic, Dacian could see the *T* on his shoulder blade, a scar only just healed over. The sight of it made his stomach lurch. "The moment I set eyes on her . . ." Wynne said lowly, remembering.

Dacian's brow furrowed. "Are you talking about Cinder?"

"Just the sight of her took the blindfold from my eyes." After a moment he added, "Dacian, I was like you. A traitor. Under Ardara's power, I too betrayed my squadron. You and I were the only high ranking guards under her spell, because we are Enma. All the other soldiers were already supporters of her dark cause. All the slaves' minds are fully manipulated, just because they are also Enma, prisoners here. Granted there are only about a hundred or so of us left, after the dungeoners were freed, but Ardara doesn't believe she can trust them . . . I digress.

"I was her favorite henchman for a while. But then she found you. She was fond enough of me to keep me around, but she always favored you.

"Then, after I freed Cinder and the other prisoners, as you know, I'm just a slave now. I guess I'm still the favorite slave, but that's beside the point." He turned back slowly, giving Dacian a look of absolute seriousness. "You need to leave, Dacian. You *need* to. You know you don't want to stay here."

"But neither do you!" Dacian reasoned defensively.

"I am bound here by my own ambition. My father is still trapped here. Not to mention I'm useless with *this* around my neck." He tapped the hunk of metal at his throat, veins blue and bulging all around its edges. "Most of all, I stay for Cinder. I know she's here. The poor sweet thing must be exhausted from being captured so much. She was never meant to be caged.

"As for *you*. You need to help Celina's squadron. You owe her that much."

Dacian sniffed. "When the time is right . . . I will rebel. And then I will."

Wynne turned to return inside, then stopped to look over his shoulder. "Dacian, I understand. Just as a star is brightest just before its death. As the sun is most brilliant just before it sets. Never forget her."

Dacian looked away, new purpose filling his being.

When Cinder awoke, she was suspended in some strange liquid like opaque, bubbly gelatin, with a reddish hue. She wore nothing but a revealing series of leather garments and straps, identical to the jumpsuit Ardara wore beneath her many flowing robes. Her wings, unhidden in her disability, were restrained tightly against her back.

She groggily opened her eyes. She was dismayed to realize she wasn't breathing, but relieved to find that she didn't seem to have the need.

Her vision was choppy, but in blinking a few times she saw that she was held inside a sealed vat of the odd gelatin. A few more blinks, and the figure of Dacian diffused into view.

He pressed his palm to the outside of the vat's glass containment. She eyed him with an odd acceptance.

"I'm so sorry." He whispered, pressing his forehead to the glass ruefully.

Her eyes closed.

The sun was rising.

Orphenn dropped down to rest and stretch his wings. He'd been flying for days. Only a few short hours and he would reach Ardara.

He leaned over, hands on his knees, catching his breath.

He was in a meadowed clearing, surrounded by orange-leaved oaks, their colors falling, blown about by the chill of the autumn wind. Just beyond a break in the trees he could see the landscape become more desolate farther out, the border of the Ardaran wasteland.

He prepared to take a running leap. When he rocketed into the air, he flew, but was only able to flap his wings a few times before colliding with a wall of water.

The sky was gone, and everything was cold, and he was floating.

Bubbles erupted from all around his body as his true body thudded to the browning grass, out cold. They sprouted from his mouth and nose and fluttered about him as he thrashed in the frigid gray water.

Above, a thick sheet of ice like powdery stained-glass stretched out of view on all sides, an enormous frozen lake.

A low *clud* came to his water-pressed ears, vibrated in his chest, again, again, again.

It was Eynochia, on hands and knees several feet over him on the other side of the ice, fallen snow scraped and pushed about her palms, a clear window to her face; she was banging on the sheen, flaky surface.

Orphenn struggled to reach her, flapping his arms, kicking his legs, wings floating uselessly.

Finally his palms rested flat against the freezing barrier, his body levering up horizontally to meet the ice.

Each movement seemed in slow motion, maddeningly far away, out of arm's reach.

Eynochia cried and banged the ice with her fist seemingly forever until the clud of her effort became the dying beat of his heart, became the only thing he could hear, encompassing him, and his eyes rolled back, and he sank and sank, and sank, then was smacked in the face with a gush of chilly air.

He cried out, curled in the crunchy autumn grass. He took deep, desperate breaths, awoken from a nightmare.

He cried again, seething, "*Ardara*."

He was weak, and he knew Ardara could sense it. Her Dreamhold would soon overtake him. When it did, his sight blotched with black and he fell into darkness.

Ardara came to stand beside Dacian, startling him. She never looked at him, or acknowledged him in any way, not even a sniff in his direction. He backed away from Cinder's vat silently, never taking his gaze from Ardara's back. When she did nothing but glare into the red plasma, he calmed.

A hand landed at his shoulder.

Dacian swiveled his head the see the reassurance in Wynne's warm, rosy eyes. One look at his face and Dacian knew he could depend on him unfalteringly. He was grateful too, as Nyx stepped out of the shadow of a tall iron pillar and stood close to the blonde. The red hue of the luminous vat highlighted her violet hair, her one golden eye like a shining beacon. Somehow, Dacian knew she was there for him, and only for him.

This occurred in quiescence, completely beyond Ardara's notice, who was absorbed in examining the crimson plasma gurgling in the vat, so each of them jumped when she finally spoke.

"Look at me." Her chilling voice reverberated about the metal hall.

The three onlookers saw moments later with relief that she was speaking to the one inside the vat.

"I know you're awake, Cinder."

Blue and green irises met Ardara's gaze, a look of absolute defiance radiating through the plasma.

After a contemplative moment, Ardara said, "You can just hold your breath forever and not die, can't you? You feel perfectly comfortable inside, do you not? Apart from the newly fashioned wing restraints I imagine."

Cinder could only leer through the layers of gel and glass, listening. Ardara tapped the surface of the glass with a rude knuckle. "Normally this plasma is a viscous and acidic material, completely toxic. I had Dacian fuse it with a sample of my blood cells." Lifting her sleeve, she revealed a deep burgundy gash across the palm of her hand. "Now anyone who shares my DNA will be unharmed, in fact protected by the otherwise hazardous fluid. Aren't you thankful?"

Orphenn will come. Cinder assured herself. *I know he will.*

As if triggered by the thought, Ardara added, "And our dear brother could have turned out to be quite the hero-if he ever made it as far as my castle. He's on his way now, getting close. The death of our sister has hollowed his heart and halved his strength. I have discovered already how weak his mind has become. In moments he'll be in the grasp of my Dreamhold, and entirely immobilized. Then I intend to send Dacian to kill him as he sleeps."

Wynne shook his head, *no* mouthed on his lips, and Nyx released a shocked gasp. The Master gave no sign that she had heard.

For Dacian, this was the last straw. His teeth clenched.

"I'm afraid I can't do that." He said simply.

At this, Ardara's eyes widened, her mouth tightened to a straight line.

"I knew it . . ." She spoke slowly, almost whispering as she pivoted to face him. Then she shrieked, her wrath emanating from every inch of her. "*I knew it!* I knew it, killing Celina at your own hand has opened your eyes!" Her gaze narrowed, beginning an attempt to regain her power over his mind.

The recoil knocked her to her side like a punch to the head. She lay prone on the tier where the vat stood. With no small effort she grunted and heaved herself onto her elbows, head still drooped so that her face was hidden behind her straggling onyx hair.

"Nice try." Dacian smirked.

Enraged, her head flicked back to grimace at him, drops of blood flinging from her face at the movement. It streamed from her eyes, red tears down her cheeks. Her breath hissed viciously between her teeth as she turned her blood streaked face to the newest Enma. "Nyx," she warned, "if you do not-"

"I *will* not." The violet intercepted.

Ardara could no longer think past the wrath that burned her.

"Get out." She whispered at first, and when there was no comply, she screamed, "*Get out! Both of you! I never want to see your faces again!*"

They hesitated, but only just. Together the ex-henchman and the neophyte dashed for the double-doored entrance, and made for escape at a speed they never thought their legs could achieve.

Wynne remained.

Ardara blinked the blood from her lashes. "I'll have to resort to an alternative." She clicked her tongue in disappointment. "What a shame. I wanted his death to be special. Squad nine will be given the mission.

"Slave! Wine!"

Wynne was quick to dart after the other two, still sickly and limping. When he caught up to them, he was lost for breath.

"Nyx, Dacian!" He gasped, stopping the renegades just before the grand entrance of bolted steel.

He leaned over with his hands on his knees, struggling to catch his breath. "You must go to Orphenn." He told them amidst sucking in air, the infernal device at his neck wheezing with him. "Nyx, you still have his golden feather, I assume? Find him. Ardara has sent Squadron Nine to uphold the mission. Get to him before they do!"

The other two had never looked so stricken.

Dacian grabbed Wynne's shoulders in desperation, pulling him upright.

"Wynne, come with us! You don't belong here any more than we do!"

"I can't do that." He shook his head. "I am the Enma's strongest hope."

"What do you mean?"

"With me on the inside, we have the advantage."

"You don't have to do this, Wynne!" Nyx whined.

"I can start a revolt among the slaves." Wynne debated. "And then move on to the soldiers. They trust me. We can take Ardara from the inside out!"

"But won't Ardara read your thoughts and find you out?"

"My mind is protected, like yours is, Dacian." Wynne grinned.

Dacian released the other man's shoulders. "How?"

"A certain powerful mutant, whom I like to call my father. You might recall, you made an attempt on his life under Ardara's control. You wouldn't remember him otherwise, because if memory serves me correctly, you were a last minute mutation, like I was. You weren't there when he shielded all of us, all at once. All hundred thousand of us." His eyes glowed with pride and admiration toward his adopted father at the memory.

"Sven was the one who shielded me . . . ."

"We will discuss this later!" Wynne cried, mood changing. "Now go! Protect the young one! You *cannot* let him die!"

Dacian and Nyx nodded and reluctantly complied.

"Go!" Wynne urged, and watched after them as they exited through the massive door, running across the rugged terrain as he had so longed to do.

He watched them hotwire a hover craft and take off at full speed. At length, he slammed shut the door and bolted the steel.

It was time to fetch the Master's wine.

Chapter Twenty-six

~

Across the Meadow

It was cold, and it was dark. Droplets could be heard, pattering heavily on the city which came into view above, towering and luminous skyscrapers, his face turned up to catch the rain.

After Orphenn's eyes had opened, New York was instantly recognizable, even at night, in the rain.

His head levered to gaze ahead, his eyes meeting like a collision with the brick and iron marquee that read *Kinder Rose.*

He was suddenly aware of a weight about him, and once again, as his gaze lowered, his eyes collided with a heart wrenching sight.

He held Cinder across his lap. She was unconscious, and unresponsive when Orphenn shook her and touched her face. "Cinder?"

Her skin was bruised and deathly pale, scraped and badly bleeding. Her unhidden wings flayed across the puddled pavement.

The rain soaked him, and came down in torrents from his forehead and the tip of his nose, splashing on Cinder's face as he leaned over her.

When she would not awaken, tears mingled with the raindrops.

"Cinder . . . You're hurt . . . Wake up . . ." He pushed wet strands of hair from her emotionless face. Her eyes were still behind her lids, blank and dreamless.

Drops of red plopped on her cheek, to be dispersed by drops of rain.

Orphenn looked down at himself to see his own injured form. His blood stained his white uniform, and dripped from his face and onto Cinder's.

"Sam, get the door."

Orphenn began to shake, and not from the cold.

Light poured over them where they lay on the dripping doorstep.

Orphenn looked, nearly blind from the brightness, up into the doorway.

This is how it started. Orphenn realized. *Except that we've swapped places.*

Instead of Orphenn's young body in Cinder's shaking arms before the orphanage as the beginning had been, the tables had been turned.

A shadow passed through the light, but rather than the silhouettes of Sam and Lora, there stood one single figure, petite and robed in slight red linens.

Orphenn seethed, and without another thought he withdrew his silver pistol, the one that never misses, and took aim.

"*Ardara!*"

He fired.

Ardara was again atop her throne when Wynne found her, carrying a wine bottle and a glass. He was afraid he might be scolded and punished for taking so long to return, but as he approached, the master was unresponsive.

She sat straight and motionless, her eyes closed and breathing heavy, but calm, as if inside a focused dream.

Cautiously, he set down the glass and bottle, mentally praying she would not awake. When she remained undisturbed, he swiftly made his way to the pillared storeroom where Cinder was being kept prisoner.

When he reached the containment unit he dashed immediately to Cinder's sealed vat. Like a fish in a tank, she felt the shudder vibrate through the vat when his palms met the six inch glass.

Her face slightly brightened. Wynne's eyes bore into her like two fuchsia flames. She could see how feeble he'd become, only a semblance of what he'd been the first time she laid eyes on him. Nevertheless, his voice was as strong and as certain as ever.

"I always knew you were special." He intoned deeply. She could hear him clearly, reverberating through the vat much less obscured than Ardara's had been, as if Wynne's voice was the only one the plasma would allow to permeate. His words warmed her like a ripple of heat from the sun. It was as if its rays shone from his eyes, and each word was a separate wave of heat. "Since the first moment I saw you, I knew we would meet again." Then he gave a rueful sigh as he examined the vat. "Once again . . . We are both prisoners here."

Cinder would have sighed with him, had she been able. She was overjoyed but also fearful when Wynne began to analyze the sealed vat's controls.

He's trying to set me free.

The side of her that feared for him was soon confirmed.

Ardara was there behind him, and advancing quickly. Cinder could do nothing to warn him.

No . . . She fretted, heart filling with dread. *If Ardara is awake, does that mean that Orphenn is . . . ?* She could not bear to even think it.

She could only watch in despair as her deranged sister pinned Wynne against the glass and commenced to attack him. She beat at him with her fists and her knees, slamming him on the glass, ramming her knuckles into his ribs. She relented when he keeled over, giving him a last stern kick once he was down.

He began to wonder why no one else ever seemed to get beaten up.

Breathing deeply, Ardara descended the steps off the tier, and lightly picked up her wine glass and sipped, as if cooling down after a workout, and then spoke. "Orphenn has proven himself more resistant than I first thought. On top of that it seems now that I will have to babysit the slave." Her body swiveled to sneer at Wynne, lying bruised ad bloody atop the tier, as she herself had been only hours prior. "Even so, I expect Squadron Nine has already reached him. By now . . . It is not unlikely that he is already dead."

Wynne spat out blood, painfully lifting his head. "No . . ."

"Though now I have no way to be sure until both of you are under control." She said this as if chiding a couple of misbehaving kindergarteners as she lifted her palm, and with it, Wynne's body. He levitated at her will, and she brought him from the tier to floor level, dropping him savagely at her feet. In the next moment, lightning cracked from her fingers and darted straight for him.

He shouted and flinched, but the lightning only flickered around him. It formed a cage of blue bolts to trap him in the small space from which he couldn't escape.

Then he watched in horror as Ardara stomped back upon the tier and pumped Cinder's vat full of anesthetic. As the Drifter's eyes rolled back, Wynne yelled, "What harm is she to you?!" But his objection was cut short when his skin met with the burn of electricity by a misplaced hand, and was out cold at the shock.

When Orphenn's ears began to function, everything was muffled. He still couldn't see.

He heard the grass crunch beneath his head and the breeze across the meadow. Then he heard shouting, voices he knew.

"We know everything about Ardara."

He recognized Dacian's voice, timid and breathless.

"If you're planning on an invasion, you're going to need us."

"I say we only need one of you." Came Sven's unmistakable grumble, accompanied by the click of readied firearms.

Finally, Orphenn could open his eyes.

The first thing he could see was a glint of silver.

"Eynochia . . ." He breathed.

She stood over him protectively, as did Sven, she with claws and fangs bared, and he wielding numerous summoned weapons in defense.

Eynochia looked down at him in surprise, but was immediately forced to return her focus ahead.

"Need *you?* Need *you?!*" Xeila shrieked from a few paces in front of Orphenn. "You've done enough! Now I think it's time to return the favor!"

Scales and spines rose on her skin as she screamed, and her fangs enlarged in a hiss. She charged at Dacian, claws unsheathing with a deafening battle cry.

And then she was upon him.

Nyx screamed.

Xeila hesitated.

Dacian, from his point of the ground, angrily exclaimed, "Do it!"

She raised her claw.

"Xeila, no! Wait!"

She halted at the plea. "Orphenn?"

The boy dizzily stood. It was then that he saw the nine or ten corpses of Ardaran soldiers, strewn lifelessly across the meadow. He pointed shakily. "Who are they? Please . . . What's going on?"

Jeremiah came beside him, crystal armor crackling around his hazel and lavender eyes. "Yes, do explain." He said sourly.

Nyx helped Dacian to his feet and stepped forward. "These are the members of Squad Nine. They were assigned a mission to take the boy's life."

Sven put in, "We were fightin' them off when these two barged in, and *helped* us. Killed their own men. Sounds *familiar*, doesn't it, Dacian?"

"We couldn't let Orphenn die." Dacian defended.

"What do you want with him?"

"It was Cinder!" Nyx cried. "Don't you see? Wynne sent us to protect your Orphenn. He loves the boy, as Cinder does. Because, well, Wynne loves Cinder more than anything."

Everyone was brought to silence at this statement.

"Wynne . . ." Orphenn whispered, his voice suddenly dissipating.

"I remember now!" Sven gasped. "The Sandman! My Wynnie boy! My Lord, I swear this memory a mine's gonna be the death of me . . . ."

Orphenn could catch none after that, for yet again, the Dreamhold swiped dominance.

He fainted.

Chapter Twenty-seven

~

His Own Darkness

"**M**ama." Said the child in the back seat. Two of the triplets sat on either side of him, the third in the passenger seat.

"Yes, Keiran?" Kella Avari replied from the driver's seat.

"Are we going to see Papa?"

"Not quite yet, dear."

What's going on?

"Owie . . ." Little Keiran rubbed his eyes, as if suffering from a headache.

"Oh, there's no need to cry." His mother criticized, mistaking his painful tears.

A hand rested on his shoulder as the car pulled into the driveway of the family's dinky white house.

"Does your head hurt, Keiran?" Came a soft, excruciatingly familiar voice.

When the boy first turned to look up at Cira, he saw the sweet, blue-eyed, pig-tailed girl, wearing the floral summer dress that matched her sisters'.

The next instant, she was Ardara, in her red robes and purple leather, lines of anger and insanity where kindness and understanding had once been, so long ago.

Lightning flickered all around her.

"*Does your head hurt?*"

He looked to the driver's seat again. His mother wasn't there.

With no driver, the car careened out of control and crashed into the house, stopping halfway into the living room. Destruction and debris fell all around them, window frames through the windshield, dust and broken glass everywhere.

Orphenn's mismatched eyes stared back at him from the rearview mirror. He went tense and rigid in the back seat as his own name echoed in his head, the two of them rocking around his mind like a one-word argument.

Orphenn. Orphenn Keiran . . . . Orphennnn . . . .

Celina was her recent self as well, gone from third grader to white-robed Supreme Commander in the passenger seat.

Keiran . . . . Orphenn . . .

But she wasn't moving. Blood leaked from her onto the gray upholstery.

Orphenn whimpered. "K-Or-Orphenn . . . Keiran? Orphenn, Orphenn, Orphenn!" he wailed. "My name is *Orphenn!*"

Ardara's hand was still on his shoulder. Now so was Cinder's on his opposite side. He looked at Ardara and screamed, and his head twitched to look the other way. He put his hand on the top of Cinder's.

Half of her was gone. Nothing but white bone and hanging entrails. The remaining half was blackening flesh. "Immortal." She kept saying. "Immortal . . . . Immortal . . . . Immortal . . . ."

Orphenn screamed. Without thinking, his hand had reached for his silver pistol. He fired maniacally. Soon the ammunition ebbed and the trigger made a fruitless click. No more bullets. Even so, each one had hit its mark without fail.

The homunculus that bore Cinder's face, and Ardara both lay motionless in the awkward stillness that death brought about. A few bullets had even gone all the way through leather and plush of the passenger seat, lodged into the already lifeless corpse of Celina, making the blood flow even faster.

His breath calmed, and he reloaded his pistol before replacing it in its holster.

Any second now. I'll be free of the Dreamhold. He thought, and his eyes widened at the realization that the bodies of Cinder and Ardara had disappeared, leaving him alone in the totaled vehicle with the carcass.

"Immortal."

Orphenn hadn't spoken.

He began to tremble violently and desperately clambered out of the car.

He quickly crossed the devastated living room and stamped up the stairs, heart hammering. When he reached the landing, he folded his arms to try and hold back the biting cold that had crept into him.

He slowed as he reached the second flight of stairs, feeling an ominous energy intensify as he climbed higher. He stopped completely when he reached the top, suddenly, dangerously second-guessing his own judgment.

Was this really the Dreamhold? Or had he truly just murdered his sisters?

"No!" Orphenn needed to hear it out loud. "No!" He stomped. He clenched his hands through his hair, pulling as if it would peel away the ache in his skull. "Let . . . Me . . . Go . . ." His teeth bared, hunching over in agony. "Leave . . . Me . . . Alone!" He shrieked.

He looked up briefly, then stared at the Supreme Commander standing only inches away from him.

It took tremendous energy for him to stand up straight and look her in the face.

She was bloody, torn through with bullets, white robes red-stained and ripped, though she didn't appear to notice. Her face, blood dripping from it in waterfalls as it had when her essence had been stolen, was serene. She showed no sign of pain; in fact she had a certain shine about her, almost ethereal.

She said nothing, only held open her arms.

She held him like she had when she had lived, arms around his neck.

Orphenn wished he could have returned the embrace.

She fell away, run through with crystal, for he had thrust his lance into her middle. He grew sick with shock as she gurgled and slid off the blade and onto the hardwood, finally gone.

He looked down at his Ardaran uniform, felt his heart compress and crack inside him. He dropped the lance and it landed with a clatter.

Not him. "No!" *I'm not . . .*

"*I am not Dacian!!!*"

Orphenn screamed.

Dacian felt his stomach lurch.

"What did he say?" Jeremiah hushed, carefully stepping to stand by Sven after setting the Day Star to auto pilot.

Sven held a seizing Orphenn in his arms, trying his best to restrain the boy's fretful thrashing. "Orphenn, come on, come on, it's alright. Wake up!" He shook Orphenn, trying desperately to reach into his mind and calm him. He seemed to be running against a brick wall.

He screamed again. "I didn't kill her! I didn't, *it's not my fault!!*"

"Come here!" Sven demanded savagely. He grasped Orphenn's head between his hands and butted his forehead to the other's. "Little Bird!"

Finally Orphenn's eyes opened, and the thrashing quieted, but the sobbing and shouting did not. He clung to Sven like a child.

"Celina, wait!" He wailed. "*Nnot . . . Youu . . .*"

"Orphenn!" Sven snapped him awake with a violent jerk. "You're right, Orphenn! It *wasn't* your fault!"

"She's . . . Not . . . . Here!" He writhed.

Eynochia cried into Xeila's shoulder.

Nyx sat silently in the corner.

Dacian could not take his eyes from the bawling boy, traumatized by the sight.

"Don't dwell on her passing!" Sven shouted, his arms growing more and more tense around Orphenn's trembling. "Remember the way she lived! My Little Bird, remember the way you loved her! Do you remember *why* you loved her?!"

Now everyone let the tears come, even Nyx, even Dacian.

Dacian remembered.

I remember. That smile, that laugh. How happy she looked whenever it rained. The way she never failed to make my heart beat faster. She never let me stay sad . . . She could never do wrong in my eyes . . . She never hurt me, the way I . . . .

Before he began to blubber as badly as Orphenn, he escaped to the gondola to let the wind swipe at his tears. He leaned against the railing and sobbed into his palms.

Ardara had never been smacked harder in her life. The retaliation of the intercepted Dreamhold flung her across the room as if she'd been in a collision with a speeding vehicle.

Wynne watched her as he slowly came to. He curled into a ball to best avoid connecting again with his electric entrapment, aching viciously from his beating.

She rolled across the floor, moaning. Grunting with the effort, she lifted herself, only managing to get to her knees. Whining in pain, her fingertips touched the blood coming down her face. Her eyes bled, even more profusely than they had last. "I can't reach him! No!" She pounded the floor. "He's becoming more stable . . . This can't be happening . . ." She spotted Wynne heave up his leaden head, and threw her wine glass in his direction, to shatter to pieces far from its mark. "Slave! More wine!"

Unable to comply, he could only watch. Ardara disregarded it anyway, for she fainted from the retaliation's fatigue.

Cinder watched with a mixture of pity, fear, and disappointment. Her head sloshed through the plasma as she turned her head to look back at Wynne, her hair floating weightlessly and trailing behind every movement.

Her eyes held only love for Wynne. He looked up and their eyes met, like a crash, a burst of everything they felt, colliding in the distance between them.

Full of new intent, Wynne began to tinker with the device at his neck.

When Dacian could finally breathe without difficulty, he wiped his face and closed his eyes. He felt the zephyr curl around him and let the sun touch his face.

He heard the door hinge squeak behind him, but didn't bother to look at who it was. He knew exactly who it would be.

Nyx stepped forward and leaned on her elbows at the railing close to him, their shoulders touching. He did not acknowledge her, only watched the dark inside of his closed eyelids, glowing red from the sunlight.

"Dacian." She said. He tilted his head slightly, still not opening his eyes. "There's been something on my mind." His silence gave her incentive to continue. She took a deep breath, looking down at her hands. "I hate to see you in all this pain . . ." She sniffed. "All this chaos Ardara has created for us . . . Makes me realize how grateful I should be for the things in this world that have the power to shine through everything else. Such as . . . Love for another." She looked at him expectantly, with a look of hope and knowing. His eyes had creaked open, but only just. "Dacian." She said, as if it was just a simple fact, "I love you."

His eyes opened wide, and fierce.

"You love me?" He spat. Suddenly he straightened, his old temper flooding into him. "You've only ever known a shell of who I am! You've only ever known the Dacian that Ardara created! How dare you confess your 'love' to *me* now?!"

"Ardara loves you."

"*What?*" He hissed.

"Why do you think she chose *you* to control?" She fought, her own temper flaring now. "She was envious of Lady Celina for having you. For her own sick revenge she manipulated you into murdering the original White Herons! I knew it had to be true. For what other reason would you eliminate your own squadron!?"

"I was merely a toy, a plaything! How is it that you think you know Ardara well enough to know who she loves?"

"I've been serving her my whole life." Nyx calmed, remembering, anger abating. "All because my parents were supporters."

Now Dacian also relented. "Who were your parents?" He exhaled.

"Vivana and Rammes Cain."

Dacian started. His features became gentle, concerned, recalling the man that Ardara had shot to death and thrown into the castle moat. "Rammes Cain . . ."

"Yes." Nyx confirmed. "Ardara killed my father." She looked at him, and for a moment it was silent. Her one golden eye, again was like a beacon cutting through his own darkness.

"I had no idea, I-"

She looked away. "Don't bother yourself with it."

She turned and left him alone on the lofty gondola, the door slamming behind her.

Chapter Twenty-eight

~

Turncoat

At last, Orphenn's breathing calmed, and Sven's grip on him loosened. He touched the boy's face, gingerly. "You'll be okay, Little Bird."

Orphenn nodded.

"Poppet, fetch this trooper a cold compress, will 'ya? He's burnin' up somethin' fierce."

Xeila nodded. "Sure thing Dad." She left Eynochia's side to head into the kitchen, just as Nyx stormed in, the slamming door making a great *bang* to vibrate through the main hold.

She ignored the stares and sat at the center table, silently fuming.

Curious, Eynochia wiped her arm across her face and stepped cautiously to the metal door that led out to the gondola.

"*What. Now?*" Dacian griped angrily as he heard the door open again. He turned to see it wasn't who he thought, and became instantly apologetic. "Eynochia . . . I'm sorry, I . . . Thought you were someone else."

She said nothing in reply, only came to stand beside him at the railing as Nyx had. Her eyes were still swollen from tears.

It was a long time that she stayed there before she finally spoke.

"You saved Orphenn's life, Dacian. You and Nyx both, protected him from those Ardaran soldiers. But don't think that makes up for anything."

"I wasn't expecting it to." He sighed, turning away, and plunging back into his depression.

Eynochia looked at him. He looked old. Old, and tired, like he was carrying the weight of an elephant on his back. "But even so . . . I think I can find the courage to forgive you."

Their eyes met. They shared a smile.

The sunlight warmed the twin smiles, and the matching slash scars they both gained in turn. They realized in the same moment, despite the circumstances, how connected they all were. To each other, and to the skies that joined the worlds.

They walked back inside together, not so deep in despair as they had been.

"Hey Pigeon." Sven called upon their entrance. "Little Bird's restin' it up in his quarters. Why don't you go see to him?" Her father had a certain instinct concerning Eynochia's heart. He kindly gave her every opportunity to be with whom she loved. Some things, daddies just knew.

Eynochia nodded and crossed the main hold to disappear down the hall.

"Sven." Dacian addressed him in deference. "I must speak to you."

Sven's only reply was an intent stare.

"You say that Wynne was your adopted nephew." Dacian came closer. "And that he went missing the day your brother was murdered."

"You tell me, boy. You were there."

"I . . . . So many have died by my hands, sir, and not of my own will . . . . I can't say that I remember. I'm sorry, Sven . . ."

Nyx came to stand confidently beside him. "Please," she said, "it wasn't him, it was Ardara. We've told you."

Sven nodded inwardly, avoiding eye contact. "I know, Ace, I know." He paused when Dacian gasped at the utterance of his old nickname. "Cut an old man some slack . . . It's a might harder to accept things after so much has been done. But my Oriana taught me forgiveness." He looked Dacian in the face. The pain was still there in his eyes, but the distrust had been replaced by compassion. "And that's how I intend to honor her." He smiled. "What was it you needed to say?"

Dacian continued enthusiastically. "Your nephew is on the inside. He is a slave in Ardara's castle."

"And you didn't take him with you?" Jeremiah chided, recalling his childhood friend, and battle partner.

"He wouldn't let us." Nyx chimed.

"He stayed behind to give the Enma advantage." Dacian explained. "He said if he stayed, we could take Ardara from the inside out."

Sven's face lightened. "Lord, that boy." He shook his head. "He needs an award or something."

"What will Wynne do?" Xeila queried. "What's his plan?"

"I don't know." Dacian admitted. "But he'll find a way. I'm sure of it."

"We need to give him a sign!" Jeremiah enthused. "We must attack as one!"

Xeila stepped forward. "I will go to him."

"Yes!" Sven agreed. "Go, and take a communicator. Wynne will tell us his plan through you." Now his tone became more serious. "At your signal, we initiate a call to arms."

Eynochia softly tiptoed into Orphenn's quarters, scared that the hydraulic door might already have woken him.

He remained unshaken, so she allowed her feet to advance.

She sat in the plush wingback chair at his bedside, and removed the cold compress from his forehead, exchanging it for a damp rag.

"Don't want your brain to freeze." She chuckled, as if he had heard her, trying to lighten her own mood with mild humor.

Then again, maybe he had heard, for his eyes peeled open, that striking red and blue at contrast with his pale face. When they met with Eynochia's green and black, awareness smacked him in the head.

How selfish I've been. He thought immediately at the sight of his beloved friend. He sat up in the bed, the damp cloth falling to the floor at the movement. "Eynochia . . ." He whispered, sending chills up her arms. He looked at her as if he had not seen her for years, which might as well have been so. It was the first time he'd truly seen her since Ardara's tainted essence had taken him. He remembered they we she had kissed him.

If I don't hold her in my arms this moment, I swear I'll die.

So he saved his own life.

He pulled her from the chair and took her forcefully in his arms, his fingers in her hair. She held him tighter than she thought possible, burying her head in his shoulder.

"I'm sorry." He whispered, unable to speak above a hush, or to find any more words to say. To himself, however, he vowed to make it up to her, as he kissed her and held her close.

Stop messing with it! Cinder wanted to scream. She just knew, at any moment, that outdated contraption would react, but nonetheless, Wynne fidgeted and tinkered with it, searching for a gap in its mechanics, an oversight in its construction, anything.

He remembered when he had stopped time temporarily and been able to safely remove a prisoner's device. If only he could find a way to remove his own. Somehow the device reacted to a change in its wearer's blood flow, the change that came about when an Enma used his gifts, like some sort of chemical reaction. It would kill him if he tried to stop time again. It was rusted and corroded, but still functioned to kill at an attempt to unlatch it, by means of electric shock. Although, upon fussing with it he discovered that that first shock from unintentionally connecting with the lightning of his cage, which had left him unconscious, seemed to have weakened the device's bolts and fittings.

Wait . . . Electric shock . . .

Then an idea struck him, gazing intently at the cage he was curled beneath, white-blue light dancing on his skin. What if . . . .

Cinder banged her palm on the glass of her own entrapment to get his attention, shaking her head, no. She looked desperate. *I know what you're thinking!! Don't do it!!* Her eyes shouted.

"I have to." He told her. "I have to try."

She continued her protests as he held his breath, and reached up to touch a burning blue bolt.

He felt the charge all through his bones, and his body began to seize, but he remained conscious. With immense will power he kept the surge constant until finally, the device cracked up, and flew apart, small pieces flying. The lightning had canceled out the device's energy and demolished it.

Wynne released the bolt and fell limp. To Cinder's relief, his eyes stayed open and blinking. Breathing heavily, his heart hammering faster than he'd ever felt it, he sat up, hunched as much as the cage would allow. Face twisted in repulsion, he painstakingly tugged the broken off spines out of the back of his neck and let them clatter like pins to the stone floor.

His head was pounding and his body shook like a dry leaf. Despite this, he gave Cinder a triumphant grin.

The next thing she saw, he was standing on the outside of the lightning cage, free. As if time had stopped and started again.

She grinned back at him.

Xeila left the Day Star, making her way to the castle on foot, so as not to be spotted. She let invisibility descend on her, her gift of camouflage, just as Orphenn and Eynochia made for the main hold.

Orphenn stepped out carrying two white uniforms, neatly folded in his arms. He stopped before Dacian and Nyx at the wide window. The sunlight played across their bodies like spirits of gold and their shadows mingled.

"For the turncoats." Orphenn said, smiling bashfully. He held out the uniforms like a gift from a secret admirer. They were White Herons' uniforms, matching the rest of the squad, and they were stark and bright in comparison to their existing Ardaran ones.

Orphenn placed the smaller size in Nyx's arms, the other in Dacian's. "That one would have been Cinder's uniform, had she not refused to wear it." He laughed. "The other's just a spare I found in the store rooms."

With this act, Orphenn wanted to show them that he trusted them both, and to put forth to the others that they would all need to fully support each other if they ever wanted a chance of surviving the imminent conflict ahead of them.

This gesture of acceptance had left the former Ardarans speechless, and in turn, exceedingly grateful.

When they reemerged several minutes later wearing white, the difference was staggering. Even their sharp headgear had been abandoned, leaving their faces to look brighter and more open. Their appearance was no longer so sinister, and matched their new attitudes and renewed allegiance.

Orphenn smiled approvingly in their direction, but then stopped to ponder, his features puzzled. "Where's Xeila?"

Cinder's grin faded suddenly-Wynne's brow furrowed in question when her gaze flickered to the space beyond him. Her eyes were wide and foreboding, and her lips mouthed one single word that Wynne couldn't interpret. He turned round to see for himself what had captured her focus so raptly.

He jumped and nearly flinched back from the figure that had partially appeared next to him.

Like a veil had been lifted from her, she bubbled into visibility.

Wynne, hand on his heart as if he was unsure that he could take much more excitement, calmed himself down and looked more closely at the smirking woman. She looked him over, noting the burns that ran up his arm, and the ring of bruises around his bare neck.

"Xeila?" He started. "How long has it been?" Cinder smiled giddily in the plasma.

"A decade at least!" She replied. "But there's no time to reminisce, my friend. Dad sent me to fill you in, so that we can attack as one strong force. When you're ready. At your signal, the invasion will begin."

He nodded with vigor, then looked up at Cinder's vat. Xeila followed his gaze. "Cinder . . ." She muttered. "Why don't you just teleport? This is an easy escape for you!"

"Alas, Xeila." Wynne answered for her. "There are countless psychic wards within both the glass, and the plasma that block her teleportation powers. We'll have to free her some other way.

"Tell me, has Orphenn recovered? He is the only one remaining that can safely break her free. The plasma is toxic to anyone not sharing Ardara's DNA sequence. If any other were to touch it, they would perish within the hour."

She shrugged. "I'll send for him." She lifted her wrist communicator to her mouth and spoke. "Poppet to Day Star. I'm here with Wynne. He's curious if Orphenn's condition has improved."

"Affirmative." Jeremiah came in. "He's up and walking, stretching his wings."

"Good, good." Wynne said, relieved.

"We need him."

"We'll send him off right away. His wings will carry him to you quickly."

Wynne took hold of Xeila's wrist and spoke into the outgoing speaker. "In the meantime, I give my signal. Initiate call to arms."

Jeremiah gave Sven a meaningful glance. The other nodded, and set to contacting the refugee camp, as Wynne's voice ceased to crackle through the helm.

Wynne released her wrist to give her his arm. "You must come with me, Mistress. I will need your help." She took his arm, and he looked again at Cinder. "Be patient, Cinder! Orphenn is on his way!"

Orphenn flew on wings of gold, and was one with the wind.

Chapter Twenty-nine

~

Fatal Minutes

The slaves were easy to persuade. After Wynne freed them of their restraints and devices, they took to him quickly, admiring his power and his compelling presence.

"An invasion is beginning!" He boomed. "Now is the time to rise!"

Countless different colored eyes stared back at him, each glowing like a spectrum of starlight. He drew them in with the mighty atmosphere he seemed to bring about, and they vowed their loyalty to him, to Denoras, and to the Enma, the essence that ran through each of their veins.

The faithful soldiers however, would not be convinced, glowering beneath their headgear.

"We owe you no allegiance, traitor!" One squad captain scoffed.

"Dispatch him!" Cried another.

There were dozens of them. They gave no warning before they charged at their opponent in unison, an uproar of cries erupting from them. Before they ever touched him, Wynne raised his palms, and they froze, their cries abruptly ceased in the halting of time. By his own will, the Enma behind him remained un-stopped, their numbers in the hundreds. The Ardarans, merely around thirty in number, stood congealed, mid-attack.

Wynne knew he could not allow them to live. This was war. "Do as you must." He said to his comrades. "Show no mercy."

He took a step back and the Enma surged ahead of him, emitting growls and hisses and the like, eager to exact their revenge.

Wynne looked away, unwilling to witness the slaughter. Xeila stayed beside him always, at his side as each Ardaran's throat was slit, abdomen run through, eyes clawed out, having no ability to fight back, for stopped in time, the soldiers stood no chance. Still there were many more after them, in the lower reaches of the castle, mostly low-ranking privates on duty, at least five hundred on the floor below.

"Xeila." He said mutedly, bending close to her, persistent to avoid looking across at the butchering so close to him. He was almost tempted to raise his hand to his eyes, but resisted. "Take them all outside the castle, and feign a riot. It will lure the rest of the guards outside. Then commence attack. Reinforcements are on their way."

"But why?"

"The rest of the comrades lack your mapping skills and sense of direction. They don't know the castle as the Ardarans do. Outside lies our advantage."

"But *you* know the castle!"

"I must go to help Cinder. Maybe I can make sense of her vat controls before Orphenn arrives, yet more the advantage." He sighed, and touched her shoulder. "This battle will be long. Now go! Lead them!"

Xeila did as she was commanded, and Wynne sped in the other direction to the containment unit as quickly as possible.

By the time he arrived, he could already hear the commotion outside, a battle several stories below. Xeila knew the castle better than he thought.

It appeared he came just in time. Ardara had gathered the energy to stand, starting to walk drowsily toward the tier.

Wynne acted swiftly. He dashed to the tier and blew from his palm the glittering sand which earned him Sven's nickname. It snowed down on her like shining starfall, and had her back to sleep in seconds.

He had no time to specify its potency, so he had no way of knowing when she would wake again. He had to plan his actions.

It was then that a golden angel soared through the broken window.

"Orphenn," Wynne beckoned, "I can't decipher these controls-" He cut himself short in astonishment.

It had to be Orphenn, yet how could it be? An aura of some great gravity seemed to surround the boy, and his eyes were even brighter than the typical Enma glow. There was something in them that chilled the air. What was most shocking was that feathers had sprouted all about his skin, golden like his wings. They spackled his knuckles and the backs of his hands, some even poked through the fabric of his uniform. They were set on his forehead and circled his eyes, some mingled with strands of his hair, like some human bird of paradise.

Nonetheless, he understood Wynne's intent and made for the tier, his face stoic and wordless. Slowly he scaled the steps, his hands raised up to touch the vat's glass. Wynne could see he was rigid with power, clamped up within him, and he shivered when the boy's fletched hands pressed against the glass.

Cinder looked down on her brother with hopeful, yet frightened eyes. *What's happened to him?*

The vat began to shine and gleam, as if with an internal light, at Orphenn's touch. It glowed brighter until it was almost blinding, and then it exploded in streams of gold. The blast of fireflies that had once been Cinder's prison floated calmly, fading and dispersing halfway to the high ceilings.

Meanwhile, the uncontained plasma remained cylinder-shaped for a millisecond, then gushed out across the unit. Orphenn stepped back on the tier, and easily waded through it to get to Cinder's inert form, wheezing and coughing up plasma.

Wynne, on the other hand, did not get out of the way fast enough, and the acidic liquid sloshed about him before receding down the waste drain. He hissed as the skin on his arms and legs was scorched, and began to swell with bloody blisters. *Orphenn is unhurt because he shares DNA.* He groaned. *Just my luck.*

Orphenn pulled off his trench coat and laid it across Cinder's shoulders. She gratefully accepted the chance for modesty, and for warmth, as she was absolutely soaked with plasma and shivering violently. Her brother helped her to stand, then looked at Wynne. The feathers outlining his eyes glinted in the dim reddish light.

He came down from the tier and approached Wynne, his face unreadable. His expression was strange. He looked almost angry, and yet still blank and placid, as if he'd been possessed.

Wynne nearly feared for his life as Orphenn advanced, unable to be certain of the boy's intent.

Then Orphenn touched him. Wynne flinched, but Orphenn did nothing more than place his hands on the other's arms. Light glowed beneath his palms, making visible the red in his fingertips, like touching a bright light bulb.

Wynne marveled as the light traveled to every hurting place on his body and destroyed it. Not only were the burns from the plasma and electrocutions completely healed in less than a second, but every other bruise, scrape and cut on his skin disappeared, followed by the ache in his left leg, which before had left him limping. Now it all was gone, and Wynne felt new and ready for anything when Orphenn pulled away.

"Orphenn." He said, in his voice like iron. Cinder wobbled over to stand beside them, and before Wynne could say "Thank you," she had wrapped her arms around him.

While they enjoyed each other's embrace, Orphenn spotted movement in the darkness. He stared as the shadows rose, eyes becoming angry and intense. He gasped silently when he saw Ardara's drowsy lethargic figure.

Without preamble, he took up the fabric of the others' clothing in both his fists and pulled them apart. To their amazement he leapt several feet into the air and swooped out the broken window with them both in tow.

He soared above the wasteland, Wynne and Cinder dangling from his hands in shock. They both had caught a glimpse of Ardara trembling in rage just before Orphenn took flight, and they now witnessed the flashes and jolts of angry lightning flickering about the tower. Neither of them demanded an explanation for Orphenn's sudden retreat.

They gazed up at him, casting about the land like a hawk on the hunt, feathers, hair and uniform curling around in the wind.

"Orphenn!" Wynne shouted above the gale. "What's happened to you?" *He's carrying the weight of two others without a single drop of sweat.*

The boy gave no reply.

"It's the essence." Cinder whispered to him. "Ardara injected him with tainted essence . . . It changes him . . ."

Orphenn swerved to the right, his great wings across the sky like a shining banner. Clattering and screaming and various cacophonies of battle could be heard as they drew closer to ground level.

"The battle has already begun." Orphenn said, his first words since he left the White Herons' ship.

They flew above the battlefield, a gut-wrenching sight. Seven allied airships, including the mighty Day Star, hovered overhead and let fall missiles, bombs and gases on the enemies. Each ship had carried as many refugees from the camp at Denoras as possible, any individual old enough and healthy enough for battle. Ardaran vessels came to combat them, just as formidable.

"Cinder!" Wynne called. "Port us back inside the castle!"

"What!" She screeched. "Are you crazy?"

"Xeila has just signed to me from below! Rebels still await me in the throne room! Hurry!"

Nyx piloted the Day Star, shouting at the helm, the others engaged in the fight along and inside the ravine.

Where water once flowed, now only grayscale dirt and stone remained-ideal battle conditions. That is, of course, until it began to rain.

Sven glanced across the gorge for his squadron as the Day Star shot down an opposing ship. It plunged to the rock, throwing up dust and debris for miles, and collapsing in on itself in an explosion of noise.

Sven was sure there would be no survivors on that ship. He caught sight of Eynochia and Dacian, fighting side by side like old friends, their teamwork unavoidable. Dacian, forming his poisonous crystal lance into two lethal blades, slashed with toxic potency at any enemy within reach. The poison bubbled on the wounds and left none who faced it alive. Eynochia bit and clawed savagely in her anthropomorphic state, silver fur flaying in a mane down her neck and spine.

Xeila, evidently, was nowhere to be seen, thanks to her flawless camouflage, but could sure enough be spotted by a keen eye when soldiers were beaten by an invisible opponent, and footprints trailed in the dust.

Then the ground rumbled in answer to Jeremiah's powerful blow. It tore the ground apart. He threw boulders, and remnants of airships and bomb casings, to fall on target in the center of the enemy's battalions, deathly, absolute. He was fierce and brilliant, so like his diamond armor.

Suddenly Sven lunged to the side and fired his shotgun into the chest of his opponent, who he almost forgot about. *Not lookin' so good.* Apart from Jeremiah, none wore armor and scarce had weapons. Before he became too discouraged, a breathtaking event came to uplift him.

A giant darkness had gathered at the center of the battlefield, a portal taller than any man. At first there was nothing. In the next second, Orphenn came gliding through the blackness on golden feathers, carrying Wynne on his back, Cinder behind them on her own freed wings. After them, hundreds stormed outward, pouring into the ravine to join the fight. The portal swirled closed behind them. They charged with the collective ferocity of wolves, and attacked with a maelstrom of ability.

Sparks literally flew, every gift and power put to use in these fatal minutes.

Sven was immediately placed in good spirits. "Whooo!! Look at that!!" He cheered, firing two pistols triumphantly. "What now?!"

An enemy battalion advanced on him, cutting short his one-man rally.

"Ah." He chuckled. "Time to get down to business then."

Orphenn dropped down onto the ravine's left bank, Wynne stepping down from his back, trying to calm his heartbeat.

"Wynne." Cinder grabbed his arm. "There is still one prisoner yet to be released."

They looked at each other for one sharp moment, and then, once again, were taken by Cinder's darkness, into the heart of Ardara's dungeon.

Chapter Thirty

~

Falling Stars

Music Man's brown and orange eyes seemed to light up the dark cell, with an air of comprehension, like he knew exactly what must be done.

Cinder kneeled at his stockade (a new one, built of reinforced steel) and held her palms against his cheeks. Wynne kneeled behind her and placed his hands on top of hers.

"Work to be done, eh?" Ira said. He clicked his tongue. "S'about damn time."

Sven's valor in battle outshone all others when he made his next move. A frightening war cry was its precursor, every single weapon in his armory, almost innumerable, hung in the air for miles above and behind him as they were summoned. The glittering dust shrouded the sky below the clouds. A swarming ocean of enemies was visible, churning within the ravine.

Sven raised his arms.

His entire armory rose with them, with a collective clattering and din of metal, firearms readying.

He threw his arms down, and the chaos descended, a crusade of every weapon imaginable plunging into the sea of opponents.

A clamor of death blew across the wasteland as Sven commanded his inanimate army, circling up, and swooping back down, throwing his body into the motions.

From yards away, to Ira the scene was full of promise, a kind of meaning no one else felt. Wide-eyed, and free once again, he felt a rush of emotion staring at the storm of blades dancing in the gorge.

"My brother." He whispered before breaking into a sprint toward the bank. He took off without thanking Cinder for porting him out of prison, thinking of nothing else but reaching out to his brother.

Wynne and Cinder watched after him. Unfortunately, his dash was intercepted and he was forced into combat.

"Why don't you stop time, Wynne?" Cinder cried, grimacing at the discord and death all around them.

Wynne answered decisively. "No. I must wait, for precisely the right moment."

And at that moment, many things seemed to happen at once, and Orphenn, who watched over as a sentry soon became overwhelmed. The following events, only lasting a few minutes, felt like years.

Eyeing the onslaught, he took flight and soared over the battlefield, evidently just in time.

A wicked-looking missile dropped through the air beside him. It was like it fell in slow motion, staying adjacent to him in the air slightly longer, as if it paused to say to him, "I dare you."

Orphenn watched it plunge for a millisecond, until he spotted Eynochia, engaged and clashing below, in its path like a silver bull's eye.

Like a bird of prey he dove, and snatched her up like a fish from the water, heartbeats before the missile met its target, and left a deep, yawning crater on the bank.

She squealed in his arms, cleaving tightly to her own guardian angel. Then she shrieked, a more painful noise.

Orphenn followed her gaze to the bank where the dance of weapons had disappeared, back into arraigned dust. Each faded without the command of their summoner, for Sven had been caught in the missile's blast.

Ardara rocked back and fourth in her lonely throne, crazed and shaking violently in a fit of panic. She bit her nails savagely, her knees huddled up to her chest. She had no one, and nothing was going her way. She had nothing left in her favor. Electricity blinked and flashed everywhere, even lightning in the clouds outside as a result of her uncontestable wrath.

She began to whimper, knowing her army's numbers were dropping rapidly, and already aware that all her castle guards were dead.

She had woken to the wretched escape of Cinder and Wynne. Not long after, a soldier came to her with a message.

"All our colonies have fallen," he'd said, gurgling from the poison that Dacian had dealt him in battle. "All of them, burned to the ground . . . . I came as fast as I could to relay this . . . ." Then he had fallen over, dead. His body still lay there, and she stared at it, thinking, *It's all over . . . The battle and the war will be lost, and with the colonies gone . . . I will never be able to rise from the ashes.*

Her face contorted with desperate tears, breathing in short gasps.

Suddenly, her twitching, back and fourth movements abruptly ceased, and she held her breath, her face blank and far away.

She was seeing something else.

A vision; she saw Denoras rebuilt, a woman again at its head, a lady of light. Everything about the woman was white, to match the city she led. She was young, yet her hair was a shining shock of white, as were her fantastic robes and pale skin, even her eyelashes bleached like snow.

Cira blinked the premonition away, sure now of her own defeat. Denoras would rise again.

"Face it!" She argued schizophrenically with her own thoughts. "There's no way you'll ever possess the power those God-Beings had those years ago. That Mother Sun, and her daughters that came to the aid of the mutants . . . Shut *up*, it's your own fault! And now you'll never be immortal! Cinder is gone, and it's all because of you!" A gasp. "Cinder . . ."

The woman she had been shown, she now realized, had her face. Cinder, Cinder was that amazing woman in white that she had seen. How it would come into being, she would never be certain, but she was determined, despite her imminent defeat, to prevent her vision from passing into truth.

"Cinder is immortal."

Ardara clutched a bulky metal contraption between her vicious fingers. "But that doesn't mean I can't steal what her life is worth."

She smiled.

Orphenn could not contain the dread swelling in him as he and Eynochia were sent rolling on the bank upon his rash landing.

Frantically, he crawled as quickly as he could to where Sven lay face down in the dust.

The man wheezed as Orphenn turned him over. He was hurt badly, struck with shrapnel and covered in his own blood, his eyes glassy and wet.

"Dad!" Eynochia wailed.

Orphenn wasted no time. In seconds, light entombed Sven from the boy's palms, and was gone again just as swiftly.

Sven blinked several times and took a deep, grateful breath, all afflictions healed by Orphenn's light.

"Whew . . ." He breathed. "You had me scared there for a minute."

The three had no time to rejoice, thanks to Cinder, there for only a second, when she used her gift to take them to shelter behind a huge steel panel, leftover from the destruction of an Ardaran ship. Xeila, Jeremiah, Dacian, and Wynne were already there, and did not greet them when they arrived-they only stared beyond them into the sky with tears in their eyes.

It was only when they looked skyward that they saw her reason for porting them to shelter. Their great behemoth, the beloved Day Star, had been shot down, and was falling to her doom.

The boom resonated in their chests and shook their bones when she met land with a colossal mushroom cloud. Sorrow filled their hearts, not from one loss, but from two.

Dacian mourned. "Nyx." He whispered.

Ira parried with a sword he swiped from a corpse, fighting back diligently, when out of the blue, he looked directly in the other's eyes, and started to sing.

His opponent froze.

The voice he heard was layered, sweet, and golden, with an unreal harmony that echoed in the ears. He wanted to follow it to the ends of the Earth, as long as he could keep hearing it.

The Ardaran slit his own throat and collapsed.

Then Ira began to sing a different song, that only his enemies heard.

His voice split the air, their thoughts, their souls were his.

Like the pied piper, they danced to his tune, his velvet words filled their every fiber.

"Move the skies I do
Walk for me, children
I am within you . . ."

The whole battalion proceeded to exterminate each other, and soon all of them had either taken a comrade's life, or their own.

When the song ended, still more enemies came forth.

Ira ran, until he was backed up against a giant slab of metal. They started to charge, when before him the first line fell one by one to the dirt, stone cold.

The lines behind slowed to a stop, timid. They too began to drop dead little by little, then a few at a time.

Thus encouraged, Ira charged and attacked any that did not die mysteriously on their own.

Orphenn, still a bit stricken, peeked out behind the edge of the steel panel to see a man pressed back against the other side, about to be butchered by an entire battalion.

He was shocked at the realization that this was the man that he had helped free from Ardara's dungeon when Cinder had been kept there. It seemed so far away now.

His head snapped around and he yelled over the noise, "Eynochia! Hold me!"

"This is hardly the time!" She scolded.

Though he did not hear her, his body had already fallen limp across her lap.

Eynochia, the only one able to perceive him in the Halo form, gawked as the glittering entity separated itself from the flesh and lingered in the air in front of her.

He bore into her with those molten eyes of gold. She felt a circle of warmth on her forehead when he touched his spirit lips to it.

"Orphenn, what are you doing?" She never said it out loud, but he heard her.

His mouth moved slowly, but the words came quickly, from several different places, repeating in echo, each one different tone and volume.

"I know . . . ."

". . . We've just lost the Day Star, and another . . . ."

"Comrade, but . . ."

"And the enemy is foolishly . . ."

"Courageous. They think they . . ."

"Still can win . . . . But they . . . ."

"Forget . . . ."

"We are Enma."

"Are Enma."

The words were still in her ears when he left her, floating like a phantom above the battalion. He softly descended and placed his ghostly hands on one Ardaran's jaw, and twisted his head with a crack, snapping his neck, and the soldier fell.

In this way, and many others, he commenced to invisibly kill off the battalion.

"We are Enma." Eynochia whispered. She looked at her sister. They had matching looks on their faces.

"We are Enma." Xeila nodded.

Eynochia cautiously laid Orphenn's body down in the lee of the metal and stood, the others following suit. Jeremiah encircled the boy's body in an adamant barrier, cracking and crystallizing into a dome around him, protecting him indefinitely.

"We are Enma!" Sven roared, and soon they all had run into the battle, abilities raging.

They forget.

We are Enma.

The words stayed and would not be let go, for it kept them going. With those words, they would survive.

Chapter Thirty-one

~

Between Dimensions

Eynochia and Xeila clawed, slashed and bit; Cinder twirled, kicked, punched, ported to dodge an attack and repeated the pattern; Sven had a crossbow in one hand and a spiked mace in the other, knives and blades flashing around him; Jeremiah took out dozens at a time with one fist; Wynne put to use for the first time his most potent slumber, sweeping his assailants with black sand, which peacefully took them into death; even Nero proved his worth this battle, though he stayed close to Sven, firing a borrowed machine gun with great skill. Meanwhile Dacian, in desperation, exhausted of his lance, had found a new way to utilize his gift of changing the state of matter.

His hands were clamped on an enemy's shoulders. The Ardaran was weaponless, already on the verge of defeat, when he started to reel and writhe and twitch in Dacian's grip.

Like the table so long ago had been reduced to a puddle of table-colored liquid at his touch, the man he held, screaming, became shorter and shorter until he burst into human-colored fluid, ending his life as a puddle in the dust.

Dacian gulped, very disturbed by it, and made sure to breathe. No one else approached him, the Ardarans slowly backing away from their ex-superior, extreme fear in their faces.

"There 'ya go, Ace!" Sven encouraged, blowing them all down with a bazooka.

Just then, a stray Ardaran crept up behind the fourteen-year-old, and bashed him in the head with the butt of his spear. Nero collapsed dizzily but held fast to his firearm, pulling the trigger and killing his assailant. Then the machine fell from his grasp and evaporated in summon-dust when he fell limp, unconscious from the blow to his head.

Jeremiah witnessed the scene, and came in a flash to the boy, heaving him onto his rock-hard shoulder with ease, and nodding assurance to Sven.

At that moment, Eynochia froze in place, staring upward at Ardara's tower.

Her eyes widened in terror and she exclaimed, "Orphenn!! Orphenn, Get back to your body!"

Sven felt his mood improve slightly, no longer so deep in the battle-state solemnity, when he saw Orphenn rush into the battle with the pistols he had given to him, eons ago it seemed.

Sven's mood changed completely when his blade clashed with another's. Beyond the crossed blades, the face that stared back at him was one he never thought he'd see again.

His own face brightened, eyes wet, brows turned up with emotion. Time seemed to stop for Ira and Sven to search each others' faces.

"Ardara's on the tower! Ardara's on the tower!" Someone shouted.

Then time really stopped.

Wynne, staring intently with eyes like fire at the tower's peak, hushed first, "This is the moment!" Then after a second he howled, "I want her to see her world, crumbling around her!!" He raised his arms high, and Time followed his command.

Every Ardaran froze, every single remaining soldier motionless as every clock stopped ticking. Even Ardara, miles above them, was paused, looking down on her land. The Enma were left unfrozen. Immediately, they all took to slaying each Ardaran soldier one by one.

Sven's sword burst into dust, sparkling through his fingers. Ira's clattered to the soil. Both their faces dripped with tears. Knowing there was no time for embrace, Sven's head hung low, emotionally exhausted. His eyes clamped shut to push out the tears, and he hummed a melody, chin quivering. Shaky words followed in the same tune, and their eyes met as Ira joined in.

"I never saw the light
I never saw the sun . . ."

They sang louder, and Sven summoned two long swords, handing one to Ira.

Their song boomed across the time-frozen battlefield and urged the ending of the fight. They continued to sing as they walked side by side and slashed every congealed enemy they passed, taking their sweet time and sending their voices into the melody, harmonizing exquisitely.

"Knowing you has changed me
When loving you begun

No tale can be told
Without a word from you
No question can be answered
Without telling what to do

When all seems lost
I'll hold you to the sky
No matter what the cost . . ."

The brothers turned to face each other, stabbing the last soldier together, and relinquishing the blades.

"There will always be you and I."

It was over.

Cinder no longer had to touch a person to port them, and so, as the White Herons and their three companions turned up their heads to the tower, lightning stilled in place all around it, they were thrown into darkness and taken wherever Cinder willed, which at this time, was the tower's faraway peak.

One second, Ardara was staring bleakly down on the scene in her wasteland, noise everywhere, inescapable.

The next second, it was dead silent, but for the wind in her ears, and now there were eight pairs of mismatched eyes staring right at her.

For a moment she glanced beyond them at the evidence of her defeat. Every one of her soldiers had been cut down. She closed her eyes. Her hand tightened around the bundle of cloth she carried in her fist.

"So. It's come to this."

When she opened her eyes, she stared straight at Cinder.

The Drifter stepped forward.

"It's all over, isn't it?" Ardara asked, almost innocently.

"Looks that way." Cinder replied lowly. "Knowing you, though . . . I bet there's a trial to endure yet."

"You know me well." Ardara took the black cloth from her bundle like the lid of a gourmet dish, and held the metal mechanism to display. "But do you know what this is?"

Instantly, Wynne made to rush forward; he'd seen it before, watched her build it-he knew its purpose.

Ardara only looked at him, and he froze. They all did, save Cinder. The other eight were terrified to find they could not move their bodies, not a budge-they could not even speak. Her power stilled them in place, and they could do nothing but watch what unfolded, Wynne trapped in the frame of a run.

"This. Is *my* affair." She told them, then transferred her harsh gaze back to Cinder. "This is a device with a function quite similar to Dacian's diffusion ability. It extracts the mutations of the Enma it attaches to, and if I will it, takes their life. Do you know why?"

"Why what? You're not making sense . . ."

"Because moments ago," she blurted, "I had a vision. I will do anything to keep it from happening. Anything. I realize now that I was wrong to search for any other power but yours."

"Mine?" Cinder's face took on a look of concern, pity and sorrow for her psychopathic sibling. How had it gone this far? Where was her only living sister now, the sweet one that loved chemistry and lemonade? Far away from here.

"*You will live forever!!*" Ardara screeched without warning, giving Cinder a terrible start.

"What?" She cried, eyes brightening with hopeless tears.

"At first I thought you were merely unable to die by injury, but I was mistaken! My visions have shown it to me, you will never grow old! You will never die!" *But I can change that.* "I may be defeated, but I'll be *damned* if I let you win!"

Screaming, Ardara wrestled with her sister, trying to affix the device, exerting herself to the point that lightning flickered around her, and both their wings unfurled, feathers flying. Fire ignited on Cira's plumage, the flames spreading down her arms, catching the trench coat that Cinder wore ablaze. Cinder shoved her away to hastily rip it off her arms and tossing it to land softly on the tower's metal roof and burn out. She was left wearing nothing but the revealing leather strap suit. She took a few steps back.

Ardara snickered. "Look." She flung away her billowing gown to flaunt an identical suit, in deep burgundy. "We match." *Just like we used to.*

"I won't fight you, Cira!" Cinder bellowed.

Just as Ardara was about to throw a punch, Cinder leapt to her and they were hurled through a door of twisting, writhing nothingness. With the device, they disappeared, to somewhere no one else would ever know. As soon as they did, Ardara's psychic hold faltered, and Wynne fell forward. Nero awakened and hopped off Jeremiah's shoulder, rubbing his head.

"Cinder!"

Orphenn, whose power had been welling up, pent up inside him, ready to burst while he was trapped in the telekinesis; now he trembled and shuddered on his knees, snarling and growling like an animal.

"Orphenn!" Eynochia fell to him and clung to his arm, shaking him. She could feel his withheld power and rage. She saw him changing. The golden feathers that fletched his skin, and covered his wings were dripping with black. It was like Cinder's darkness, and yet, entirely different . . . . This blackness had a wickedness to it she couldn't describe, something menacing. It frightened her as it spiraled around his body. It was pressing on him, possessing him.

"The essence!" Dacian reveled. "It's taking him!" He ran to the boy, and said to Eynochia, "Move, I can diffuse it before-"

"GET AWAY." Thundered a strange voice that came from Orphenn's mouth. The words were not his own, nor his actions; he rose and waved his arm. The power sent a gush of wind across the roof. They all went sliding across the metal. Dacian slid off the edge, only just catching the ledge to stop himself plunging to his death. He cried out, but Jeremiah was there to pull him to safety with one mighty hand.

When they looked back to Orphenn, he had changed almost completely. He cackled and wriggled painfully, driven insane by tainted mutation, as it took him into its raging hatred. The thing that stood there had Orphenn's face, but his eyes were nothing but two flaming orbs of yellow, and the black hugged to him like a cloak. He moved with his head bowed lowly and tilted nefariously to eye them all with a horrible bloodlust. He looked at least two feet taller. The blackness trailed like dust behind him with every movement, and it had formed two horns that floated above his temples, his inhumanly wide smile bright and fanged. His breath rasped.

The scene was haunting. The breeze blew over them, an almost tranquil moment before he attacked the closest person to him, with a frightening scratchy cry, like something straight from Hell.

"Jeremiah!" Dacian shrieked.

Before Wynne was crushed beneath Orphenn's careening blow, Jeremiah did as Dacian willed, using his amazing speed to bring Dacian between Wynne and the demon that was Orphenn.

The dark thing ran right into him.

Dacian grabbed at it, and began his attempt to diffuse the tainted essence from the monster, to filter it out and abolish it, and to bring back the heart inside.

Wynne had tried to stop time to aid them countless times before this, but failed. His gifts were acting up again, curse it.

Dacian shouted with the pain and the effort, his hands burning. Orphenn screamed in an angry fit, like a child's tantrum.

Here, Eynochia knew she could help. *You're like her.* She heard her father's words again clearly, and she felt her mother was close to her when she pressed her hands on top of Dacian's.

Finally, her power, the strength of her mother's and hers added to Dacian's efforts and refined them. She was intensely pure, and it fortified them both, brought Orphenn to his knees and sucked the dark poison from him. The flames of his eyes went dark, burned out, and his squirming ceased. They let go of him, stepped back carefully. His head hung low. The darkness fell away, purified, hissing as it went. He dropped to his side looking utterly spent, exhausted. He sighed.

Eynochia kneeled by him, and hefted him onto her lap, touching his face, stroking his hair, now free of feathers. His pearly eyelids lifted to see her beautiful face. Stunning, even after battle, her silver hair tangled and dusty, covered in soil, and scrapes and blood, uniform torn, about as beaten as they all looked by now.

Orphenn frowned. "I'm so tired." He griped, brow furrowed peevishly. "I'm so sick of the pain . . ."

"I'm sorry." Eynochia whispered.

"You don't care . . ." Orphenn whispered back, trailing off.

"I do!" She countered bluntly. Her next words she whispered as if it was the greatest secret. "If I didn't, would I be here holding you? This isn't like you, Mr. Optimist!" She spoke so soothingly, that Orphenn nearly drifted as she did. "I'm always by your side, always will be, partner. Know why? You're my best friend. And I love you more than anything."

Hearing this, he was no longer tired. He squeezed her hand, eyes big, hopeful lights. They shared a short smile.

It would be a long time before they could do so again.

It was then that the portal returned.

"Where have you taken me?" Ardara demanded.

There was nothing but endless black, though they stood on solid ground, like a room with no walls. Fathomless, yet still somehow contained.

Cinder watched her sister for a while, as she argued and muttered to herself, pulling at her hair and shaking her head. Then she spoke, though it did not seem that the other was listening. "This is the space between dimensions. The very darkness between the worlds." Cinder answered, thinking, she'd never stayed so long in between portals. She didn't like this unwelcome feeling, but she set aside her paranoia. "You have no power here."

Ardara turned, the parasitic new device falling from her hand to the solid darkness. Those eyes could have cut Cinder apart, had they been knives.

"How dare you?" She spat.

Cinder unexpectedly gasped and choked. She knew she should have heeded her first feeling of foreboding. And now, something was threatening to consume her altogether.

They were both shocked at this, Ardara already aware of what was happening.

"Your own darkness will consume you! It seems you can die after all!"

Fear gripped Cinder like cold strangling hands, and in an act of last resort, ported back to the tower.

But once there, the portal did not close again. It grew, and it wanted to absorb her, and keep her forever.

She clawed the metal trying to escape it, but hands clawed at her. She looked back to witness the frenzied face of her sister.

Wynne went to help her, but Orphenn stopped him with a firm hand. "No, you'll be taken too! She'll be okay!" *I hope . . .* He shivered. *Please . . .*

"No!" Ardara squealed, grabbing and tugging at her back, pulling her back into the darkness. "You will not leave me to die!"

From the shadows, Cinder created a long abyssal mallet and swung it backward. It connected with Ardara's skull, and knocked her backward benumbed, stolen by the oblivion, where she would stay.

Cinder still tried to make for escape from the terrifying abyss, but it would not release her.

Now Orphenn was the one to leap forward, regardless of his own words of caution, and no one stopped him. Cinder's fate, had he done anything otherwise, would have been infinitely different.

Cinder was almost swallowed entirely, when strong arms held her, more unwilling to let her go than even the darkness was.

Orphenn had pitched right into the darkness to take hold of her, and it twisted and seethed in protest, knowing its end was near-for from the boy came the brightest kind of light, growing larger and mightier than any nothingness, and pushing it back into its place. It grew so bright that it filled everything in sight, so blinding it might have been the sun itself, and the others were forced to look away, shielding their eyes.

To those below on land, it looked like a falling star had taken rest atop the tower, burning white.

Like a supernova, it stayed bright until its own power burned it away and fizzed itself out.

The light receded, and the White Herons slowly showed their faces again to look upon the boy and his sister.

Orphenn had saved her, but even still, Cinder would be eternally different.

Chapter Thirty-two

~

Peaceful Place

When Cinder woke, it was inside her own tent at the refugee camp. Though the only way she knew this was the memory of being asked to port everyone here, when she had not even had the strength to open her eyes, and passed out soon after.

When she opened her eyes, it was just as dark as when they were closed.

She sat up shakily in the canvas cot, blinking vigorously, hands reaching out for nothing. "I . . . I can't see . . ."

"Cinder?!" Orphenn grabbed her hand after rushing to her from the other side of the tent. "Oh God . . ."

"Orphenn." She said, relieved, already placid, as if the loss of her sight was as trivial as a paper cut. "I'm blind."

"Damnit! Cinder! I'm so sorry!" She heard him sob, felt him press his cheek to the back of her hand. "I feel horrible!"

"Orphenn." She said firmly. "I'd rather be blind than dead."

She couldn't see his grateful smile, but she held is hand tightly.

"Princess Cinderella!" Came Sven's unmistakable rumble. "You've awakened!" He paused. "Aw, damn, kiddo. You've gotten so . . . White."

It was true. The others came to see her, and marveled at the difference. Cira had seen even detail accurately.

"You were white after the light faded, but I didn't think it would stick . . ."

This woman, who from the first day had always worn nothing but black . . . It was hard to imagine her in anything else, and astonishing to see it.

Now her hair was whiter than Xeila's, bleached by Orphenn's light, just like her eyelashes, and, sadly, her eyes. Her pupils could still be seen-right slitted, left split-but even they were

190

clouded with white, her irises almost transparent. The only extra clothing they could find for her was a spare infirmary gown, also white.

Ironically, she was quite a sight.

"Even you're skin is twice as white!" Xeila joked. "I didn't think that was possible!"

After a bout of laughter, Wynne chimed, "I think she's twice as beautiful."

Cinder smiled in the direction of his voice. "I have to go back . . ." She said reluctantly.

"What? No."

"I have to see her." She insisted. "Just to see."

No amount of disapproval could stop her, either.

Cira had come to inside the smothering darkness, and realized that this is where she would die.

She was forever, completely, utterly alone.

Just as she had this thought, a soft, white light appeared, warming her skin, and through to the bone. It started as a little firefly, then blossomed out, and became a woman. The woman did not look at her. She stood out against the darkness so harshly, and she even had a subtle glow, like a goddess of moonlight.

"Cinder?"

The woman answered by following the voice and kneeling beside her. Now it didn't matter how long she stayed between. No darkness could touch her.

"Cira." She laid a tender white hand on Cira's forehead. "I can take you back." She said without preamble, pleading. "You can be my sister again." Cira's chin quivered and a little whimper escaped her throat. "Come back to the light. You don't have to be alone anymore."

"Neither do you."

"What do you mean?"

"I'm not your sister."

"What are you talking about, you will always be my sister!" Her hands clamped around Cira's.

They both cried, tears of unbelievable grief.

"You'll never be alone." Cira said. "In my vision. You will always be surrounded by people that love you. Forever."

"What are you saying?"

"If I was meant to come back . . . I would have seen it." Cinder heard Cira's other hand searching for something, find it and grasp it, metal clinking. The device. "In my vision . . . I wasn't there."

"No, Cira! Please! You don't have to do this!" Cinder tried to hinder her in any way as she clipped the metal thing around her own neck, but everything is harder when you're blind. "We can change all that! We can change it together! I've already lost one sister, Cira!"

"It will be better this way. I promise."

Those were Cira's last words.

The device drained her of everything, starting with her mutations, moving on to her body heat, and finishing with her heartbeat.

The Lady of Light mourned inside the darkness until she felt her heart would decay, and her tears would fill a lake.

Cinder carried the body of her sister to the River. Her eight companions followed behind, and behind them a procession of all the camp refugees, Nero at its front.

When she reached the River's bank, she said not a word. No one did.

Cinder stepped into the water and waded through it until it soaked up to her hips. Remarkable, that she found her way without her sight, as if someone was leading her, as well.

Its warmth and its sparkling colors twinkled and twirled around her, knowing her, remembering her, welcoming her. Silent tears mingled with it, like a quiet, sad hello.

Cinder felt one last time the face of the Cira she'd always known, kissed her forehead, held her tightly.

Then she let the water take her.

Like it had for Oriana and Celina before her, the River cradled Cira, lifted her into the air to face the sun, its light glittering through the ripples.

Something amazing happened then.

Before the water rained back down, it formed two shapes beneath Cira's upraised pyre, two figures like water sprites, river spirits. They were forms of two women, and they held hands and danced, their bodies waving and dripping across the surface.

Cinder could not see it, but still, she knew, and let out a surprised sob.

The forms were embodiments of the last two to perish in this River.

They spun and circled around Cinder and took her hands, and she joined the dance.

She cried and blubbered, and they lifted away, Cinder's hands reaching blindly up for them as they ascended.

Celina and Oriana held Cira, cherished her. They sustained her spirit, lifted her soul. They helped her to her peaceful place.

Still reaching up, Cinder closed her eyes, and felt the water rain back down.

That night Cinder could not sleep. Her stale cot held no comfort, her humid tent no shelter.

That night Wynne had come to her, and that night he kneeled beside her cot.

That night he kissed her.

He sprinkled, like sugar from his fingers, kind, glittering sand about her head. Floating down, it sparkled on her skin and hair like diamond dust. Her eyes closed.

That night she slept.

Recovery from such war and such loss would not come quickly. But restoration would have to. The people of Denoras could only live in tents for so long.

The time had come to go to the ruins to sum up the damage and make plans for rebuilding.

The White Herons all had gone to the destroyed capital, plus Wynne, Dacian, and Ira, and even young Nero came along by request of Lady Cinder, who had finally accepted the role of Supreme Commander. She wore Celina's coronet with unhidden pride.

They traipsed about the center of the ravaged city.

"I would like a new monument to be sculpted as well, to be outside of the front of the palace, like it was before . . ." Cinder listed off her desires for renovation and renewal, merely from her memory of the ruins, while Wynne took notes and Nero led her by the arm.

The sun started to dip behind the mountains, turning the clouds orange and lavender.

A ray of sunlight lingered at the spot where the angel monument had been, and they watched it curiously, all but Cinder, who could only feel its warmth.

Then the sun gave a sudden flash, and she was there, as big as the monument used to be, more beautiful than the new one would ever become.

Orphenn marveled, awestruck and staring in wonder, as did the rest of them, like a matched set. In disbelief, he said, "Mother Sun."

"*I am here.*" Said she.

She looked just as she had in Celina's Dreamfast, like a spirit of the sun, celestial and brilliant among the ashes. "*I have watched your journey, Cinder Avari, of Earth.*" Her voice was like honey and molasses, like the wind and the rain.

"Yes, Mother?" Cinder acknowledged reverently.

"*You are the only sister left alive, my child. I have mourned for your losses. Had the other two lived, I would have given the three of you my intended gift, as reward. The gifts I bestowed when first we met were given to save my daughter Earth, and that you did. Now you have not only bettered the world you left, but also brought peace to this one, twice.*

"*But alas, I am at a loss now as to your reward.*"

For a breathtaking moment, she paused in thought.

"*Oh, Cinder. You are immortal.*" She recalled. "*But how are you to rule this world peacefully, forever, without your loved ones beside you?*"

Cinder took a deep breath, and sighed. She had been thinking the very same thing.

"*When the sun sets, all of you will be blessed with immortality.*"

A collective gasp rose from the group, all their faces changing simultaneously.

"*The nine of you will have each other here for the rest of eternity. That is my gift, it is your reward.*

"Ah, but Cinder . . ." Added Mother Sun, "*However will you rule your people if you cannot see them?*"

The colossal being took one step, and just that quickly had shrunk to average womanly size, waving hair floating weightlessly around her. She held Cinder's shoulders. Two maidens of light, brought so close.

Mother Sun kissed Cinder's forehead. She felt like she'd be warm forever.
Then the sun set.
And Cinder could *see* it.
She let fall tears of joy.

Epilogue

~

The sun was low in the sky. The sky was painted with hues of vermillion and violet, and the clouds were a pink that reflected Wynne's eyes. The eyes that looked upon Cinder with everlasting love.

"You know . . ." Cinder grinned, gazing adoringly at him with eyes like white diamonds. "On Earth, it's bad luck to see the bride before the wedding."

"Well," He debated with mirth, "we're not on Earth."

The wedding party was only beginning beyond the balcony, background noise.

Someone called to them from the clamor. It was Xeila.

"Time to dance!"

Cinder gave a reluctant sigh and gazed at Wynne with beseeching eyes. He urged her on, and they began to move back toward the celebration.

The two of them wore magnificent robes of Denorasian white for the occasion. Wynne, with half of his platinum blonde hair tied back, looked like a fairy tale elf, and he fit the part. Cinder wore the same formal robes that Celina had once worn, and today was without her coronet, for this was also a crowning ceremony.

After opening many wedding gifts, Cinder stood at one end of the Circle of Union, and Wynne at the other. The horde of guests surrounded the circle in the traditional Verlassian style to watch, and Ira, the father of the groom, stood in the center. Wynne and Cinder walked slowly as rehearsed to meet him in the middle.

Ira held Celina's coronet on a cushion in his left hand and its twin in his right. Long pendants, also twins, hung from both his wrists.

Wynne smiled. He formally picked Celina's coronet from the plush velvet and slipped it gently onto Cinder's forehead. Its gem matched the luster of her hair.

Cinder did the same, regally placing the corresponding headdress on Wynne's blonde brow, with a prestige that Orphenn had never seen her wear.

Next, Ira lowered the pendants over their heads. They were both made entirely of shining white crystal, and sparkled around their necks in the frothy twilight.

They faced each other, and lowered, bowing to one another traditionally.

Now that they matched, Wynne raised his right arm for Cinder to place her hand atop his elevated palm.

Ira gave the queue to a player of an odd instrument that looked like a combination between a Chinese Erhu and the gears within a music box. The music it produced was instantly tear-jerking.

They flowed effortlessly with the melody in ceremonial dance, spinning, twirling, bowing, never taking their eyes from each other.

When they inched closer, and Cinder sensed the song was nearly done, she whispered to Wynne ruefully, "I'm so happy. I never want this moment to end."

In the instant the musician played the last note, his fermata was stunted.

They stopped dancing, and with a subtle wave of Wynne's hand, everything was slowed, and the world came to a dead silent stop.

He and Cinder were the only two things alive, the surrounding wedding frozen in place. To them, all that existed was each other, and all time was stilled around them.

"It doesn't have to." Wynne said.

The only noise in the world was the beating of their hearts. The only movement was their embrace against the sunset, in this moment that was only theirs forever.

Cinder had taken the title of Supreme Commander with valiance, and dignity. Celina's memory was always with her, as well as Cira's.

It took twelve years to rebuild after the war. Denoras took the longest to restore, but it became the most beautiful city on Aleida. It was more breathtaking than it had ever been, with ten times the size and grandeur. Lady Cinder ruled over it with strong, yet gentle wisdom, with help from her eternal companions, and with Wynne beside her every step of the way.

And they wore matching coronets on the day of their wedding.

Plenty of other interesting things happened that day.

"Okay." Now twenty-nine year old Orphenn said, dragging Eynochia behind him. He pulled her beneath a white gazebo in the garden, away from the noise and chatter of the post-wedding party in the courtyard.

"What is it Orphenn? Why'd you take me out here?" Eynochia giggled.

"I have something to say." He said, with a secretive smile. He took her hand. "You're my best friend." He told her, beaming like a laser. "But not just that. I've never felt this way about anyone but you. I mean there was this one girl in third grade, but that doesn't count." She laughed and he went on, "Point is . . . You are my first and my last. It's always been you. And if I had to choose anyone to spend forever with . . ." his voice caught as he reached for something in his pocket. He swallowed and said, ". . . It would be you." Warm tears spilled from her eyes and she smiled. "Now, I'm going to do this the Earthling way."

He lowered to one knee, and flipped open the lid of a tiny box. Inside, it held a gleaming diamond ring. (Probably provided by Jeremiah, who finally married Xeila a couple years back).

"Eynochia." He intoned deeply. "Will you marry me?"

Her answer mirrored a reaction that might have come from her father.

"Damn straight! Thought you'd never ask!"

So now, Cinder's wedding guests had another couple to congratulate.

"Dang, everyone's gettin' married, ain't they?" Ira exclaimed.

Sven held Orphenn close to him, then held his face in scarred hands and kissed his forehead. "Ah, Little Bird." He said tearfully. "I always knew you would be my son."

After everyone had taken their turn to embrace them, Orphenn stopped, and looked at them all. Just looked at them. His sister Cinder and new brother Wynne; the new-ish couple Jeremiah and Xeila, now his new brother and sister; Nero, who might as well be a little brother, and Dacian, who he already considered a brother anyway, knowing how much he was still in love with his sister Celina. It was the best, and biggest family an orphan could ever have dreamed.

He could see. They all had loving eyes, smiling faces, happy hearts. Wide open, warm, accepting arms. Laughing into the sunset.

Yes. He said to himself. *These are the people I want to spend forever with.*